Dixie Noir

DIXIE NOIR

KIRK CURNUTT

FIVE STAR
A part of Gale, Cengage Learning

GALE
CENGAGE Learning

Detroit • New York • San Francisco • New Haven, Conn • Waterville, Maine • London

GALE
CENGAGE Learning™

LIBRARY OF CONGRESS CATALOGING-IN-PUBLICATION DATA

Curnutt, Kirk, 1964–
    Dixie noir / Kirk Curnutt. — 1st ed.
        p. cm.
    ISBN-13: 978-1-59414-821-7 (alk. paper)
    ISBN-10: 1-59414-821-X (alk. paper)
    1. Ex-convicts—Fiction. 2. Forgiveness—Fiction. 3. Self-realization—Fiction. 4. Montgomery (Ala.)—Fiction. I. Title.
PS3603.U76D59 2009
813'.6—dc22   2009027523

First Edition. First Printing: November 2009.
Published in 2009 in conjunction with Tekno Books and Ed Gorman.

For Diane
and for the real lifers at the real-life El:
Jim, Bart, Bubba, Wayne, Warren, Knox, John,
and Clay, who named this book

"This definitely is not Montgomery, Alabama. Tell me. What would you do if it was? If this turned out to be another Montgomery?"

"Buy a plane ticket."

—A conversation between Milkman and Guitar
in Toni Morrison's *Song of Solomon* (1977)

Saturday, 2:37 A.M.

You know how it is when you drop a guy who thought he had the drop on you. He gives you that "Et tu" face, like you betrayed him by having more smarts than he ever thought to credit you with.

For High C, the shock was double. That's because this was the second time I had shot him when he was convinced he was about to kill me, and he couldn't believe it had happened again. Frankly, I couldn't either. I had cost him a yard of lower intestine once already, and that's not a danger likely to slip most men's mind, not even if it was ten years ago. The only consolation was that C could slump in peace knowing he wouldn't make that mistake thrice. It was clear to us both he would be dead before he got the chance.

"I reckon you'll bleed out in seven, eight minutes max," I said, pulling up a chair. "I'll stay until you do."

His hands fluttered sort of like flippers on a seal when it's rolled on its side. I couldn't blame him. I wouldn't want to go out with half of me hanging over an armrest either. I tugged him by the ponytail until he was upright in his recliner. By way of thanking me, he went, "Always the humanitarian, ain't you, Ennis?"

I stared at his beard. It was his pride. He grew it long and combed it wide so it hung to his navel like a big gray arrowhead.

Only now a black circle marred the lower third of that immaculate expanse of silver. That was the spot that the bullet had burned through on its way to his stomach. As we watched together, blood dribbled out.

"Make them patch that before the funeral, will you? No cheap filler like filings or steel wire, though. Make them go to a barber and get real hair. It can be women's so long as it's human. There'll be folks that'll want nothing more than to see me stretched out for visitation with strands from a jackass tail hanging off my chin."

I closed my eyes and tried to swallow a bad smell floating between us. I wasn't sure if it was bullet smoke or singed beard or some combination of the two.

"There's a copy of *Tosca* in the CD player, too. Maria Callas's last stage performance. Flip it on."

"You're wasting a lot of breath making demands. Maybe you should pray instead of giving orders. It might do you better in the long run."

He wanted to laugh, but it came out a gargle.

"It's not polite to deny a man his dying wish."

" 'Wish' is singular, as in one. One is all you got time for. And saying that's not rude when the man dying has only himself to blame for his predicament."

"That's how you see it, huh?"

"You came after me, remember? Don't tell me you don't; it hasn't even been a week yet. I was looking forward to my anonymity, but you had to bring it all to a boil."

"What kind of bullet do you have in that gun, killer?"

I popped open the cylinder of the Charter Arms and told him. C pried a smile across his lips.

"If I'm not mistaken, you claimed self-defense the last time you parked a Hornady in me. Saying it was my fault didn't work a decade ago. What makes you think it will now?"

"This time you won't be around to testify otherwise."

His smile widened until he looked like a tranquilized lion.

"Touché . . . I guess I hadn't thought that far ahead. No reason to, is there?"

He tucked his beard over his shoulder so the blood wouldn't stain it any further. We both looked at the wound. It was easy enough to see—C was shirtless, wearing nothing more than a swimsuit. The wound sat an inch or two above his belly button. The diameter didn't seem much wider than a finger, but I could tell it was deep. I almost expected to see straight through to the recliner.

"I got to know," he said with a wince. "Did you aim for my sternum, or were you just on the shaky side? You were kind enough to plant me in the gut the last time."

"I've grown up since the last time. Your line of sight changes when you look at things with a higher moral eye. I'm still getting used to the angles up here."

"Don't flatter yourself. You've always looked down on people. Famous son of a famous father—why wouldn't you think you were better than everybody else? You thought you were better even when you were nothing but a ten-cent junkie."

He laughed again. Again it came out more of a gargle.

"A ten-cent junkie with a two-dollar whore," he went on. "No wonder you landed in the clink, Ennis. That math won't work however hard you try to square it."

"I never thought I was better than Faye. I wanted to save her because I thought she could've been better than you and me put together. Now, granted, you and me put together didn't add up to a whole lot of good back in the day, did it?"

"From the way things have turned out, I'd have to say no." With his beard thrown over his shoulder and his eyes all scrunched up his whole face looked askew. "You've got a lot of growing up left to do. I hope you stick around long enough to do it. I'd hate to think that all the betterment a ten-cent junkie can manage is to make himself into a ten-cent savior."

We looked at each other for a long time. Then we heard the girl downstairs. She was singing to calm herself: *"En-nis, won't you come out and play?"*

"What do you know?" C shrugged. "There's the proof in my pudding. You better go get her. Don't worry about me. I'll let Jesus know I forgive you. That's not something I would usually do. Forgiveness is personal. Who kills who is just business."

"It hasn't seemed like business with her," I said, nodding toward the ghostly voice. "I've never heard you get so personal."

"That's the real lag in your growing up, my friend. Admit it. The only reason I'm sitting here with my lifeblood gurgling into my rectum is because of what I said about Dixie. If you were forward-thinking you'd realize that therein lies a solid line of defense. You could say I baited you by calling the daughter of your two-dollar whore a waterhead. You lost your marbles, you shot in anger. It wouldn't be so far from the truth that the forensics would contradict you. As you've been kind enough to note, I won't be around to woo a jury to the contrary."

"You're forgetting one pretty important detail."

I pointed to the dead body next to the bookcase. It lay crumpled on its side, the head buried under a pile of hardbacks. They had toppled off the shelf when the body fell. It hadn't taken three or four minutes for that one to bleed out. One shot had dropped that one dead.

C went to shrug again, but the movement pumped a thicker gush of blood from the hole. I saw dizziness flush through his face. *"En-nis,"* Dixie continued to sing. *"Won't you come and stay?"*

"That's a Lapua in him," C pointed out. "Easy enough to explain: my gun, not yours."

"If you're that willing to confess maybe I should stanch you."

"You're about a pint late on that offer." He was sweating hard and had to stop to grimace every few breaths. "Boy, I sure would love me some Maria Callas right about now. Nothing against Dixie, but she's no Maria Callas."

"Take back what you said about her and I'll think about it."

"Hey, if that's all it takes . . . I'm sorry I called Dixie a waterhead. I meant it as a term of affection."

"En-nis, won't you come and stay? . . . En-nis, won't you come and play?"

C sighed. "I've never been anything but a crazy check to her, Ennis. None of us have. You're lucky her whore mother didn't have her hooks into you like the rest of us. It's not like the brat will miss me when I'm gone. You watch."

"Too bad we won't be able to watch together."

He let out another wet rattle of a laugh. I never knew a man to get so much entertainment out of dying.

"That may not be as farfetched as you think. We might just get to watch it together. From there."

He cocked a wrinkled finger at the floor and then jabbed a few times, in case I didn't get the point.

I almost didn't.

It was a good ten seconds before I realized he was pointing to Hell, not downstairs.

★ ★ ★ ★ ★

The Monday Before

★ ★ ★ ★ ★

CHAPTER ONE

I told Dad there were two things I wanted when I got out of Kilby. I wanted my teeth fixed, and I wanted to see Faye's grave.

I expected the latter to happen a lot sooner than the former since from what I had read a full set of implants can run upwards of $30k, and I didn't have a job yet, never mind insurance. I should have figured Dad would greet me with a plan as well as a hug. He had probably been working the details the whole nine years, four months, twenty-one days and two hours of what he gingerly liked to refer to as my "time away." I no sooner squeezed into his truck outside the discharge gate than he handed me an envelope with ten $100 bills.

"Of course, dentures aren't as chi-chi as implants, but plates will have to do until we can save up the scratch." He looked at his watch. "We'll have to gun it to get to the South Boulevard, though. Your appointment's at eleven."

It made him nervous that I wasn't more talkative. To fill the dead air he showed off the satellite stations he was newly subscribed to. We listened to Hank Williams sing "My Bucket's Got a Hole in It." Not five miles into the heart of Montgomery, still on Wares Ferry Road, he snapped the radio off.

"You'll have to shave that beard to get you work, you know. Nobody will hire you all hairy and such."

"They'll probably be more scared by what's underneath. Do you know I haven't seen my face since I went in? My last glimpse of it was the mug shot they kept flashing at the trial. I looked like I'd had a meat tenderizer taken to me. I grew the beard out to spare others what I've been sparing myself."

"You're not so rough. You look to be twenty pounds heavier than when you were using. I reckon the weight's filled in the craters and evened out the lumps. I bet you get rid of the briar patch and the ladies will come running. At the very least, chop these things off, lest you want folks calling you Swami."

He flicked one of the twin tails I had braided into the bottom of the beard. They looked like leather shoelaces dangling midway down my chest.

"These are my conversation starters." I started to smile but then I remembered my teeth. Smiling was something I could bear only a little better than looking to a mirror. "See, I can show people how hard you have to scramble on the inside for something to keep you occupied."

"You finished your college degree while inside. That says your time wasn't too unoccupied."

"You can only study twelve, maybe thirteen hours a day. That leaves a whole half of one to fill up. Sleep's no good—there's too much noise. You end up lying on a bunk waiting for your life to crawl by. I can't tell you the hours I killed combing these suckers straight and then re-braiding them. One joker tried nicknaming me Rapunzel, but I put the kibosh on that. It would have sent the wrong signal."

I regretted bringing up the part of prison life Dad didn't know. I could tell he dreaded learning more than what his nightmares had taunted him with, so I shut up. He flipped the radio back on. Now Hank was singing "I'm a Long Gone Daddy."

It seemed to us both that truer words were never spoken.

Soon we came to the east side of Montgomery, the commercial side. Franchise restaurants and big discount retailers gleamed like bejeweled palaces where the strip malls and mom-and-pop car lots had once been. "The whole damn town is moving this direction," Dad said. "Nobody knows where the center of the city is anymore. It keeps drifting east." Then he started pointing to various places, telling me we would lunch here on this day and dine there on that one. I stopped listening when I saw exactly what I didn't want to: a big sparkling Lamar advertising billboard with the words ROLL TIDE in blood crimson.

Goddamn if that wasn't the last thing I needed on my first day of freedom.

"Bama's supposed to have a pretty good year," Dad said as we passed the giant letters. "They got a good shot not just at the SEC west but at the SEC championship. Been a long time coming. You know what else has? You and I may just take a game in together. I was thinking the time may be right for that. Just to prove to ourselves we've got no worries."

"No, sir."

He sighed and changed the subject. "You're coming home at an interesting time, son. Tuesday is Election Day. We may have a new mayor, or we may get four more years of Amory Justice. The paper says it's too close to call."

"Amory Justice is still mayor? Jesus. He's been mayor since I was a kid."

"If he wins, it'll be his *seventh* term—the longest ever in Montgomery history. But you know what? It'll be historic even if he loses. He's up against Walk Compson. That's right, Ennis. *The* Walk Compson. Montgomery may finally have its first black mayor. About time, don't you think? It's only been—what?— *fifty years* since Martin Luther King and Rosa Parks walked these streets."

As if on cue, we passed another billboard: TIME FOR A CHANGE. I recognized Walk Compson's face next to the slogan. He was grayer and jowlier than I remembered, but still recognizable. He should have been, given what a big part of my childhood he was. Once upon a time Walk and Dad had been tight—almost brother tight. In the sixties they both had been big players in the Civil Rights Movement.

"This has been the ugliest goddamn election I've ever seen," Dad was saying. "It's exposed a lot of old wounds people thought were healed. All over black vs. white, of course. . . . Hey, what do they call that computer program people jimmy up pictures with?"

"I wouldn't know, Dad. It's been ten years since I've seen a computer."

"Photoshop—that's it! See, one day Amory's campaign puts out a brochure with a picture of some of his constituents. Just to show he's a diverse guy Amory has one little old black lady in the group. Well, Walk's people go out and track this woman down, and what do you know? Turns out she never posed for that picture! Amory's campaign Photoshopped her into it!

"That's not the crazy part, though. The crazy part is that once Amory's people get over the embarrassment the bad press socks them with, they gather up all of Walk's campaign literature, and what do you think *they* find? Sure enough, in the picture of folks supposedly voting for Walk, all the white people have been sliced in. . . . Like I said: *crazy.* Crazy and ugly. We should be better than this . . ."

I wasn't paying attention. I was listening to the radio. Hank was singing "A Mansion on the Hill."

I could identify.

Bypass traffic was thick, so it was after eleven before we made it to the Troy Highway. Now this was the Montgomery I remembered: RV parks with cheap plastic flags flapping in a hot breeze, rent-to-own rip-off joints, a tattoo parlor called Love Hurts with a boiled-peanut stand at its curb. No BAMA NATION bumper stickers. We pulled up to a row of rubicund offices that looked like garden homes. They were all brick and identical, right down to the cedar chips rimming their hibiscus and St. John's wort. Across the feeder road was an Alabama Beverage Control store, and I wondered if it was the reason Dad chose this particular dentist.

"I'll wait for you out here," he was quick to say.

It wasn't my place to make an issue of how he had spent the past decade, so I went inside and filled out the paperwork. I had almost fallen asleep when the doc strolled in with a clipboard. I could tell right away my appearance shocked him.

"You're Ennis Skinner?"

"That's my name, but I'm not him."

"Ennis Skinner's not too common of a name. If you're not him, I reckon you must get awful tired of answering for him. I sure wouldn't want to share a name with the biggest washout in Alabama football history."

"When it gets annoying I think of how much worse I could have it. My name could be Charlie Manson, you know. Or Jeffrey Dahmer. Or Adolf Hitler. Those names help put mine in perspective, wouldn't you say?"

He tossed the clipboard to a counter. "Well, then, open up, Mr. Skinner. Let's see what we're dealing with."

"I got to warn you first. It's not pretty."

"It rarely is."

It was all of eleven-thirty. It seemed awful early to be so world weary, especially for a dentist.

"I won't be winning any gold stars for dental hygiene," I told him.

"The sooner you let me in there the sooner you'll be strolling out with a kisser full of piano keys. White ones only, of course—no black."

As I figured, he lost the smart-aleck when I gave him his

21

gander. I had all of six teeth to my name—four top incisors, a back molar, and a single bottom canine. I considered telling him that I was a freshly minted baccalaureate, but I doubted that would make him think better of the rot. There's only one way you denude a mouth like mine, and I could see from the way the dentist's brows went all wormy he knew it as well as I did.

"How long you been out?" he asked, a little flutter in his voice.

"Out or off?"

"Whichever you prefer."

"I've been out of prison for all of ninety minutes. But I've been off the stuff since before the war, before 9/11 even. I spent the millennium locked up. I've walked out into a whole new world, haven't I?"

None of this was reassuring him, so I reassured him.

"I want a set of teeth that are as clean as I kept myself while I was in the pokey. You might say my teeth are my reward, but I got a lot of amends to make before I can pat myself on the back. Either way, you're safe, Doc. You're the one with the weaponry, you know."

I nodded to the tray of scrapers and picks next to the cuspidor.

"You prefer gas or a needle?" he asked, both of us eyeing the tray.

"Gas."

"Thank God."

I think he gave me an extra squirt just to make sure I was immobile. I guess he was afraid I would jump up and gum his jugular with my six remaining teeth. Well, I couldn't blame him. I'm sure he had read in the newspapers all the hysteria about how violent tweakers can be. Maybe his wife nagged him about getting out of the one-day denture business because a racket that once made its gravy off gramps and grannies now attracted mostly lowlifes. Who knows? I just wished he had believed me when I said I was off meth for good.

The incisors came out easy. A little wiggling with the elevator and two yanks of the forceps at most. The canine was tougher but nothing like the molar. For that the dentist had to bust out something that looked like an apple-corer. In Kilby I had yanked out two molars myself using nothing but a fork. Most guys stole silverware from the cafeteria to file tines into shivs, but I bent mine into a customized extractor.

The doc clamped the tool over my tooth like a ratchet and rocked it up and down until I thought my jaw would bust in half. Sweat droplets started beading his forehead, and he had to call in a nurse to swab them before they burned his eyes. When the root wouldn't give he hunched over and threw his weight into his front foot. His whole fist was practically in my craw. I heard a pop and my tongue instinctively shot into the socket. Of course, I couldn't feel a thing, but I didn't need to. I knew what hollowness felt like; I had felt hollow for a long time.

"We'll have to wait for the bleeding to stop." He packed gauze along the gum and then left for a while. It was such a while and I was so gassed I dozed off for a long time. When the dentist returned he carried a pair of horseshoe-shaped pans filled with pink goo. I caught him looking at the tray of tools, making sure no scrapers or picks were missing. We stared at each other until he realized I was still glazed from the nitrous oxide. That seemed to give him some confidence. He jammed the first pan into my mouth, not gentle at all.

"That's for 1988," I expected him to say as he took an impression of my top plate. "That's for what you cost Bama all this time hence."

He didn't let out a peep, though. Even numb I could taste the goo, which sent saliva streaming down the back of my throat.

When I gagged, the doc gave me a Dixie cup of water and disappeared with the pans. This time I thought the office would close before he came back. This time I waited at least three hours.

When the dentist finally came back, he carried a set of acrylic teeth.

"These are called economy dentures for a reason," he said, bonding them into my mouth. "They'll make you look pretty but they won't take much stress. Stay away from tough chews. No kickboxing, either. If you give them too much of a workout you'll have to come back and upgrade to our custom brand. You can catch bullets with those."

He reached into a drawer, fishing for a mirror.

"Say hello to the new you."

I must have been his first patient ever not to primp and pose. He didn't know how to react when I shut my eyes and rolled out of the chair toward the door. Apparently, the doc didn't think I deserved such a clean getaway.

"It's a good thing you're not the same Ennis Skinner that got Bama in all that probation trouble years ago. This way I don't have to embarrass you by not asking for your autograph."

"You know how you can rest assured I'm not *that* Ennis Skinner?"

I gave him such a sarcastic grin I thought the PoliGrip might snap and shoot my new dentures straight out of my face.

"I pull for Auburn. War Eagle, Doc."

Outside I discovered I had guessed right. Dad had walked over to the ABC store for a bottle of Conecuh Ridge. It sat on his truck hood, right out in the open. I didn't need to look at it to see how much he had downed. From the way Dad was leaned up against the car I knew he and the bottle both were two-thirds gone.

"Conecuh Ridge is the official state spirits now," he sputtered. "Pretty funny, huh? State spirits from a state-owned spirits shop. God bless the ABC board. What's next? Maybe Goody's Headache Powder can be the official Alabama hangover remedy. Ooh, wait, what am I thinking? Your teeth. Smile for me, child."

I brushed past him and grabbed the bottle. You could hear shards plink on the windshield when it exploded against the brick wall. That's how hard I chucked it—glass bounced all the way back over the sidewalk, showering the truck like hail.

"Today's not easy on either of us," Dad said, sheepishly.

"No point in making it harder than it has to be. I know you resent what I've put you through, but there's better ways of communicating it. You wouldn't appreciate me going phooey this fast."

I thought he was going to cry. I had only seen him do that twice, first when I was sentenced and then when the board granted my parole. Dad shook off his tears, though, when he remembered for a second time that he had forgotten all about my teeth.

"They look good, Ennis. Real good. Almost natural."

We left the broken glass and the whiskey splatter on the wall before anybody came rushing out of the dentist's office. When we made it to the bypass, Dad started back toward the residential east side, but I told him to turn left toward downtown.

"You don't want to head up to Oakwood? I thought you said you wanted to see—"

"Pull in here real quick."

I ran into a Walgreen's and bought some toiletries. When I came out I didn't tell Dad what they were, which only made him more anxious. I caught him eyeballing the bag.

"Don't worry. It's not Sudafed. Those days are done."

"Oh, I know," he lied. "They've got laws for that now. You can't buy a drop of cold medicine or anything with ephedrine anymore without signing a phone book's worth of paper. Nothing like a law to save folks from themselves, eh? Next you know some Joe'll figure out how to extract a high from Preparation H and the government will start tracking sales of that. Us honest ones will have to hand over a driver's license just to take the itch out of our hemorrhoids."

I did my best to ignore the bitter edge in his voice. I figured I deserved it. I decided to change the subject, so I told him I would like to see the new house. Of course, it wasn't new to him. He had sold the one I grew up in only a short time after I went into Kilby, right after my mother died. She just flat-out collapsed three weeks after I was sentenced. Heart attack, they said, but I knew better. She died of disappointment.

To spare himself having to live with the memories, Dad had moved into a little two-bedroom a couple blocks on the boho side of Felder, down where the college kids threw block parties where they played Jarts ironically and did earnest keg stands until four A.M. When he first showed me pictures of the place I had to laugh. The thought of Dad trying to hit the sack in the middle of all that coed revelry was a gut-buster.

"We'll have to share a bathroom," he told me as we pulled onto the gravel drive. "I couldn't see any point in getting a two-seater when it's only me."

"You weren't thinking you might like a woman to share your place? No woman will ever settle for one bathroom."

He wasn't sure if I meant his woman or mine. "Let's give it some time before you start having company over."

I ignored that swat, too. *Go ahead and let the Conecuh Ridge do your talking,* I said to myself.

Then I went inside, and first thing I saw the two picture frames. The first was so huge it damn near dwarfed the house.

It filled an entire wall. I could've handled that if what Dad had framed was a baby picture or some memento of my dead mother's but, no, he had gone out and made a shrine of my old jersey. The one from my sophomore year, no less—1988, the season it all went phooey.

As if that weren't bad enough there were pictures tucked in the corners of the frame. They were from my last game, the Sun Bowl at which Alabama beat Army 29-28. I stared at my last name and my number (12), and I thought *Even in my old man's eyes I'm never not going to be that guy. Even in my old man's eyes I'll always be a screw-up . . .*

"Look at the floors," Dad said. He was nervous, afraid I was going to make a stink. "I think this place was a painter's studio originally. The floor had dribbles all over it. I started to put some carpet down but the wood was too pretty to cover up. I sanded and re-stained them myself. You can't tell I didn't have it professionally done, can you?"

I didn't answer. I was looking at the second picture. This one was of Dad. The picture that made him famous and put him in the history books. In 1961 he and Walk Compson were Freedom Riders alongside the great John Lewis. When they rode into the Montgomery Greyhound station they were jumped and beaten by a mob of angry whites. An AP reporter happened to catch the mess the pummeling made of Dad's face, and the next day his picture was in every major newspaper in the country. Since then not a Civil Rights book in print had failed to reproduce it. It made for a great story, even if the picture was far from flattering. In it blood streamed all the way from Dad's jaw down to the belly of his black tie and white shirt. He was fishing a broken tooth off his tongue, too.

Teeth were a big motif in our family, I realized.

"I'll take your frame down if you want," Dad said. "It was just my way of saying I'm still proud. You were a good person,

Ennis. No matter what happened. You just went astray."

I was already in the bathroom by the time his voice trailed off. I threw a towel over the mirror before I saw my reflection. I rinsed my face and then took out the Barbasol and disposable razors I had bought at the Walgreen's. I wrenched the plastic safety edge off one of the razors to expose the blade and then sawed the braids out of my beard.

I knew Dad wouldn't have scissors handy, so I grabbed a fistful of hair and hacked as close as I could get without gouging skin. By the time I finished the sink was piled with curly gray clumps. I couldn't believe how little of my natural almond-brown was left. I was thirty-nine, for Christ's sake, and gray as a ghost.

I spread the Barbasol over my face and scraped away the whiskers. It had been so long since I was clean-shaven that I had to put on a second layer of cream and go over the stubborn areas again to get them smooth. Because the razor was cheap blood dribbled down my cheek and chin. I dug around in Dad's drawer and found a styptic pencil. I wished I had the dentist's gas handy to take away the sting—it about doubled me over.

When I came out it was Dad's turn to look stung. I figured it was because I had carved my face to ribbons.

"You look sixteen," he said instead. He was welling up even. I wanted to tell him his sentimentality was just another way of reminding me what I had put him through, but that seemed ungrateful. I decided to walk off my irritation. That irritated Dad right back.

"You're hoofing it up to Oakwood Cemetery? We're in the worst heat wave in Montgomery history. This is our eighth straight day of hundred-plus weather. There's an alert on. Even if you make it up there you won't be but a puddle."

"I haven't stepped fifty straight paces without coming to razor wire since I don't know when. I'm looking forward to every one of those hundred degrees. It'll be just like two-a-days in August. I want to remember the feeling of those. I'd like to earn my sweat for a change."

"I'd feel better if we stuck together."

"I'd have to be pretty stupid to start trouble less than twelve hours out."

"It might take stupid to start trouble, but it wouldn't take but bad luck for trouble to find you."

I was already to the door. "Do me a favor and don't go buy more Conecuh Ridge. I'd hate to bust a bottle on your new floor."

But Dad wasn't about to let me get away without getting the last word.

"You remember what I used to say about expectations? I used to say you were a victim of too many high ones. You were just a kid. I put them on you, and you cracked. Everybody deserves redemption. But redemption is about expectations, too. I don't want you feeling like I'm putting pressure on you, but you need to know my expectations for you are plenty high. You'll only ever get one second chance, Ennis."

I figured he deserved his say after standing by me for so long, so I took my licking. Only when I was sure he was through did I walk out on him and his expectations.

I didn't take the direct route to Oakwood Cemetery. That would've been some kind of stupid, because the direct route would've taken me past the neighborhood where all my trouble started. That neighborhood was centered upon Fifth Street, which back in the mid-nineties I would come to know as Recipe Row. It earned that nickname because nearly every one of the little shotgun shanties on Fifth Street cooked its methamphetamine according to a different formula sold to them by High C, the man I had tried to kill.

I had no clue exactly where in Oakwood Faye was buried, and the guard shack was locked up, so I had to hoof the hills of burnt grass searching out the newer sections of gravestones. Along the way I passed Hank Williams's grave. I had never once seen old Hank's memorial without there being empty beer bottles littering the marble coping. It's supposed to be a tribute, but all it does is provide folks an excuse to mythologize their benders. I might have scooped up the empties and pitched them in the culvert on the cemetery's back lot if a pair of tourists didn't wander up on me. They caught me reading the date of Hank's wife Audrey's death. Otherwise I would've shuffled off before they could start in on the small talk. They asked directions to the place that inspired "Kow-Liga." I fudged some directions up Highway 231 that would get them to Blue Ridge and out of my hair. After they left I regretted shafting them. I realized I was mad because of what they'd said:

"Anywhere you go in the world Alabama is famous for three things: Hank Williams, Martin Luther King, and football. Roll Tide!"

To find Faye I had to pester a Mexican gardener I came across. He radioed the sexton's office for her plot number. No wonder I couldn't spot her on my own. She didn't even have a goddamn headstone, just a cheap little marker that didn't seem any bigger than your average brick: ALICE "FAYE" JAMES, it read. 1964–2004. Nothing else. She was thirty-nine when she died, I realized. My age now. Somehow keeling over dead from heart failure made her life seem incomplete. I decided that whoever paid for the brick must have been on the skids. That was the only acceptable explanation for not springing for at least a line of Scripture.

I sat next to her grave and talked to her for a while. I told her I only remembered the good things, which was a lie not even a dead woman would fall for. Still, I recited what few memories didn't make me wince. I remembered her ginger-colored skin. Her jet-black hair. The curves of her body when she danced. How she always smelled of talcum before we got hooked so bad we stank of ammonia. She perfumed herself with it. I remembered how after a hot bath she would let me rub her down with it. I thought about those rubdowns so hard I imagined I could smell the talcum. That was about the one good memory I had to cling to.

Maybe it was the nostalgia, maybe the heat, but before too long I felt nauseous, so I left Oakwood and hoofed it down to the boho. Along the way I passed the church on Dexter Avenue where Martin Luther King, Jr., preached during the Montgomery bus boycott of 1955–56. Every single bank sign on the block screamed 108° IN THE SHADE! except for one that said DON'T ASK—YOU DON'T WANT TO KNOW.

Even though I tried to keep out of direct sunlight, I was plastered in sweat and needing water by the time I crossed under the interstate and hit the boho. In my day there was only one real bar down here, a dump called the Gypsy Wrangler. It was a stupid name considering the last time either a gypsy or a wrangler was seen in Montgomery the president was probably Chester A. Arthur or somebody. I had wasted enough life and money in that snake hole, so I crossed to the restaurant side of the street. A new joint had opened mid-block, a nouveau Mexico place if the sign was any indication: EL REY BURRITO LOUNGE.

What the fuck is a burrito lounge? I wondered.

It had been a long time since I had eaten Mexican, much less fancy Mexican. I wouldn't be eating it today either for fear of losing my dentures to a quesadilla, but I damn sure could enjoy the smell of free man's food. I went inside.

Right away I wished I hadn't. I wished I had sucked it up and settled for the Gypsy Wrangler. The guy who used to tend bar there—a guy I had hoped to avoid for a while—now tended bar here.

Bubba Burch and I stared at each other, neither blinking.

"You serve sweet tea?" I finally said.

"We serve it sweet and unsweet."

"You'll serve me?"

His rubbed the sharp V of his chin until I thought it would wear down to a U. Then he shrugged and started wiping fingerprints off a smudgy Captain Morgan bottle. "We're not allowed to discriminate—not until we're given a reason, anyway. The far booth is open."

From what I could see, every booth was open. There were exactly two customers in the place.

"You don't want me sitting at your bar? You afraid I'll gab your ears off, Bub?"

"There's only one thing I want to hear you say to me, Ennis. Since I doubt I'm any more likely to hear it today than I was ten years ago, I'll pass on the conversation. Like I said, far booth."

As I headed to that far booth I saw him tuck his tip jar behind the counter, out of reach.

Well, I deserved that, so my feelings weren't too hurt. They were, though, when Bubba stopped his waitress from coming to my table. She was a stomping redhead in satin gym shorts and knee-high socks. As if that weren't enough she sported pigtails bunched together with fat red rubber bands. All that was missing was a lollipop, but the eye candy wasn't what interested me. I was more curious what she smelled like. I was trying to exorcise the memory of talcum. Instead, I had to contend with more than a little whiff of Bubba's irritation.

"You don't trust me around your girls?" I asked when he delivered my order.

"I've known a few guys to get sent away, but I've only ever

run into two after they made parole. You're the second. The first is a dingle we call the Bicycle Rapist. I didn't let him through the door when he came calling for sweet tea, much less offer him a back booth, so enjoy what hospitality you're getting. However little it is, it's what you're due."

He started to walk away. I was wiping up the ring he had spilled when he set my glass down none too welcomingly.

"What's got you slinging hash these days? The place seems a little staid compared to the Wrangler."

"A better quality clientele. This one's more trustworthy." He didn't bother looking over his shoulder. "And there's no hash on the menu, Hardboil. We're upscale."

"You do know I'll be paying you back, right? Don't think I forgot. Not ever. I plan on making my amends. I just have to get a job first. You're not hiring, are you?"

Bubba was back behind the bar, almost smiling. Not a humored smile, mind you. It was one of those *what-shit-I-got-to-endure* ones. A tolerant smile. The bare minimum kind.

"You owe me two dollars for that drink. Anything else is too past due for me to care about collecting."

So that's how it was going to be. Well, I didn't want to feel that bitter, so I took a slug of tea and was glad it was sugared enough to wash the bad taste out of my mouth. Meanwhile, I did some quick math. At ten percent interest annually compounded I figured the five Franklins I had pilfered from Bubba's tip jar the night everything went phooey and I shot High C now added up to an even grand. I watched Bubba wipe down a fat decanter of orange juice and I thought, *You'll get your money and then some, pup. You wait and see. And when you do you won't be able to look at me like I'm something you wipe off a shoe.*

I had finished my drink and was contemplating something stiffer when they waltzed in. Two punks, one itchy and young, the other a good ten, maybe even twenty, years older. Tubbier, too, with creased skin and worn features that made me think of a bald tire this side of showing its threads. They were both in oversized surfer shorts and identical ROLL TIDE T-shirts. Comedians, both of them.

I knew right away they weren't here for the hash, upscale or not. They kept flicking their eyes my direction as they pretended to study the menu. Try the guacamole, I wanted to call out. Instead I motioned over the stomping redhead with the pigtails and knee-highs. She didn't want to come, but she did.

"Bubba said I'm not to wait on you. Not even for a refill."

"Bubba's got his hands full with Chip and Dale up there. I don't want a refill, anyway. I'm cashing out."

I handed her the last two $100 bills in my pocket.

"That's a lot of change to ask me to make over a two-buck tea."

"Your job is to sneak one of these into Bubba's jar without him knowing. The other hundred is yours. Consider it commission for being asked to be sneaky."

She was looking at my face, but not into my eyes.

"Did you just start shaving today? A guillotine might've done less damage."

"No need to square your shoulders on me, Red. There are no strings here; I'm just trying to help you out. What with Bubba quarantining you from tables, you can't be making your tips."

"Yours is the only table he's quarantined me from. Ever. That means you must be some sort of bad boy."

I started to smile, but stopped. I didn't deserve to smile yet.

"You got any tattoos to go with those freckles?"

"Not anywhere I can show you here. Health inspector, you know."

I rolled up my sleeve and showed her the face on my forearm.

"St. Jude, in case you don't recognize him. He's the patron

saint of desperate causes. I got this back when I thought I was one, but I'm saving up to get it altered. What would you think of St. Dominic Savio?"

"What's he the patron saint of? Big tippers?"

"No. Choirboys."

She smiled slyly as she tucked the bills in her apron. "I hope for your sake Dominic Savio has some muscle. You need a savior, I can tell."

"I'm doing all right on my own. Only one thing the saints can't protect me from."

"And what's that?"

"Your perfume."

Her brows shot up. For a second I thought she was going to hurl my money back in my face.

"So much for no strings, eh? A line like that's more than a string, dude—it's a rope. And I don't let myself get rope-a-doped, not even by choirboys who claim to have found religion."

"You see Augie and Doggie up there as well as I do," I said. "In about thirty seconds, I've got to get past them and through that door without besmirching the reputation of this fine establishment. It's better for everyone here if they run me out rather than your real customers. A pretty scent makes for a nice send-off, that's all I'm saying. It'll help me not begrudge having to go."

She peeked toward the bar. The two punks weren't pretending to read the menu anymore. They were pretty much gaping at us. As for Bubba, he wasn't so much gaping as glaring. Red leaned into my booth, pretending to make sure the woozies of hot sauce hadn't been squeezed dry, and buried my face in the curve of her neck. Suddenly, you could've said talcum to me and I would have thought you were speaking Taiwanese.

"Go for the alley, not the sidewalk," she whispered. "There's a fence on the far side of the parking lot that backs up to a neighborhood. If St. Jude can get you over it, you ought to be able to lose them among the houses."

Only when she strolled off did I realize I was sitting on my hands.

I stood up and tried to make it by the bar as nonchalantly as I knew how. At least the punks didn't start anything inside. I would have hated to be banned from Bubba's before I got to sample something more than the sweet tea.

Two steps outside and to the alley I realized Red wasn't the only one who knew about that jumpable fence. The punks had it blocked with a cherry-red SUV. For a second I thought I was hallucinating. In 108-degree heat a cherry-red SUV looks an awful lot like a juicy strawberry.

I stared at the SUV's hood, thinking I could use it as a vault to get over the fence. Then again, I had to make it up there. It had been twenty years since I last measured my vertical leap.

"Don't make us chase you," said the older one with the bald-tire face. "It's too damn hot to run."

I threw up my hands and turned. They came at me slowly, swimming through the humidity.

"You're missing one, aren't you?" I said in lieu of bolting. "Where's Dewey?"

"Don't talk," the twitchy one went. "That's the second rule after don't run. It's too damn hot for talk, too."

"I figure you for Moe," I told Treadface. "Your buddy here looks like Larry, but there's nobody in the SUV. I figured that's where Curly or at least Shemp would be, soaking up some air conditio—"

The heat got the better of Twitchy. His fist shot straight into the consonant coming out of my mouth. The punch was such a stunner I thought he had knocked my tongue out the back of my head. My neck snapped back and my crown bashed into the brick wall.

"That's for 1988," the younger one said.

I lost balance and keeled over onto my hands and knees. I tried to gather my senses, but only one thought came through the pain coherently: I should have gone ahead and had that dentist upgrade me to custom dentures when I had the chance.

That way I might have been spared the sight of my bottom plate, busted in two, lying in the ant heap where I hocked it and several runny gobs of blood.

CHAPTER TWO

I didn't need my college degree to figure out where I was being shanghaied to. At least, that's what I thought until the SUV ripped straight past Recipe Row without so much as a flick of a blinker.

"You know," I said from the backseat, cradling my bottom plate in my palm. "All day I've had this feeling that it would take a mighty stroke of luck to make it to dinner without hearing from High C. A guy can forget a lot of things in ten years, but where he did the deed that he got sent away for usually isn't one of them. If we're not headed to his place, you mind telling me where we are going?"

Twitchy wasn't just the more hotheaded of this Heckle and Jeckle—he was the more succinct, too. "Cork it," he grunted, "before you get another stroke of luck in the teeth."

At least his buddy wasn't so averse to conversation.

"C hasn't lived on Fifth Street in a long time. That neighborhood's not good for anyone to live in anymore. Real estate on the Row sucks right now."

So much for small talk. I crooked my head to stanch the blood flow from my lip and tried to predict our route through the tinted windows. We rode I-85 east toward Atlanta for about ten miles before getting off at an unfamiliar exit called Chantilly Parkway. I remembered what Dad said about the whole town heading this direction. Sure enough, we passed a bunch of Winn-Dixies and Wal-Marts and Home Depots until Treadface

38

cranked us left into a gated community. WELCOME TO "THE WOODS," a sign said. What a fucking name for a neighborhood, I thought. What was its slogan? A GREAT PLACE TO DUMP A BODY?

We pulled into the garage of a gray stucco McMansion with a Kelly green door. I hoped I never had to pick this house out of a lineup because it looked like every other goddamned one on the block. As the garage door chugged to a close behind us, Twitchy yanked me out of the SUV and shoved me through a back door that opened onto a back patio with a kidney-shaped pool. The water appeared to be just as Kelly green as the front door.

"Black algae," High C said, shaking his head at the pea soup. "It's come closer to killing me than you ever did, Ennis."

In nothing but a hip-hugging, Euro-style swimsuit, he looked heavier than I remembered, although he was just as hirsute. Mountain-man beards haven't really been fashionable among the criminal element since Grizzly Adams and that guy from the Oak Ridge Boys made them seem more silly than scary, but guys like High C don't change their style. C had been growing that beard ever since he joined the Outlaws Motorcycle Club. That was forty years ago, when he dropped out of UC–San Diego three credits short of a chemistry degree to become a star methmaker for the most notorious bike gang this side of the Hell's Angels. I remembered C telling me that he had only been clean-shaven once in all that time hence, and only then because he had caught a bad case of lice off an Ozark stripper.

"How's the baby?" I asked. When he scrunched his eyes in confusion I pointed to the long horizontal scar that bisected his navel. "You look like you've had a Caesarian section."

He smiled. "And here I figured your sense of humor was a product of all the crank you used to do. Tell me, squirt, how's your old man?"

"Let's leave my old man out of any conversing we do. In fact, let's not converse at all. I'd really rather not get my parole revoked my first day out. I was told not to consort with known felons."

That wounded him. "I've only ever been locked up once, and it wasn't even a felony. Smart guys know how not to get caught. That's the difference between you and me. By the way, how did you manage to spend your whole time at Kilby? It's supposed to be a receiving center. You should've done your time down in Holman."

I didn't much feel like answering.

"Let me guess," C went. "The warden grew up in Lee County. What Aubie wouldn't want the privilege of saying he had Ennis Skinner locked up in his population?"

"Not quite. He wasn't from Alabama at all. Starkville, through and through."

"Mississippi State, huh? Well, I wouldn't have thought one of them would have had the gump. Go figure. But back to your dad. I hope you know ole Quentin Skinner needs a lot of nursing. That Civil Rights crowd has had a tough time growing old. It can't be easy to have been so certain that you changed the world in your youth, only to find it's still a shitpot all these years later. Have you heard about this mayoral election that's going on? A shitpot, Ennis."

He smiled from under his beard. "The whole time you were away I was worried for Quentin. You getting hoosegowed put him over the edge. I can't tell you how many DUIs he would have by now if the police didn't feel sorry for him. I was going to send my boys here over to Huntingdon to keep an eye on him, but by that point Quentin was done professoring. Tell him why, boys."

"Quentin got fired from Huntingdon College for teaching drunk," the younger punk said with a grin. "He passed out right in a lecture hall."

"Slept through his own puke, they say," the fatter one added.

Of course, this wasn't news to me. I had heard the story.

"I appreciate your not hassling Dad while I was in," I told C. "Not everybody in your position would have accepted that the bad blood between us was our business, not his. If you want me to say thanks for watching over him in my absence, then here you go: thanks. But that's all you're getting out of me. I don't know what point you're making by hijacking me here, but I've done my time and I want to be left alone. I've got plenty of amends to make but yours aren't one of them. The way I reckon, the bullet you took from me was pre-payment for what you let happen to Faye."

"And just what do you think I let happen to Faye?"

"You let her die."

We traded stares. Then C harrumphed and plucked a robe off an Adirondack lounge chair. He tried to cinch the terrycloth belt around his waist, but the hump of his gut stuck out too hard and too far for the robe to cover much. Swear to god, he looked like he had a Volkswagen bug parked in that belly.

"Come inside with me. You need to see what I've been up to while you were sitting out your sentence."

I hadn't taken two steps sandwiched between him and Zig and Zag before C abruptly stopped. He stuck his face into mine, so close I could smell dinner. The comb strokes in his beard looked like plough troughs in a tilled field.

"Just so you know, ten years for the three feet of sewer line they had to cut out to keep me from going septic doesn't seem like justice, not to me. While you're deciding what you will and won't thank me for, you ought to think about the fact that I didn't make a victim impact statement at your parole hearing. I could have, you know. The D.A. was after me to. I'm pretty sure I could have convinced the board that a decade isn't enough time to rehabilitate an attempted murderer."

There wasn't much I could say to that, so I didn't argue. We went through a sliding glass door. Just the two of us, though: C ordered Archie and Jughead to keep to the patio, even though the concrete couldn't have felt hotter if you'd stood over an open grill with steak sizzling up your nostrils.

Inside my first thought was that High C must have robbed a Pier 1. The whole place was outfitted with throw rugs and accent tables and spiffy couches and chairs done up in colors you would probably need a dictionary to recognize as a shade for green and beige. That's not to mention the candles and sconces and chi-chi lamps crammed into every cranny. Yes, C had gone suburban. It was a big step up from his old shotgun shack on Recipe Row when what passed for décor was a powder-wigged portrait of Handel thumbtacked to the wall. Back in the day, if you wanted to tick C off, all you had to do was ask if it was a picture of his mother.

"I bet you've never heard of *Fidelio,*" he said, flicking a remote control. Suddenly, the room shook to the sound of a quavering soprano. The more C thumbed the volume button, the more I thought the vibrato in that voice would shake the sconces right off the honey-blush peach walls.

"It's the only opera Beethoven ever wrote. Did you know that? Of course you didn't. You've got a college degree now, but what do you really know? All you know is that you feel guilty about screwing up your life and the lives of every football moron within two hundred miles of the Black Warrior River."

"You didn't have to bring me to Hearst Castle to insult me. You could've had your boys knock out my teeth and be done with me."

He was listening to the music, not me. He was an opera nut. That was how he'd gotten the nickname High C. It had nothing to do with the drug formulas he cooked up in that chemistry kitchen he called an imagination. Instead, it referred to the musical note two octaves above middle C. According to rumor, that was the highest one he could hit when he sang along with his favorite arias and recitatives.

"You'd like the plot of *Fidelio.* See, what happens is that this Spanish noblewoman, Lenore, dresses up as a man so she can get a job as a prison guard to be near her husband, Florestan, who's a victim of political prosecution. Only when she assumes the identity of Fidelio, this other local gal, Marzelline, falls in love with him—or her, as the case may be. There are all sorts of hijinks and hilarity, of course, but the important point is that at the climactic moment Lenore rips off her costume to save Florestan from certain death. So, you see, it's all about how we men are redeemed by the love of a good woman. Now that I think about it, I should've sent you a CD of *Fidelio* while you were in the pokey. You could've passed the time wondering which of the guards up there at Kilby was Faye in disguise, waiting for the opportune time to spring you."

When he could tell I wasn't amused he clicked the music off, disappointed. Even so, the soprano's quaver rang in my ears.

"Maybe I'm nothing but a screw-up," I admitted. "But at least I know it. No matter how high culture you want to think you are because you know Vivaldi isn't a brand of motor oil, you're just a methmaker. Even among lowlifes that's the equivalent of a short-order cook flipping eggs in lard. You're the same two-bitter you were when you rolled into this county twenty years ago showing weak-wills how to boil the pseudoephedrine out of their Sudafed."

"I didn't 'show' them my wizardry for free, you dope. I charged them for the opportunity to learn those secrets. You're just jealous because your football boosters never gave you the $10,000 you needed to enroll in one of my classes. Why don't you drop the Prince Galahad routine and admit that's why you shot me: you thought that with the cost of a bullet you could get hold of my recipes."

"You know why I shot you. I did it for Faye."

He rolled his eyes. "That snatch again. Goddamn, you're just naive enough to believe your own bullshit. Well, if that's what it takes to ride your hobby-horse. In the meantime, I can rest comfortably knowing that not too many short-order cooks ever made my kind of cake. Chefs, yes—cooks, no."

"What's with the past tense business? Are you trying to tell me you're retired?"

"Not retired, no. Reconfiguring the market, something smart businessmen know is inevitable. You didn't read many newspapers upstate, did you? Well, go try buying that Sudafed you were talking about and you'll see. Nowadays you can't find it or Actifed on a store shelf. It's all kept under lock and key by the pharmacists, who have to keep a record of your name for anything tougher than a cough drop."

I didn't let on that Dad had mentioned this earlier. I didn't want C thinking we'd talked about my old life.

"You'll be happy to know your tax dollars don't pay for much imagination," he went on. "The law's called the Combat Meth Act. Congress voted it into law about two years ago. They lumped it onto the ass-end of the Patriot Act, as if meth were some sort of bin Laden plot. Of course, the law hasn't stopped anybody from doing the shit—it's just made it harder for home-cookers to get their mits on the precursors. And you know what that means, don't you? The Mexicans have swooped in to corner the market. Jesus, the government couldn't have done a better job of sending the manufacturing over the border than if they'd made it an official part of NAFTA. But that's okay. I saw it coming years ago. When grandmas started making meth at their crochet clubs, I knew the glory days weren't going to last. It was only a matter of time before the jackboots marched into action.

You gumming up my intestines got me thinking about the need to diversify. I decided a smart guy would find a legal way to flog his wares. It took a while to put together a business plan and find a reliable First Amendment lawyer, but I wasn't in a hurry. I knew the market was there, just waiting for the right guy to make it happen."

He walked over to a mocha-brown bookshelf that probably smelled mocha-brown, too, and plucked off what looked like a Sears catalogue. Only when he tossed it to me did I catch the title: *Mysteries of Methamphetamine Manufacture: Exposed!* And in almost the same sized letters: *By High C, The Galloping Gourmet of Psychedelic Cookery.*

"You're kidding me, right?"

He wasn't. His pride had him glowing like kryptonite.

"All those years I was teaching goobers how to synthesize reagents for $10,000 a pop—I had to do that on the down low, you know, because you get caught with a Bunsen burner and a beaker of phenyl acetone and to the narcs you're Al Capone. But a book—Jesus, the things you can get away with. Seriously. Look at the disclaimer on the copyright page."

He was insulted when I tossed the book to his coffee table without flipping a single page. C slapped his hand over his heart and recited what he wanted me to read like it was the Pledge of Allegiance: *"This book is sold for information purposes only. Neither the author nor publisher intends for any information herein to be used for criminal purposes."*

"Freedom of speech, baby. The blackshirts can't touch me."

"You want me to believe you're some kind of author?"

"I'm not just the author—there's no money in authoring. I'm *the publisher.* About four years ago I bought out a little imprint house here in Montgomery. Who knew we even had one? It was putting out all these dark and dreary gunk novels by one-nut professors nobody wanted to read. I went in and told the staff,

'Anybody here who can't take the heat of Uncle Sam wanting to sew his lips shut better pack up and head to North Korea right now to live in tyranny. Because we're going to stand up for the Constitution. Anarchy ahoy!' I liked that line so much that's what I renamed the imprint: Anarchy Ahoy. *Mysteries* was our first book. We sold out the initial press run in two weeks. We did a second edition right before the Combat Meth Act, and we did another 250,000 copies at $19.95. You know who else sells 250k a year? *To Kill a Mockingbird*, that's fucking who, and my book's not even assigned reading for eighth graders. Of course, in-store retailers won't touch me, but who needs them when we have the Internet? Any crankhead with computer access can find us with two clicks on Amazon.com. Before that damn law, we never ranked less than the fortieth most popular among technology books. We used to average right around number nine, in fact."

"So you got to build your very own kidney-shaped pool thanks to Amazon.com. Too bad the feds made your book obsolete. Maybe if you'd been able to do a third edition you could've afforded some algaecide to clear it up."

"Oh, my business is doing just fine. I figure even with Combat Meth Anarchy Ahoy can still do fifty thou or so a year of *Mysteries*. It's not like pseudoephedrine doesn't exist anymore; you just have to go to the black market instead of smurfing CVS to get it. Plus I know how to diversify. I do sixteen or so books a year, each for a different market segment. We also do *The Everyday Guide to Guerilla Warfare, How to Create a New Identity, The Hit Man Handbook*. God bless the American free enterprise system. Like I said, it's all in the disclaimer."

"Bully for you. Now that we've caught up, I should be going. Speaking of CVS, maybe Yogi and BooBoo out there could run me by one on the way back. It'd be nice if they kicked in for some Krazy Glue since they kicked in my face."

I showed him my busted bottom plate, which was still in my palm.

"Hey, that gives me an idea for a new title," C said with mock excitement. *"How to Stomp the Crud Out of a Moron without Leaving a Mark."*

I didn't laugh.

"Don't act so pained," he said to me. "Did you really think two guys with our kind of history could live in a town this small and stay out of each other's way? We have a connection few people have: shooter and shootee. I hate to say this out of respect for ole Quentin the Pukedrunk, but that's a bond thicker than a father and son's. And that's not to mention things that tie us together that you don't even know about . . ."

He gave me a wink.

"For example . . . Faye. How well do you really think you knew her, Ennis? What if you'd never met her at all? I know my life would've been different without that tuna. She's the reason you shot me. Notice I said 'different,' not 'better,' though. Because in the end, you shooting me changed my life in a lot of positive ways—"

"I don't want to hear anything more about Faye. Not even her name. Not out of you, not out of anybody."

He took a step toward me. Stroking his beard, he looked like a devil.

"See! That's defensiveness I hear in your voice. And defensiveness means you have feelings you don't want to expose—like *regret,* maybe. Let's face it: if not for Faye, our worlds never would've collided. We would be perfect strangers to this day. I understand what havoc she wreaked on you because I'm a victim of it, too! If you can't share those feelings with me, Ennis—those *what-I-might've-been-if-not-for-that-gash* feelings— well, then who can you share them with? Your dad? Shit—the boys can tell you what ole Quentin said about Faye while you were at Kilby. He used to say it, drunk and out loud, in the damn lecture hall in front of all those little Methodist girls. . . . Yes, I'll be happy to tell you, but I've got to warn you: you'll learn a new word or two."

"I'll deal with my memories myself. I don't need a therapist. Especially not one who used to be a two-bit junk cooker."

He shook his head. "I keep telling you that 'cook' and 'chef' are two different things. Fortunately, I don't take things personally. Maybe that's one of the few ways we're different. But let me ask you this, Joe Namath: in all that time you spent getting high with Faye, did she ever once tell you she had a kid?"

It might as well have been a rhetorical question. The look on my face told him she hadn't.

"The kid is nineteen now. Her name is Caroline, but Faye never called her that. She nicknamed the girl Dixie. Kind of hokey, I know, but Faye had a lot of Southern hokum in her. Now Dixie's a pretty little thing, no thanks to Faye. Faye's parents took Dixie in the first time Faye got busted, probably right around the time she met you."

He stopped to enjoy the additional surprise I couldn't hide. During the whole seven or eight years of our joint downhill ride Faye had told me repeatedly she was an orphan. She blamed that for her susceptibility to drugs. "I've never felt loved," she used to say.

"It's hard to protect kids' innocence today," C sighed. "Come upstairs with me."

He was halfway up the circular stairway that led to the loft above us when he realized I hadn't budged. It never entered C's mind that after nine years in prison a guy wearing nothing but a clingy swimsuit and a robe was the last person I cared to go upstairs with.

"You're not my type either," he smirked. "Never fear. This isn't the bedroom. Up here's my office, where I write."

The first thing I saw upstairs: a fat white safe the size of a mini-fridge. Next to it was a fat white paper shredder of almost exactly the same dimensions. It was enough to laugh. I could almost imagine C's giddiness at hitting Office Depot to stock his office with supplies.

He was already at his fat white computer tapping the keyboard. "Look at this," he said, twisting a wide monitor my direction. They were pictures of a girl. Black thatchy hair that looked clipped with a cleaver, slim shoulders, a hint of baby-fat in the cheeks. A disturbing face: remote, displaced even. The kid was naked, of course. The positions were all the ones you'd expect—on all fours, on her back, bent over, etc.—but there was an awkwardness to them that let you know right away that none of the poses came naturally, much less willingly. It was as if the photographer had staged each with all the delicacy of contorting a rubber doll.

"It's been a long time since I've seen female flesh, but these aren't anything I care to look at."

"Look at her eyes, not her body, doofus. She's cockeyed, wouldn't you say? That's because Faye was using the whole time Dixie was in utero, and the kid paid the price. She's a shortbus, Ennis. Not quite retarded but slow, which makes her easy meat for the sharks. She doesn't know any better than to get herself hooked up with a wannabe cretin who would do this to her."

If the pictures themselves weren't so depressing, it would've been enough to make me laugh. Like C ever cared what cretins did to women.

"How did you find these? Surfing porn?"

"A week ago an anonymous e-mail showed up at my Anarchy Ahoy box. 'Hey Scruff-Bunny,' it said. 'Check out this link.' I would've marked it as spam if not for one thing: 'Scruff-Bunny' was Faye's nickname for me. I figured it had died with her, but apparently not. Apparently she shared it with someone."

He looked at me.

"I haven't sent an e-mail in a decade," I said. "And remember: I didn't even know there was a kid in Faye's equation."

C stared back at the screen. Back at the crotch shots.

"Dixie is the only good thing that ever came out of Faye. And now she's disappeared. I called her apartment for two days before I sent my boys to check it out."

"How close are you to this kid?"

"Before Faye died I only knew Dixie from a distance. Since then I've taken an interest in her well-being. I helped her pick out some of the furnishings for her apartment. Now the furnishings are there, but she's gone. Whoever posted these has her, I'm sure of it. You're going to help me find her, Ennis. Her and the wannabe who's spreading these shots all over cyberspace. Because you owe me. All I had to do was testify at your parole hearing and it would've been another ten years before you'd be hanging in the boho sniffing burritos. The way I figure it, if you help me find Dixie, the debt is paid. Every bit of it. I'll even forgive you for this."

He drew his thumbnail across the scar that bisected his belly.

"None of this makes any sense." I shook my head. "What do you care about Faye's kid? You never cared about Faye. You let her die."

C turned his head toward me, slow and mean. Even in a Euro-clingy swimsuit and a terrycloth robe that couldn't contain his gut, he didn't look anything like a publisher. He looked exactly as I remembered him, exactly like the drug-dealing biker kingpin I had once agreed to kill.

"Don't you get it, you dumb fut?" he spat. "Dixie is my daughter—mine and Faye's."

Chapter Three

Red came skipping out the back of El Rey, cell phone in hand. The good cheer she felt upon clocking out faded when she saw me. I was leaning against the wall I never made it over, my head still swimmy from my visit with C, my tongue floating in an ocean of spit. Between the Krazy Glue holding my newly fixed bottom plate in one piece and the PoliGrip bonding it to my gums, I was slobbering like a dotard.

"St. Jude and St. Dominic both failed me," I confessed.

"I told you. You need a savior—a saint's not enough."

"I'm hoping you might do me a favor. My old man's waiting up for me. He's going to be ticked that I've been out all night. I thought maybe if you swung by his place with me and assured him I was with you and not out raising hell he would go easy on me. He doesn't live far from here."

She cocked an eyebrow and nodded at my mouth. "You want me to lie and say I gave you that splitter?"

I tried to grin, but the blood on my lip had dried so hard it cracked when my lips bent. The best I could manage was a grimace.

"You can tell him I shortchanged you on the tip."

She gave me a wary look. Then her cell rang. I recognized the oldie but goodie that served as her ringer: Tom Petty, "Don't Do Me Like That." From the way she frowned I was happy to know there was at least one person in the world she was even warier of than me.

"Oh, hey, Eric—yeah, I'm off, but listen . . . there's no need to come get me tonight. I'm going down to the Wrangler with Denita and the girls for a little while. I'll call you tomorrow, how's that sound? . . . Don't get mad, dude. It's a girls' night out, that's all. . . . No, no, no. No boys, I promise."

"Boyfriend?"

"Ex." She stuffed the phone in a funky little purse that didn't look big enough to hold it. "Eric was a little on the possessive side, so I had to punt him. You know what sucks about being a chick, though? You find out that no matter how independent you think you are you still have to rely on guys. Lately I've had to ask him to follow me back to my apartment when I leave the El. I don't know if you've heard, but the boho's not safe anymore. Prisons are letting all kinds of pervs run free these days."

"I'll assume you mean the Bicycle Rapist," I said hopefully.

Red gave me a sly smile. "Promise me you can give a perv a splitter as well as you can take one and I'll let you walk me home. I may have some beeswax there. You ever try Burt's Honey Lip Balm? They have the sweetest tagline: 'Honey-kissed lips look as sweet as they taste.' That's not a come-on, though. Just so we're clear."

"Couldn't be clearer, Red."

"That's not my name, but I'm going to let you call me that. Maybe when I know you're not a perv I'll tell you my real one."

We started up Boultier Street, past the junior high where I first made a name for myself in football. The school had been deteriorating as long as I had been. Now it looked to be abandoned, with only a handful of Goth kids loitering outside its doors begging cigarettes off strangers.

"By the way, I owe you this." She pulled a $100 bill out of her purse. "Bubba caught me slipping the other one you gave me into his tip jar. I'm afraid I'm none too good at sneaking."

"Bubba probably thought it was a con. He probably checked his wallet to make sure I hadn't picked his pocket while he was distracted. He doesn't trust me much—and for good reason . . . I stole from his tip jar once."

"He was surprised, for sure, but in a good way. I vouched for you. I said you seemed genuine enough."

Four blocks north of us we saw the gated campus of Alabama State University, Montgomery's historically black college. Turns out Red and Dad were practically neighbors. We no sooner passed Westmoreland, the street where his little two-bedroom sat, than we turned on Felder Avenue and walked a block west to the corner of Dunbar. Every telephone pole and utility box we passed was decorated with competing stickers and fliers advertising next Tuesday's mayoral election. JUSTICE DOESN'T LIVE UP TO HIS NAME, some said. VOTE FOR COMPSON. Others, DON'T GET WALK-ED ALL OVER. KEEP THE COURSE WITH AMORY. I couldn't have cared less.

"Guess what famous person used to live here," Red went. Ahead of us was a spooky Georgian half-hidden behind the pink blossoms of a lurching magnolia tree. We walked up the semi-circular drive to a glass-fronted vestibule.

"Let me think: Rosa Parks. Or Martin Luther King, Jr. No, wait. I bet it was Jefferson Davis, president of the Confederate States of America. It used to be that if you asked about famous people in Montgomery, you had a one-in-four shot of getting it right. Have there been more than four famous people from here yet?"

I no sooner said it than I remembered my own unwanted place in the history books. Apparently, so did Red.

"You don't include yourself in that list? Bubba told me about your QB career at Alabama. No specifics, just that you were responsible for the NCAA coming down so hard on the Tide that they're still trying to get over you in Tuscaloosa. Bubba says that makes you the second most-hated man in Alabama after George Wallace."

"I think I have George beat these days. History has been kinder to him than to me."

We ascended a creaky stairwell that carried us to a pair of apartments. Red fumbled for her keys and then had to strain in the dark to hit her deadbolt. The old house had so much settlement that the doors hardly fit their sills anymore. She had to elbow hers to get it open.

"Zelda Fitzgerald used to live here. Wife of F. Scott—as in *The Great Gatsby.* You've read it, right? Everybody should at some point, and I don't just mean in eleventh grade. Well, Zelda was born in Montgomery and met Scott here when she was two months out of high school. In the early thirties they moved back after she was locked up for a year and a half in a Swiss sanitarium. Two of the saddest novels ever written were started in these rooms: his *Tender Is the Night* and her *Save Me the Waltz.* See, this house was supposed to be their shot at a normal life after living high on the Roaring 1920s' hog. Only things didn't work out as hoped. Within six months Zelda was back in the loony bin. Schizophrenia, supposedly, but that was the diagnosis du jour back then, so who knows? They say her ghost still haunts this place—that's why I just knew I had to live here."

She flicked on the light. The first thing I saw was a face in a mirror that I didn't recognize. I ducked before I took in too many of its features.

"You have something against your own reflection?"

"I haven't seen my face in a long time," I admitted. "I don't care to, honestly. Not until I feel like I've made some amends."

I backed into a corner. There wasn't a lick of furniture in the small living room except for a single recliner and a bean-bag chair. Instead, the place was crammed full of canvases, some watercolor and some acrylic, some resting on easels and some tilted to the walls, all bearing twisted, tortured bodies so swollen that they seemed burdened by their very humanness. I tried to shake away any resemblance to the pictures of Faye's daughter that C had shown me.

"I can see why you wanted to live in a haunted house. Your vision of humanity is pretty haunting, Red."

"I'm only a waitress because the artsy-fartsy in me hasn't figured out how to earn a dollar."

She pulled the fat rubber bands out of her hair so the pigtails fell out of formation and all that red swept over her shoulders like a splash of fire. She was rolling the bands onto her wrist when she caught me staring.

"You mind telling me why you wear those? No offense, but between the pigtails and the socks, you look all of ten years old. It's a little . . ."

"Pedophilic?" She shrugged. "Welcome to a woman's world, dude. I discovered a long time ago that the Shirley Temple routine earns me better tips than if I dress like the thirty-year-old I am. You should see what I can rake in at the El when I wear my Catholic schoolgirl skirt. There are limits, of course. Bubba said he would fire me if I ever showed up in a French maid outfit."

She disappeared into the bathroom, reemerging in pajama bottoms and an oversized T. I was grateful the shirt didn't say ALABAMA. It didn't even say AUBURN. The bright orange letters spelled out TENNESSEE. "I wear it just to piss people off," she smiled. "Now pucker up."

She dabbed the blood flakes off my lip with a damp hand towel. Then she rolled balm across the split skin, her hand on my cheek holding me steady. I tasted honey, but I tried not to let the pleasure show. Being so close to her was embarrassing; I hadn't felt a woman's touch in ten years. Another ten since I hadn't been too coked or methed to appreciate the mysteries of

their touch.

"Tell me what you did that was so horrible, QB. You intentionally run out of bounds or something?"

"I wish the infraction was that minor. At the time it didn't seem like anything big. I worked hard, I partied hard. At some point the line between working and partying blurred. I fell into a bad habit of doing the second when I should've been focused on the first."

"Bubba said you hit the field high, that that's what started you on the downhill slide."

"Only a few games, but one turned out bad enough to ruin me. It was the end of my sophomore season, 1988. I had won a starting position that fall. A sophomore starting at quarterback is rare as hell, and it went to my head. Back in those days boosters were happy to give you anything you wanted—cars, booze, girls, cash, you name it. All under the table, of course. Well, one booster slipped me cocaine. I became a coke fiend at twenty. I liked it so much that I started doing lines in the locker room to get revved up for games."

"So you got caught with something white on the end of your nose that wasn't chalk?"

"No, I wasn't that stupid. Or that smart, maybe. I didn't so much get caught as I confessed. On national TV, no less. We'd just beat Army in the Sun Bowl by a single point. It was a brutal game that should have been easy. We were the mighty Tide playing nobodies. I lost my confidence in the third quarter, so I did a snort right before the fourth. After we managed to pull out the win, a sideline reporter asked what I attributed the turnaround to. My exact words were, 'God, a great coach, and the cocaine on my membrane. Not necessarily in that order.' "

Red burst out laughing.

"You can imagine how that remark went over," I continued. "By the end of day I was suspended. By the end of the week I was off the team, permanently. My getting canned didn't stop the NCAA from investigating, however. That's when the shit hit the fan. I spent a few years dodging subpoenas. Eventually, my coach was fired. The University cut ties with most of my boosters. The football program had some good years—they were national champs in '92—but thanks to me there was a cloud of suspicion over any win they achieved. Then the NCAA levied one of the stiffest penalties in its history. That's when the death threats started. I couldn't take them or reporters hunting me down for an interview on some 'Whatever Happened to. . . .' segment. I was Ennis 'Cocaine on the Membrane' Skinner. By the time I was your age, I was full-throttle nuts."

"And that's how you ended up in prison."

I shrugged. "I'm trying to believe what St. Jude and St. Dominic tell me in my dreams: that I've done my time. That even Ennis Skinner, the biggest punch line in Crimson Tide history, deserves a clean slate. But I've got to earn my redemption."

Our eyes danced deep in each other's for a moment. Then Red popped the cap back on the balm, tossing it to the built-in telephone cubby that all old houses in the boho have.

"Come with me. I want to show you something."

No, it wasn't the bedroom. I didn't deserve her yet. Maybe I never would. Maybe I was incapable of making my amends. Red plucked a book from a calf-high stack on the floor and slid open a dormer window. Before I knew it she had hoisted herself outside and was scrambling over the gable. I could hear her feet on the shingles above me, so I followed.

The night was just turning dark, but that didn't mean it had cooled. I thought of all those bank temperature signs, and I doubted they had dipped too far below triple digits. I still felt like I was standing in front of an open oven. Red plopped down on the roof's peak, flipped open a pen light, and began reading:

"In the death heat of a motionless breeze, she could feel the

temperate invitation to insignificance; the lulling, stagnant stolidity, seemingly pantomimed for her in the immobile salutes of the unwavering loblollies and pecans, summoned her in arid whispers to relinquish her ambition, her very energy even, until she would be as disrobed of mystery as the lawns of zoysia that blistered under the unforgiving sun. In her own mind she might grow as complicated as the Confederate Jasmine that draped the mossy crumbling brick walls separating the old homes on Hill Hedge; she wanted to twine in long bursts of clematis and hyacinth, weaving through arbors and trellises and statuary with the reach of flagrant purples and wine-reds that wouldn't wither no matter how the air strove to smother their brilliance in blankets of woolen calidity. But the world around her was in collusion with the swelter, and so her days became long valiant stands against the shrivel of the red clay chalking her soles and the clotting of cotton fields that evaporated in the great waves of enervation. No matter how hard she believed herself capable of lithe accomplishment, there was always a part of her that was sure she would simply and irrevocably disappear in a puff of sunstroke . . .;"

She closed the book. "What do you think?"

I didn't want to tell her that I barely understood a word. "That's Zelda, huh?"

"Nope. That's *me*. It was *inspired* by Zelda. Look." She held the book out to me. A half sheet of stationery was tipped into the binding. The paragraph she'd read was written in such a steady, gorgeous hand you would have thought it was an actual typeface. "*Save Me the Waltz* has great descriptions of Montgomery. I like to try to match them. It's overripe, I know, but I like overripe. It's way better than boring, don't you think? Scott and Zelda were overripe; it's what I love about them. They were perishable, and that's what gave their love beauty."

"And here I thought overripe just meant a bad smell."

She laughed a little. "Do you know how Scott and Zelda met? He was an officer training for World War I at Camp Sheridan north of town. He first saw Zelda at a country-club dance on a July night none too different from this one—an unbearably muggy night when the air was so thick with heat it seemed opaque."

She wasn't looking at me. She stared at the fading orange of daylight crusting the roofs. If you looked at the orange hard enough, you would swear it was dappled with ripples of heat.

"I identify with what she says in this book about things conspiring to consign her to insignificance. Whenever I feel like this town wants to keep me motionless and imperceptible, I come up here, and I read and then I write. Then I look over this town, and I think of orchids and goldenrod and pomegranates. Colors come to me, and I say to myself, 'Fuck the hot. I'm not letting it stifle me.' That's when I go and paint. I paint most of the night."

I didn't know what to say. I was also looking out to the rooftops. Houselights were slowly flipping on. They made the night seem electric with possibility. I didn't want to be stifled, either, but I couldn't shake that poor kid's face in the porno pictures: Dixie. As much as I wanted to enjoy my freedom, I couldn't. Enjoying seemed the same as not caring, and I had hurt too many people by not caring. I had left C's fancy house saying he could solve his own problems and leave me alone. Now, thanks to Red, I knew that wasn't going to happen. I may not have known the kid even existed until today, but I bore some responsibility for what she had been through.

I had failed to save her mother.

Even putting it like that was phony, though. I didn't just fail Faye. I damn well waltzed her down the red carpet of self-destruction. No matter how hard I wanted to proclaim my lack of malicious intent, I was implicated.

And all because I had let meth become my means of escaping into insignificance.

Insignificance doesn't exist, I decided. It's a myth.

Better yet: it's an excuse.

"I should let you get to your painting." I rose abruptly. "I don't deserve this view yet. I haven't earned it."

"You're right. You haven't—not yet. But you can start tomorrow. We need a line cook at the El. Bubba said he's willing to give you a shot. He'll take $200 a month out of your pay until the money you stole from him is paid back. Just don't be offended if he keeps his tip jar out of your reach for a while."

"I wouldn't blame him, not at all. I don't blame anybody but myself."

"You still want me to lie to your dad for you?"

"No. I'll tell Quentin the truth. I've stifled him with enough lies over the years. He deserves better, too."

Red tiptoed down the shingles and corkscrewed herself back through the dormer. I started to follow, but the view hypnotized me. The cream-colored houselights boiled through the dark clutch of branches, giving the green leaves and pink blossoms a tingly glow.

Fuck the hot, I thought.

I spread my arms as wide as my wingspan would take me.

For the first time in ten years—for the first time ever maybe—I didn't hit a wall.

★ ★ ★ ★ ★

TUESDAY

★ ★ ★ ★ ★

CHAPTER FOUR

As it turned out, I didn't have to explain my fat lip to Dad.

Quentin Skinner, the great white hero of the Civil Rights Movement, had passed out before I returned to the little house on Westmoreland.

I drained what was left of his Conecuh Ridge in the sink and let him crash in the recliner while I enjoyed my first peaceful sleep in I don't know how long. In the morning I woke him by promising to pick up breakfast. He had a hell of a hangover, but he wanted things between us to sail smoothly, so he tossed down a pack of Goody's Headache Powder and didn't make a stink about the empty bottle I left on the dinner table. It was my way of saying I had expectations of him, too.

After Dad showered we walked over to this place I used to love on the outer edge of the boho, Dirk's Filet and Vine. It was barely 8 A.M. and already 98 degrees, so it was clear we were headed for our eighth straight 100+ day. The half-mile hike left us plastered in sweat, but we didn't mind because it meant we'd earned our meal. I ordered a plate of biscuits and sawmill gravy; Dad went for a bacon-egg sandwich and a cup of grits. Mine came with a side serving of fat sausage sliced open lengthwise. The links had just the right amount of griddle black on their backs, so I knew the skin would pop and the juice would run when I bit in. I was so hungry I kept imagining that sound. I didn't even think to worry if my dentures could take the pressure. That's how eager I was.

As we ate I told Dad about my job prospects with Bubba Burch at El Rey. Quentin tried to be enthusiastic, but I could tell things were moving too fast for him. We switched to sports talk, but only harmless stuff. No Bama. We debated the likelihood of the Atlanta Braves making it to the pennant races only to muff their shot at a World Series for the umpteenth straight year. Then a crowd of seven or eight mover-shaker types rolled in. They were so loud we could barely hear our own conversation.

"Hey," Dad realized, perking up. "That's the mayor! That's Amory Justice!"

He made it sound like Marilyn Monroe had just sashayed into the room. I didn't get his excitement. Amory Justice looked like every other Southern fat cat I had ever seen: blue suit, white shirt, red tie, dyed brown hair so stiff and blow-dried it had the shape and texture of a helmet. Like something a Spartan might have worn during the Peloponnesian War.

"Drowning out regular Joes at restaurants doesn't strike me as a way to win over voters."

I watched him shake hands with other customers. In profile, the guy looked like he had a drill bit for a chin. His bottom jaw was so long and sharp he looked like it ought to be mining tungsten instead of greasing palms.

"Who's the filly? I bet it's at least his third or fourth wife, huh?"

Seated to Mayor Justice's immediate left was a blond in a maroon business suit toting a black binder. Her cheekbones were so angular they looked liked they had been sharpened on a whetstone. Everything about her seemed ground to a point—fingernails, elbows, waistline. Legs so shapely they plunged like daggers into her heels. If she weren't wolfing down a ham biscuit I would have thought she ate men for breakfast.

"That's not his wife *or* his mistress," Dad answered. "That's his daughter, Reese. She's the brains behind his campaign, the one who's inflamed all the racial stuff the past few months. Believe it or not, even in these enlightened days, insinuating that a black mayor will turn Montgomery majority black brings out the Republican base. She's so good at race baiting the Compson people have a nickname for her: they call her 'the Kudzu Ann Coulter.' "

If that was the case then the mayor's daughter was off her game. At first she hardly let out a peep during the strategy session. Instead, she took notes in her binder, intently scribbling down every percentage recited by her father's flunkies as they went over a new set of poll numbers. From what Dad and I could overhear as we busily pretended we weren't eavesdropping, Mayor Justice had every reason to be happy. He was leading in several precincts. Predictably, the ones he was losing were predominantly black. Still, the numbers weren't making him happy.

"None of this means jack shit if Walk's people get that 'Get Out the Vote' business organized next Tuesday," he carped. "They're going to get church vans to drive whole congregations to the polls. Bobby, I want you to drive by Appleton, Churchwood, and Nixon middle schools and see if any trees need trimming. With any luck it'll still be hotter than a warlock's asshole next week. The more direct sunlight we get bearing down on those lines waiting to get to the ballot boxes, the more Walk's folks are likely to get hot and sticky and leave. Especially the older ones—that's who Walk's people spent the spring registering, folks who haven't voted since George Wallace last won the governorship in 1982. This is what we need to be thinking: how we encourage Walk's folks to walk away."

"You know," a staff member piped up, "those three schools you mentioned are about as decrepit as you'll find facilities today. Maybe it's time we looked into their maintenance schedules. Maybe the air conditioners that are supposed to keep those gymnasiums cool next week could take a day off for an upgrade. There have been stranger coincidences."

The mayor groaned as he cracked the shell on a hardboiled egg. "No, no, no. There's no way you'll ever get Dreaden over at the school superintendent's office to sign off on a stunt like that. He's still ticked we didn't push harder on the property-tax initiative he was after me to float. He was in the *Advertiser* last week saying he was undecided. Don't think that wasn't a mote to my eye. We'd be leading in at least two west-side precincts if that son of a bitch had given me the endorsement he was supposed to."

The table settled into such a gloomy spell that Dirk's actually went quiet except for the scrape of spatulas on the griddles. Dad and I scrambled to improvise a conversation so not to seem conspicuous. Then a man in yet another blue suit whisked into the diner and strode straight up to Reese Justice. He looked familiar, but I couldn't place the face. He whispered in the woman's ear and was gone as fast as he had appeared. I watched him walk outside, light up a Marlboro, and loiter, even though he was sweating like a hog.

"Gentleman," the mayor's daughter spoke up. "I'm about to give you a lesson in opposition research. That was supposed to be your forte, Bix, but you've done such a piss-poor job of it that I doubt you could get Robert E. Lee elected to the Confederate Generals Hall of Fame if such a place existed. Would anybody like a demonstration of how inept Bix here is at his job? Let's have a little quiz: Bix, can you tell me exactly where in Montgomery my father's opponent was born in the year of Our Lord 1942?"

Everyone looked to the man at the far end of the table. This was Bix, whoever Bix was. Even under the patina of his fake tan the guy grew visibly pale. When Bix didn't answer, Reese Justice nodded bitterly.

"Just as I thought. Walk Compson was born November 15, 1942, at 808 Teague Street. It's right there on page one of his autobiography. Didn't any of you read that book? Do any of you even know where Teague Street is? It intersects Fifth Street. In fact, 808 Teague Street is *on the corner* of Fifth and Teague streets. And does anyone realize what that means? No? Well, let me tell you. It means Walk Compson was born right there in the middle of what has since that birth of his sixty-six years ago come to be known as Recipe Row. That's right, folks! Our opponent comes from the most concentrated drug neighborhood here in Montgomery, Alabama, and we've done absolutely nothing to point out the absolutely nothing he's done throughout his so-called career of public service to save the poor people right there in his home neighborhood from winos and crack skanks and methheads! One week to go in this war and we're sitting on this pot of gold like we've got a lifetime to let its interest accrue!"

She snapped the cap on her pen and threw it down on her binder.

"As y'all are heading back to your offices here in a few minutes—and this includes you, Daddy—I want you to take a little detour off Mulberry Street. I want you to turn onto Fifth Street and drive along Recipe Row. How many of you have ever done that? Well, if you haven't, I recommend rolling stops at the intersections. Those shiny Crown Victorias you're driving make easy targets for BB guns, the shooting of which I've discovered is a big pastime on the Row. Nevertheless, as you're making those rolling stops, I want you to peek at the house lots you're passing. There, among the detritus of lives that our opponent hasn't done diddly to improve, you'll see a brand-spanking new set of yard signs. WELCOME TO FIFTH STREET, they say. HOME OF WALK COMPSON. THANK YOU, WALK, FOR MAKING THIS

SUCH A BEAUTIFUL PLACE TO LIVE."

I started to think that "Kudzu Ann Coulter" was an inaccurate nickname for this woman. Kudzu creeps; Reese Justice pounced.

"Do you know the best part?" she continued. "The residents couldn't have been happier to plant those signs in their yards. They *wanted* them there. That's how fond they are of our opponent along Recipe Row. Now, do you want to tell me that folks in other predominantly black precincts don't have similar resentments? *We haven't been doing our jobs, people! We're conceding the black vote to Walk just because he's black!*"

The whole time the mayor's daughter talked I was looking back and forth between her and the man smoking outside. By the time she finished I was shriveling in my seat as much as the staff whose asses she was re-ventilating. That's because I finally recognized him.

The smoker was Treadface.

My first inclination was to tuck my head in case he spotted me. Then I wondered why I was hiding. Maybe I was the bane of Alabama football fanatics, but at least I wasn't a thug kidnapping ex-cons by night and doing politicians' dirty work by day.

As I soaked the last bites of sausage in what was left of my sawmill gravy, I tried to figure the connection between Amory Justice and High C. Surely a man like the mayor, someone who had been in power for twenty-four years, was too smart to get involved with a former meth cook for the Outlaws Motorcycle Club.

Then again, I had met a few politicians who went dumb from thinking they were too smart to get sullied by their unsavory inclinations. For a while at Kilby one of my blockmates was a former Randolph County commissioner who financed the meth habits of several young women as long as they were willing to service him. One of the women turned out to be fifteen, and still said commissioner couldn't understand why he had been convicted of both solicitation and child abuse.

Screw it, I decided. Who the mayor's daughter ran with wasn't my business. I only had two hours before I was expected at El Rey, and I hadn't even started making my amends yet.

As Dad went for a coffee refill, I tried to decide the best way to find Dixie. I was going to find her, get those pics off the Internet, and make sure neither ended up in the hands of pervs. The only starting point I could come up with was Faye's parents. Obviously, since I didn't even know they were alive until C told me, I had never met them. No clue where they lived. I went to Dirk's cash register and asked to borrow the phone book. Just what I was afraid of: 178 Jameses were listed there, and I didn't even have a first name for Faye's old man.

Then I had an idea.

"Let me borrow your cell," I told Dad when he returned with his king-sized styro filled to the brim. I looked up the number for Oakwood Cemetery and dialed.

"Yes, sir, my name is Stewart Pennington, and I'm hoping you might be able to help me. I'm chair of the Lee High School Class of 1983 25th Reunion, and I'm trying to track down the parents of one of our classmates. She passed shortly after our twentieth, and we didn't do anything to remember her. It's been bothering us for five years, so it's a big deal. Our classmate is buried up there at Oakwood, but I don't know her folks' names. I'm sure you've got them on record. I was just up at the cemetery yesterday, you see, and I noticed her headstone. It looks well maintained, so I know they still visit her. We'd like to ask them to lend us some pictures, so we can put up a little memorial for her. We're doing it for all the classmates we've lost, but this one is the only one we don't have info on. The girl's name was Alice James. She's in plot C-282 . . ."

I saw Dad flinch. He wasn't thrilled that I had Faye on the brain.

"No, sir, I'm not asking for an address or telephone number. You misunderstood me. I only want her parents' names. Just whoever you have as your emergency contact for plot C-282 will be fine. I can look the phone number up myself."

The gambit worked. A second later I was circling a number in Dirk's phone book:

JAMES, LISTER . . . . . . 1013 HALLWOOD LANE . . . . . . 36117 . . . . . . 269-5241.

Dad wasn't impressed.

"You care to tell me what you're up to?"

I copied the address onto a napkin, my excuse for not looking him in the eye. I knew he was as steamed as his coffee.

"A fib doesn't violate my parole, does it?"

He didn't appreciate the wisecrack.

"I'll tell you everything, old man. Afterward, when I know what's going on myself. C'mon, let's take a ride. 36117 is an east-side zip, right? Doesn't Hallwood Lane sound like some fancy-ass address?"

Before he could answer there was a ruckus at the mayor's table. Cell phones were blaring, a cacophony of bleeps and chimes and melodies. It sounded as if news of World War III was breaking over the wire.

The whole group, including the dagger-legged blond, hopped up and folded their reports and spreadsheets into briefcases and computer bags. Most left their plates unfinished. Good thing for Dirk's that customers pay before they get to scarf—otherwise the mayor's party would have stiffed ole Dirkus on the bill. That's how much of a lather the mayor's gang was in to get the hell out. All those blue suits, white shirts, and red ties brushed past me and Dad at the diner exit like they couldn't imagine we might have pressing business, too.

Goddamn politicians. It would never enter their minds to hold a door for a regular Joe.

It was one more reason to regret being a convicted felon. I couldn't vote in Tuesday's election.

CHAPTER FIVE

Turns out Hallwood Lane was so new that nobody in east Montgomery could tell us where the hell to find it. It didn't even show up on the GPS in Dad's Jeep. We had to stop at two different Shell stations and then a CVS to beg directions. Finally, a lightbulb went off for a clerk setting up a candy-bar display. Thanks to a customer who had fainted from the heat after hoofing it to the drugstore, the clerk remembered Hallwood Lane was the residential axis of a new subdivision called Thorington Trace. Dad had heard of that, so we set off down a country-looking stripe of asphalt called Ray Thorington Road, where patches of houses bloomed between man-made ponds dotting acres of what, just a year earlier, Dad said, had been cow pasture.

"The whole damn town is moving this direction," he complained. He didn't seem to remember he had said those exact words just twenty-four hours earlier. I didn't begrudge him his forgetfulness. Between Red, High C and Dixie, Tread-face and Twitchy, and now Reese Justice, twenty-four hours earlier already seemed a lifetime ago.

As I quickly discovered, the feeling wasn't going to ease anytime soon. Mainly because, as I also quickly discovered, 1013 Hallwood Lane shouldn't have been so hard to find.

We could have just followed the police right to it.

We saw the squad cars the minute we turned into Thorington Trace. Something about a hundred degrees and 100 percent

72

humidity lets you spot black and whites even from three blocks away. We rolled up as close as we could, parked, and jogged to the small crowd gathering around the freshly strung crime-scene tape roping off the front yard.

Cops, both uniformed and plain-clothed, were walking in and out of the house, grim-faced. A nearby camera crew filmed the surreal scene. Whenever the reporter thrust her microphone and shouted out questions, the patrolmen securing the perimeter threw up their hands and blew no-comment kisses. The fact that Dad and I were strangers didn't stop locals' gossip from rumbling around us.

". . . I *knew* something was going on. I usually see Lister at six-thirty every morning, walking his dog. Usually with the granddaughter, right up until he and Brenda put her in her own place . . ."

"I heard a dog howling on Sunday and Monday both. I never thought it was Rufus making that racket; it sounded too yappy for a cocker spaniel. I thought it was Mrs. Hoople's terrier. That damn thing is always barking its head off . . ."

". . . I don't believe he was alone. It's not possible to do that to yourself alone . . ."

"Do what?" Dad whispered in my ear. "What are they talking about?"

"Hold on. I'm about to find out."

A few houses up on the opposite side of the street sat a navy-blue PT cruiser with CRAVEN REALTY stenciled to its side. A woman stood in the crook of the open driver's side door, frantically jabbering into her cell. I knew she was a real-estate agent because I could see the fear of dwindling commissions in her eyes. When she hung up I slipped out of the crowd and hustled over to her.

"You haven't seen anybody from Rudick Realty around here, have you?"

"Rudick Realty? . . . I've never heard of them."

That wasn't surprising: I made the name up.

"My father and I were supposed to meet a woman from their office over here. We were going to look at a couple of houses. Is this 1122? I think this is one of the listings she pulled off MLS for us. . . . Well, maybe it's for the best she's a no-show. I can't imagine a crime scene is going to be good for the east-side market. Too bad. I'd heard a lot of good things about Thorington Trace, but my dad's almost seventy. I can't in good conscience think about moving him into a violent neighborhood. Crime is why I'm looking to get him out of the boho district."

"Crime? Thorington Trace is one of the safest neighborhoods in Montgomery! This is a family environment!"

I jabbed a thumb over my shoulder. "With all due respect, ma'am, you don't usually see a platoon of patrol cars like this in a family environment."

She closed her door and stepped around the PT cruiser toward me, her blond dye job as washed out as her face.

"If I tell you something confidentially, you have to promise you won't spread it around. What happened here will be public information soon enough, but you have to understand . . . my brother-in-law is a fireman. He was one of the first-responders and told me how they found Mr. James when they broke in. It's insane—this is going to destroy his law firm. It may even affect the mayor's election on Tuesday. Lister James was one of the biggest lawyers in Montgomery, one of Walk Compson's closest advisors they say, and now this!"

"You haven't told me what 'this' is."

Spilling the beans was bothering her conscience. But it was either spill them or kiss a potential commission goodbye.

"I'm just trying to reassure my potential clients nothing has happened here that would make Thorington Trace a less desirable place to live. It was an accident, that's all."

"What exactly was an accident, ma'am?"

The woman took a deep breath. "Apparently Mr. James was into . . . well, how to say it . . . *extracurricular activities.* Something went wrong and he suffocated. He asphyxiated himself."

Asphyxiation was a funny word. You only ever heard it anymore in conjunction with a certain adjective.

"You mean . . . *autoerotic asphyxiation?*"

The term brought a pucker to her face that made her look like she had bitten deep into a lemon. "I don't know anything about that business. I only know that when the first-responders went inside they found him trussed like a Christmas turkey in some sort of rubber suit with all kinds of ropes restraining him. Apparently there were two or three leashes that went from the—um—collar around his neck to his wrists and feet. Whenever he tried to move, he cut off his air supply. Apparently he cut it off once too often. Now you know why the Compson campaign may be devastated when this gets out. And don't think Amory Justice's people won't make sure the news is known. These policemen here? They work for Mayor Justice!"

I couldn't believe what I was hearing. It was enough to make me forget why I had come to Thorington Trace in the first place. Not to mention the lie I had told about why I was here.

"You know, sir, I'd be happy to show you and your father this house if you're still interested. Craven Realty is far more considerate of its clients than Rudick—if I do say so myself."

I couldn't blame her for taking her shot. A realtor still has to make a buck, even in the middle of autoerotic asphyxiation.

"Thanks, but I think we're going to have to pass on Thorington Trace. East Montgomery is a little too—um—*kinky* for our tastes. We're a pretty conservative family. We'll take our chances in the boho."

I went back to Dad, who had inched himself closer up to the crime-scene tape. "You don't want to know," he said when I asked what rumors were floating around. I scanned the crowd and found the neighbor who had mentioned the Jameses setting Dixie up in her own place.

"I'm a family friend," I told the guy. "She needs to hear this from someone who cares."

Fortunately, amid the shock and confusion, the neighbor didn't bother to wonder why if I was indeed such a close friend of the family I didn't know where Dixie lived. He blurted out the name of an apartment complex off Audubon Drive.

"That's down in the boho," I said, surprised.

"Oh, yeah. Brenda told me Dixie loves that part of Montgomery. She says the kid loves to eat at that burrito place on Felder. I can't remember the name, but you know what I'm talking about. Nouveau Mexican. Very hip. You can't miss it. . . . Oh my God, there's Brenda now!"

I turned in time to see a squad car stop in the middle of the street. The passenger door flew open and a large woman spilled out. She ran crying and yelling past us to duck under the tape and disappear into the house. It happened so fast that the patrolmen at the door didn't have time to stop her. We heard several screams that seemed loud enough to pop the bricks right off the facade. Then a group of cops escorted Mrs. James back outside. Only escort is the wrong word. Dragged would be more accurate. Faye's mother bucked to free her arms from the officers gripping her wrists. A detective with sweat streaks like branding scars all over his chest planted his hands on her broad, fleshy hips and shoved.

"Let me go!"

Her voice sliced the air like a razor.

"That's not my husband! That's not Lister! Somebody did that to him! Somebody suffocated him and put him like that!

Why won't you listen to me?"

The chief investigator in charge of the scene rushed up and tried to console her.

"Where's Walk Compson!" Mrs. James yelled. "Where is he? He should be here! He was Lister's friend! He'll tell you! *That's not my Lister in there!*"

The more she tried to wrestle herself from the uniformed cops the rougher they got. She was a big woman, and I could tell that her strength was wearing out their patience. The cops tried to get her hands behind her back. One bent down to grab for a leg. The move gave Mrs. James enough leverage to break a hand free. I wondered if she didn't break that hand breaking it free—she no sooner jerked it loose than she sent it flying across the chief investigator's jaw. It wasn't a punch but an open-palmed slap. Still, the man staggered back two paces and shook his head. Those of us in the crowd were shaking ours, too. Nobody could believe what we had seen.

Maybe if the investigator had shaken *his* head a bit harder his senses might have come to him. Instead, what he did next suggested that he didn't just lose his marbles—he dumped them right out of the pouch. The guy tackled Mrs. James. Just flat-out dropped both her and himself smack dab in the middle of the James family's zoysia grass, not ten paces from a welcome mat on the porch that said ALL ARE INVITED INTO GOD'S HOUSE.

Two other cops went down with them. The next we knew four people were rolling in a heap of feet and elbows. That brought more patrolmen rushing over. It also brought the camera crew's lens zooming in. The crew filmed the melee like it was a goddamn football game.

"*Oh, God, no,*" someone yelled. "*Not that.*"

One of the cops drew his Taser. He let Mrs. James have it, too. Just pressed it down on her back and let it rip until I couldn't tell if I was hearing more screams or the actual popping of the voltage. The neighbors were booing and screaming for it to stop. I was suddenly aware again of the heat, the unrelenting heat. I thought I might puke.

"I can't deal with this," I said, grabbing Dad and tugging him back toward our truck.

"You can't drive," Dad said when I took his keys. "You don't have a license."

"They won't yank my parole for that. Let's go."

I was cutting a turn to exit the subdivision when something sank in that amid the spectacle I hadn't even registered. I was caught so off-guard that I had to look into the rearview to make sure I wasn't imagining it. The police had Mrs. James on her feet. As they bent her over the hood of a squad car to cuff her I could still hear her voice:

"Where's Walk? Somebody please call Walk! *Walk Compson should be here helping us!*"

My eyes hadn't deceived me.

Mrs. James was black as coffee.

CHAPTER SIX

"I always knew something was—"

Dad stopped, as if suddenly aware of the implications of what his surprise was about to let fly from his lips. I wasn't going to excuse Quentin Skinner, the great white hero of the Civil Rights Movement, from admitting what he was thinking, no matter how unconscious his thinking might have been.

"Something what? Say it, old man. You always thought something about Faye was . . . off? Weird? So now you know why, huh? Because you just discovered from Mrs. James that Faye was at least half-black it all makes sense why she was trouble? That her race has something to do with why I ended up in Kilby?"

"Don't talk to me like that!"

"What if we find out Mr. James was African American, too? Will the fact that Faye's parents are both black make it crystal clear to you what led Faye to become a drug addict?"

"I said stop it, boy! I was on the right side of Civil Rights before you were born!"

"Maybe we should run to Penneys and buy you a set of white sheets. You can cut eyeholes in the pillowcase."

I thought he was going to slug me. Instead, he swatted the gearshift, popping it right out of fourth and into neutral. The clutch shrieked as I jammed on the brake. We skidded to a stop in the dead center of Ray Thorington Road. Sitting off to our right, as if by some kind of divine taunt, was a church. SAVE

AND DELIVER ME FROM ALL WHO PURSUE ME, OR THEY WILL TEAR ME LIKE A LION AND RIP ME TO PIECES WITH NO ONE TO RESCUE ME, the signboard read. PSALMS 7:1–2.

"Goddammit," Dad grunted. "I was beaten up for riding a Greyhound bus with blacks! Later I drove marchers from Selma to Montgomery with rednecks taking potshots at my head! Don't you ever tell me I'm a racist! You don't have the right to judge me until you've done something in your life besides screw it up!"

He recoiled as soon as he said it. That offended me more than what he actually said. I deserved what he said, after all. We sat for a moment, both of us startled by the heatedness of the exchange. Then I restarted the truck and we inched toward the intersection with Vaughn Road.

"You really don't need to be driving without a license," Dad said.

I drove on.

Ten miles to the west, Vaughn ended at the doorstep of the boho, and yet I never felt so far from home. That was crazy to say having just spent ten years in prison, but it was true. What stunned me wasn't the fact that Faye was at least partly African American. If I'd have known, it wouldn't have mattered. Not a bit. I could square my shoulders and state with certainty that I would have still been drawn to her. We would have still struck up our devils' death dance and destroyed each other.

No, what threw me was the fact that I had never even thought to ask about her background. I had never seen a picture of her family. Not because she hid pictures from me, but because I had never asked. Not even after she told me they were dead. I had spent hours with her and never picked up on any hints of a heritage. I had tasted every inch of her skin and never recognized a single feature or trait. I'm sure they were there. They had to be. I didn't recognize them because that's how little I knew the woman I had killed for—or attempted to kill for, anyway.

"Where are we going now?" Dad demanded.

We were back in the boho. Not heading toward Felder and El Rey, though. We were whipping through the little streets—some of them cobblestone—behind the green quad of Huntingdon College where forty-seven years earlier Quentin Skinner felt called by God to fight for racial equality. Where for nearly forty years after that he taught classes in history and peace studies until his son became a methhead and he coped by passing out in his own puke.

The quad gave way to a series of older, more rundown neighborhoods. We came to the one apartment complex on Audubon Drive. It had to be where Dixie lived, I decided. A curdle of something sour ran through my saliva as I read the last names painted on the mailboxes. How many Jameses could live in a single complex? There was no D. JAMES.

Then I remembered "Dixie" wasn't Dixie's Christian name. I had to double back before I found a building with C. JAMES. I left the car running and ran up the stairs to #23A, Dad still yelling, "Where are we going?" I pounded my fist on the door, half afraid it would creak open. I was thinking of Lister James, roped up like a dead deer ready for a hunter's muddy front bumper. If that was what could happen on a fancy suburban street like Hallwood Lane, there was no telling what I might find in the boho.

Only the door was locked. As I tried to peek through the apartment's lone window, Dad came up behind me, wiping the doorknob with his handkerchief. "You can't just leave your prints everywhere you go. All you need is for somebody to lift a partial palm and you'll be back to Kilby before you can explain why you keep turning up at crime scenes!"

"So you think Hallwood over there was a crime scene? You

believe what Mrs. James was yelling, even though she's—"

"We're not in a moving car this time. I'm not afraid to hit you now."

He meant it; I could tell.

"We're going to have to break in," I said, changing the subject. "Give me a credit card."

"I will not."

"Give me a damn credit card!"

I said it so loud a woman pulling grocery bags out of her hatchback looked up at us from the parking lot, startled. "Congratulations," Dad grunted, whipping out his wallet. "You just created an eyewitness."

He wouldn't let me jimmy the lock; he did it himself. We slipped into Dixie's apartment. The place was barren except for a few furnishings: a couch, a bookcase, and a small TV connected to the wall with a snaky coil of cable. Here and there a picture was tacked to the wall. Sure enough, there was a family one, at least what was left of the James family when it was taken. It was Dixie with her grandparents. Dad chose his words carefully this time. "It explains a few things," he said when I showed it to him. Lister James was white all right, but I wasn't looking at him. I was looking at the kid.

Dixie appeared about the same age as in the porn shots, but somehow, sandwiched between her gleaming grandparents with a red satin bow shining in her hair, she had the look of a ten-year-old.

"What's wrong with her?" Dad asked. "Is she handicapped?"

"I don't know for sure. The word is she's slow—whatever that means."

"I have to ask . . . Is she yours?"

"No. She's too old. I didn't meet Faye until 1991. I reckon Dixie would've been three then. She's nineteen now, so she would've been born around the time of the Sun Bowl—"

I stopped myself. I didn't want to bring up my "cocaine on the membrane" days.

"Around the time I first screwed up. I never even knew the kid existed until last night."

"Where is she?"

"If I knew that, we wouldn't be here." I didn't like my own sarcasm. "I've been asked to find out," I said more softly.

It didn't make Dad any happier. "You mind telling me by whom?"

"An old acquaintance—that's as much as you'll want to know, okay? The parents were the obvious starting point. That's why we went out there, to talk to them about Dixie. What happened to Lister James can't be unconnected to her. You have to trust me on this. Something is going on here."

"Whatever it is, it doesn't have to involve you. Not if this Dixie isn't your daughter."

"I wish I could see it like that. I do, but I can't. I owe Faye."

"Faye ruined your life, boy."

"And I ruined hers." I made myself stop staring at Dixie's face. "We're wasting time. We better start looking."

"Looking for what?"

"I'm not sure. I'm hoping we'll know when we find it."

He searched the books on the bookshelf while I went into the bedroom. I started with the drawers of the cheap dresser. It was all socks, panties, T-shirts—nothing out of the ordinary for a young woman. There was nothing unusual in the closet either, unless you think the sight of a pile of winter sweaters in 108-degree August is inherently unusual.

I dropped to my knees and checked under the bed. There was a shoebox there. I pulled it out and took off the top. Inside was a stack of vintage comics. *The Adventures of Supergirl,* every damn one. I pulled out the issue topping the stack and flipped through it. In every damn panel Supergirl's blond hair had been colored chestnut brown.

The same shade as Faye's.

Comics weren't the only thing in the shoebox. There were several transparent plastic baggies, all with locks of hair. Some were stiff and gray like a horse tail, others spongy and matted— African American hair, I realized. I stared at one bag whose contents were curly and almond-brown. I recognized it immediately. My hair. I could remember the day that Faye clipped it off of me. "I want a keepsake of yours, sweet pea," she had said. "Something to remember you by."

It was the day I was sentenced for shooting High C.

"Ennis, come look at this!"

I clapped the lid back on the shoebox and rushed to the kitchen. Dad was stooped in front of the refrigerator door, which was covered head to toe in pictures, to-do lists, and word magnets from one of those genius vocabulary kits: *fusillade, obsequious, concatenate.*

Dad wasn't looking at any of those, however. He was staring at a tattered slice of paper taped just above the ice dispenser. At the top was a note addressed to Dixie written in bold Sharpie strokes: TAKE THIS WITH YOU EVERYWHERE YOU GO!

Hi! My name is Caroline James, but my friends call me "Dixie."

I am not mentally challenged. I may just behave differently from you sometimes.

I am a very loving person trying to live on her own. Sometimes I need help.

Please don't be afraid. I don't mean to embarrass you. I just don't always know the right way to act in certain situations.

If at any time you think I am being a problem, please call my family at 269-5241. (That's a 334 area code).

Thank you and have a nice day!

Love, Dixie

"269-5241 is her grandparents' telephone number," I pointed out. "I recognize it from the telephone book at Dirk's."

"Well, if one grandparent weren't dead and the other buried under a pile of police, I would suggest we call them. I would be interested to know what kind of grandparent makes a kid walk around with a sign saying 'I don't mean to embarrass you.' "

"The kind of grandparents who're embarrassed, that's who."

He read aloud the line about being "different." "They might as well have taped KICK ME to her back." He blanched. I wasn't looking at the note anymore.

"Do you notice anything about these magnets?"

I drew a finger along the words from the genius vocabulary kit. Every so often among *superannuate, expatiate, egregious,* and the like there was a magnet with a seemingly random letter instead of a word: a G here, an I there, an L. Seven letters in all. Dad was squinting at *leonine.*

"I'm noticing how these magnets are telling me I need to invest in a dictionary. Who the hell uses these words?"

"One of the correspondence classes I took at Kilby was American literature. A guy from Troy University here in the Gump. Hardest damn teacher I ever had; a real writing freak. I don't think he ever gave anything above a C, but the readings he assigned were great. One was an Edgar Allan Poe story called 'The Purloined Letter.' You ever heard of it?"

"I've never heard the word *purloined.* I'm sure it's here somewhere on this refrigerator, though."

"Long before Sherlock Holmes, Poe created the first fictional detective, a French sleuth named Auguste Dupin. In 'The Purloined Letter' an evil politician swipes an incriminating note from the Queen and blackmails her over a romantic indiscretion. The French police have searched every hidden crevice in the politician's apartment, but they can't find it. Dupin steps in and locates the thing in about two seconds. Turns out the note is hidden in plain sight on a mantelpiece, only slightly disguised. It's the politician's way of showing the police he's craftier than they give him credit for. Dupin knows the guy is touchy about proving he's smarter than everybody else in Paris, see, so Dupin reasons that he wouldn't so much hide it as flaunt it."

"What do French sleuths have to do with refrigerator magnets?"

"At one point in the story, Dupin talks about a puzzle game played with maps. Contestants take turns calling out names of cities or rivers that their opponents have to locate. Dupin says that novices almost always go for the most obscure places because they're spelled out in the smallest possible letters. The idea is that looking for that tiny type will fry the competition's brains. Smarter players know to go for places where the type is big and stretched out across such a wide space that the letters don't even look like they form a word. The idea is that that type is so obvious it's like the print on street signs and placards—we overlook it. 'By dint of their being so obvious,' Dupin says, 'these words prove invisible to the casual eye.' "

"I still don't get it, but at least I know what 'dint' means."

I pointed to the seven magnets with the single letters on them. "From a distance, stuck between all these big words that distract us because we're intimidated by them, these letters look randomly arranged. That there's no obvious sequence to the vocab words encourages us to assume that the letters have also been thrown up here in no particular order. But spoon these seven single letters out of the soup and put them up next to each other, and you'll see my point. They spell out something, all right."

I could see Dad mentally arranging the G, I, L, and other letters.

"*Gilbert!*" he said excitedly.

"Elementary, my dear father. I may have to buy you a book

of Poe stories for Christmas. I'm sure you're happy to know my college degree is good for something, huh?"

"Yes, well, who does your baccalaureate tell you this 'Gilbert' is?"

"That's a whole other mystery. Hopefully, it won't take a master's degree to solve it. If I had to guess, I would say Gilbert must be the guy who has Dixie. If she's as vulnerable as this note makes her out to be, it wouldn't be hard for a sweet-talker to talk her into running off with him. She may not even know she's been kidnapped—Gilbert may have her convinced she's in love."

"Stranger things are possible," Dad agreed. "Love's been known to dupe the best of them."

I didn't ask if he meant that as a compliment. Not wanting to press my luck, I took it for one.

"What time is it? I can't be late to El Rey, not on my first day of work."

Dad didn't bother to look at his watch. "It's time to get out of here—that's what time it is. If this Dixie is indeed missing, the police are going to know about it by now. Unless they're still Tasering poor Mrs. James. Even so, we need to go. And try not to leave any fingerprints on your way out. With your luck, the police will think *you're* Gilbert."

CHAPTER SEVEN

At El Rey, Bubba clocked me in and introduced me to the line cook who would train me, a gruff and tumble guy with the chest of a grizzly that the staff had nicknamed "Wookie." What exactly I was being trained for wasn't immediately clear. For the first half-hour of my employment we stood around Bubba's laptop in the back office and watched streaming coverage of the melee on Hallwood Lane. It was breaking news on WSFA-TV, the local NBC affiliate. The camera crew's footage was so riveting that you couldn't turn away, not even after the station reran it for the fortieth time.

Something about the rocking camera angle and the woosh of the zoom made the scene even more disorienting and unreal than it had been in person. Seeing white cops pile on a black woman, you thought you were watching archival footage from 1963, even if the Taser waving in and out of the frame was too anachronistic to let you believe that this was an archived image from a shameful past. It was just a matter of time before one of us mentioned the object that, more than any remnant of the distant days of Bull Connor, symbolizes the responsibility of racial awareness in Alabama.

"They might as well have put a fire hose to her," Bubba said, disgusted.

Wookie was more philosophical. "Amory Justice must be shitting himself right about now. Never mind the newscasts— this footage will be on YouTube in no time if it's not there

88

already. This is Rodney King meets Maccaca. Those cops just cost ole A. J. the mayor's race."

"I'm not so sure about that," I said. "Watch what happens when they get Mrs. James to her feet."

It took a minute, but then we saw the shot of the police cuffing Faye's mother. "Where's Walk?" Mrs. James cried straight into the camera lens. "Somebody please call Walk! Walk Compson should be here helping us!"

"That line right there," I said. "From what I've seen of the Justice campaign, I wouldn't put it past them to make a clip out of that and hammer it home until the polls close. Take that shot of Mrs. James out of context, and you have a black woman crying out in vain for the black candidate who's supposed to be protecting her. Don't folks already think of Walk as the savior of black Montgomery? Slap a tagline on there like *Where's Walk Compson When You Need Him?* and I bet you pull in a few thousand extra votes from folks who missed the full story. Folks from black Montgomery, I mean."

My new co-workers looked at me like I had sniffed a little too much Tabasco.

"You really think an incumbent mayor would have the *guavas* to use a clip of his own police's brutality against an opponent?" Bubba scoffed. "That's pretty damn Machiavellian, Ennis. You're as cynical as you are sober these days."

I shrugged. "I happened to see Reese Justice in action this morning. I wouldn't put anything past her. She strikes me as Machiavelli in Max Factor."

Wookie wondered what the connection between the James family and Walk Compson was anyway. "It's not like Walk Compson is even an activist anymore."

I started to tell him what the woman from Craven Realty had told me: that Lister James was an advisor to the Compson campaign. That he was so close to Walk, in fact, that his death might affect the mayor's race. I stopped when it hit me I would have to explain why I was on Hallwood Lane that morning.

The Wook wasn't too upset by my holding out. He had yet to stop telling me everything he knew about Walk.

"The guy quit the Civil Rights Movement twenty years ago to sell cars. Everybody knows that. That's how Walk's autobiography ends, with him disillusioned that all these years later race is still an issue in Montgomery. 'Once I was in the business of making my city a better place for all its residents,' it ends. 'Now I'm just in business.' That has to be about the most downbeat conclusion to any inspirational story I've ever heard."

I was surprised that a line cook could quote lines from a Civil Rights leader's memoir. Apparently, I let a lot of that surprise show.

"Wookie's a history buff," Bubba explained. "Tell him, Wook."

The bearish man shuffled his feet, embarrassed. "I used to take classes up in Tuscaloosa."

"Ph.D. classes," Bubba clarified. "The Wook here is what they call A.B.D.—*all but dissertation*. Actually, they should classify him A.G.F., as in *ain't gonna finish.*"

That sounded mean, but the Wook was ho-hum about the fact that he would never be Dr. Wookie.

"The truth is I make as much money here as I can teaching. There aren't many jobs in colleges anymore. You get stuck adjuncting, man, and you're done for. Colleges treat part-timers like itinerant labor—no insurance, no benefits, no retirement. Besides, I like the kitchen better than the classroom. Nobody wants extra credit for finishing his plate."

"If you were going to write a dissertation," I asked, "what time period would you study?"

Wookie didn't hesitate. "Montgomery, 1955–1956, the bus boycott period. One of the most interesting casts of characters you'll find in American history. And I don't just mean the stars of the show like Rosa Parks and Martin Luther King, Jr. I'm talking about the unsung heroes—E. D. Nixon, Joanne Robinson, Johnnie Carr, Clifford and Virginia Durr. Back when I was taking classes I started collecting scrapbooks. You know—newspaper clippings, correspondence, handbills, and fliers. I even have photographs that have never been published before. I used to go around interviewing everyday folks who were part of the boycott, and they would let me copy heap upon heap of their personal stuff. I could never find the right angle for a dissertation, though. The story's been told so often that I didn't have a fresh take on it."

"You should interview my dad, Quentin Skinner."

"As in Quentin Skinner, beaten-to-a-pulp-at-the-Greyhound-station Quentin Skinner?"

"The one and the same. He has great stories about watching the bus boycott from Dexter Avenue, right there by MLK's church. He was a teenager then, and his family was friendly with Robert Graetz. You know Robert Graetz, right?"

"Sure! The one white minister in Montgomery active in the bus boycott! I interviewed him years ago, too, but he was already writing his own book. The Klan tried to blow his house to bits not once but three times."

"I grew up with my Dad telling me how the fifties and sixties were the most inspiring periods of his life. I envied his connection to history; there was nothing so revolutionary going on when I was in my early twenties. Occasionally up in Tuscaloosa kids would stage anti-apartheid protests, but those never took off in the same way that the Civil Rights Movement did. I would love to see your scrapbooks sometime, Wook. There may be a picture of my old man in there, watching history unfold on Dexter Avenue."

The grizzly bear smiled like I had asked for too much. "Sure, you can see them anytime you want. What use do I have for them anymore? Like Bubba says, I'm A.G.F. Or maybe A.T.E. is more like it: *Attached to the El.* Anyway, we better get hopping if we're going to get the chow done for this event. We've got a lot of quesadillas to make."

Before we set to work, Bubba had one more piece of intel to proffer.

"You know how you can find out how Walk Compson knows that Mrs. James lady? You can ask him—or at least his people. His campaign is this afternoon's special event. They're throwing a little birthday party for their deputy director. Only make sure they've got plenty of tequila in them before you start fishing, Ennis. Lexi needs to make her tips."

"Who's Lexi?" I casually asked.

Bubba and Wookie didn't answer. They were too busy laughing.

CHAPTER EIGHT

They were laughing, of course, because Lexi was Red's real name.

As the Wook and I set to work, I wished he and Bubba hadn't let her secret out, even if they didn't know it was a secret. I didn't deserve to know her real name yet; I hadn't earned the right. Now I would either have to admit to her that I knew it, which felt like a letdown, or I would have to pretend I was clueless until she shared it with me, which was worse than a letdown—that was a lie. Either way, I felt like the rug of the one good thing I had going had been yanked out from under me.

She turned up about an hour after I clocked in. Wookie was boiling rice as I chopped green onions. Even amid the swirl of odors around me I was aware of her right away. She had lost the pigtails and gym shorts but had kept the knee-highs. Now the socks snuck up toward the hem of a short pleated skirt that flounced at her hips when she walked. Her tank top said DEMOCRACY IN ACTION.

"Power to the people," Wook sighed, face flushed with either steam or lust.

"Forget peace," Bubba cracked. "Give me a chance."

I shot him a look, but he shot me one straight back. His let me know that laughing at his jokes was part of my job description.

Red only said one thing to me before the El doors were unlocked and the Compson party began to arrive: "*Save Me the*

Waltz reading tonight. Maybe a little Nat King Cole for the soundtrack if you're lucky. We can see the house he was born in from my roof. Ten o'clock. Be there or be square."

I didn't push for another word. I wasn't going to be greedy.

Because I was back in the kitchen, I had to peek through the double swing doors for a glimpse of the crowd. They were a pretty liberal-looking bunch for Alabama. I counted at least three ponytails and five pierced ears on the white guys. Even the hippier-looking ones were dressed elegantly—all khaki, no jeans.

They were no match for the African American men, though. Those guys were the spiffiest. Unlike Amory Justice's coterie, they weren't uniformly decked out in navy blue and red neckties. Their suits were gold, sherbet, mauve. Several of them wore three-piecers, and plenty of watch chains dangled between vest pockets, with shiny silver fobs poking out over their bellies.

Compared to all their razzmatazz, I looked like something stuck to the bottom of a shoe.

Not forty minutes into the shindig, Bubba came back to the grill as Wookie was showing me how to arrange a tilapia taco platter. "You're going to have to bus," he told me. "We've got plates and margarita glasses all over creation out there, and His Boy Elroy is a no-show. I know he's a friend of yours, Wook, but enough is enough. His ass is history."

"His Boy Elroy?" I asked, washing my hands.

"High-school kid," Wookie explained. "He should be in high school, anyway. He dropped out last winter claiming he wanted to make money. Hell, I used to make fifteen bucks an hour tutoring him in history before he got stupid. Honest to God, his name is Elroy, so he gets *Jetsons* jibes from here to Timbuktu. I think that's why he's a screw-up. Lotsa Hanna-Barbara fans left in the world, you know. Elroy's probably at home wondering if life would be easier if his name was Yogi."

"I've got no problem bussing tables," I assured my new boss. "There's not much work I think I'm too good to do."

"Good," Bubba nodded. "Just one thing." He tapped his forearm. "Roll down your sleeves. This is a class crowd. They don't want to see your tattoo."

I did as told and covered St. Jude up. Then I grabbed a bus tray and headed out the doors into the dining area, Bubba right behind me. He veered off behind the bar as I started stacking dirty dishes. I could feel him eyeing me like he thought I might heist the silverware. Then I happened to turn my back for just a second, and when I turned back, I caught him red-handed. He was tucking his tip jar under the bar again.

"I don't blame you," I said as I toted a load past him to the sink. "But maybe someday you'll see there's no need for that."

"Maybe someday," he shrugged.

Someone in the crowd knocked a plate over, so I had to grab a mop and wipe the floor. As I wrangled the salsa pile into a dustpan, I saw him. Walk Compson. Maybe because I was squatting at the time, he looked the way I remembered him as a kid: like a mountain of a man. Like something straight off Mt. Rushmore.

It wasn't just that he was a big guy—6'5" at least—or that his features appeared so chiseled you thought the lines in his face were groove marks from a sculptor's tooling. It was his aura. The guy had presence, authority. Not many black men his age could claim to have so intimidated George Wallace that the *Il Duce* of Alabama never failed to address him as *Mr.* Compson. I remembered my dad telling me that story years ago, back when Quentin Skinner thought his son might carry on his legacy and amount to something.

As I was walking the dustpan to the garbage can, I accidentally bumped into Walk. When I apologized, he said, "No apology necessary, son. We're in your house, and we made that mess. Thank you for cleaning up after us."

We stared at each other for a second.

"You look familiar," he said. "Have we met before?"

"Me? No. I'm nobody—just a Joe."

"Aren't we all at the end of the day?"

I almost smiled. Unlike Mayor Justice, Walk Compson was a politician who might actually hold a door for a regular Joe.

After I cleared the tables, I had to lug a Santa Claus–sized sack of garbage out to the dumpster. The son of a bitch was heavy as hell, and it leaked. As I hoisted the bag onto my back, I felt something liquid gush down my spine. I hoped it was beer or Margarita mix, but with my luck it was probably a steaming glob of *queso blanco.*

I shuffled out the rear door with my knees as bent as an arthritic's. How I was going to get the bag over the bin's top without it breaking and dumping taco flotsam over my head wasn't clear. I was trying to decide whether I was strong enough to chuck the thing overhand when somebody stopped me cold.

"Either you're Ennis Skinner or you stole his face. I'd recognize those eyes anywhere."

It was a black man, mustachioed and my age, his chest and arm muscles bulging under his blazer like fists punching their way out of a sheet. The guy looked as if he planned to toss me over the bin.

"What's the matter, Ennis? You don't recognize me?"

I did.

"Tyler Petco." I didn't put out a hand for him to shake. He didn't put his out for me, either. "It's been a while," I admitted.

"A long while," he agreed, his ruby lips drawn tight. "Last I saw of you, you were high-tailing it out of the locker room with your tail tucked between your legs, not two seconds after Coach Perkins cut you."

"I think we've just agreed that's been a few years, Ty."

During my short tenure as a Crimson Tide quarterback, Tyler Petco was my favorite receiver. The guy had pistons for legs and was about as nimble as Baryshnikov when it came to leaping for a catch. In fact, our offensive line started calling him Baryshnikov, but he objected. "More like Nijinsky," he replied. "Nijinsky had more vertical leap. Plus, unlike other cats in his time, he could perform *en pointe.*"

He then enjoyed schooling us in our ignorance by providing an overview of the career of Vaslav Nijinsky, lead dancer for the Ballets Russe back in, like, 1909. Ty was a smart guy, in other words. A real overachiever. Back then he could teach me all he wanted about ballet if it meant he reeled in the bombers I chucked him. About two months before I was kicked off the team we trounced Mississippi State 53–34, in large part because of Ty. I went twenty-two for thirty that day, and twenty of those passes were delivered straight to his breadbasket. Those completions helped earn me some of my best single-game stats—and I wasn't even high on coke.

"I guess you didn't get my letter a few years back," Ty said. "It was after the fifteenth reunion of the '88 squad. Of course, all any of us could talk about was you. I didn't even know you were in Kilby until then, Ennis. I'm really sorry—I spent most of the nineties in Ghana doing missionary work with the Presbyterian church. If I had known what happened to you, I would have written from Africa. Then again, since my Montgomery letter never made it to you, I guess one from Ghana would have had a tough time getting delivered, huh?"

"The postman doesn't ring once in prison. Never mind twice."

The truth was I had received Ty's letter. It was all about how he forgave me for ruining his senior season. I never wrote back because I didn't write anybody back while I did my time. I didn't know what to say to people I had screwed other than "Sorry," and one word doesn't do diddly when it comes to making one's amends.

"You part of Walk Compson's campaign?" I asked.

"You bet. Walk's going to make for a great mayor. He's going to bring this city into the twenty-first century. And I'm not just talking racewise. I'm talking economic development. We've got a good shot at landing a Hyundai plant in the Gump. That's an opportunity Amory Justice would never pursue. He would be afraid of Montgomery getting overrun with Koreans."

Ty slipped into a mock accent that sounded a lot like Foghorn Leghorn: *"Howevahh would ahh proud Southahhn herithhhhage survive with foreignahhhs stalking our streets and pahsuing our whomen . . ."*

"You don't have to sell me on your candidate," I said. "Ex-cons don't get to vote."

I thought my back was going to snap from the garbage bag. I swung it off my lattisimus dorsi and into my hands. I couldn't lift it higher than my shoulders, however. I had the thing at my chest but it was too damn heavy to straighten my arms. The bag might have flattened me if Ty hadn't rushed up to lend a hand. Together we pushed our elbows straight until the sack went over the top and clunked down the dumpster's gullet.

"You're going to ruin your suit," I told him, wiping my hands on the back of my grubby khakis.

"Better my suit than your back, don't you think?"

"One of those things has a brighter future than the other. And it's not my back."

He was looking for something to wipe his hands on. I offered him my apron.

"Mr. Compson told me about your father, you know. He's quite fond of Mr. Skinner. He says guys like him and Robert Graetz don't get the attention they deserve. It takes some spine for a white man to get whupped and bombed back in the day."

"I'm not so sure spine runs in my family; I don't seem to have inherited much—literally or figuratively." I stooped to stretch my vertebrae. "So you're hot on Walk Compson, Ty. Bully for you. Let me ask you something, though: if he's such a stand-up guy, why is Lister James's wife all over TV asking where your man is? There she is screaming his name as she's getting Tasered, and Walk is nowhere to be seen. Him being a no-show this morning wouldn't happen to have anything to do with the condition Lister was found in, would it?"

I could see Ty hesitate. "Politics is a dirty game," he admitted. "No matter how clean the candidate, he's only as good as his friends. And sometimes a man has to distance himself from friends who aren't as clean as a man's friends need to be. There's nothing hypocritical in not tolerating friends' uncleanliness, Ennis. Lister liked to brag he was a close advisor of Walk's, but the truth is that they haven't been close for a good three years now."

"Why? Because Walk found out the good lawyer was into rubber suits and leashes?"

"Rubber suits and leashes might make for good newspaper copy, but they're harmless among consenting adults."

"They weren't so harmless to Mr. James."

"No, but Lister had other . . . *inclinations* that, if they'd become public knowledge, could've made what happened today seem as harmless as consenting adults holding hands in the park. Personally, I think he's better off passing away as a punch line rather than a pervert."

"What are you talking about?"

Ty was impatient with my grilling; I could see it in the tautness of his mustache.

"I shouldn't go into details. I made a pledge a long time ago when I entered public service that I wouldn't gossip. A man has to keep his conscience clean when he's involved in as dirty a game as politics can get, and I have to live with myself. What's your interest in the James family, anyway?"

"I knew their daughter."

It was like a light kicked on. "Let me guess: Alice Faye . . . the infamous one. Lister and Brenda's other children are very successful, you know. One's a lawyer in Birmingham, one's a pediatrician in Auburn, and the youngest runs a Baptist mission down in Mexico. Then there was Faye. Her death would have broken her parents' hearts if Faye hadn't been breaking their spirits for twenty years. It was almost a relief to them, I think. She was definitely the black sheep of the family."

"I'm not sure that description is politically correct, given the makeup of that household."

Ty smiled. "You're right—a poor choice of words on my part. My bad. But if we could conjure up Faye from the great beyond—conjure her up clean and sober—I wouldn't be surprised to find out that race had something to do with her going to pot. The other James kids are clearly mixed race, but Faye—well, she was white as snow, now wasn't she? It couldn't have been easy for her to have the heritage she did but no visible sign of it. Imagine her bringing a boy home for the first time. . . . How many of those boys froze in shock at meeting her mom for the first time? I bet even you, the son of Quentin Skinner—why, I bet you even mistook Mrs. James for the maid when Faye introduced you."

"Faye never introduced me. Today was the first time I ever saw the mother. Faye told me that her folks were dead."

Ty smiled again. "You've just made my point, haven't you? However, we like to think we've risen above the cauldron of racial conflict—conflicts that made this city a crucible fifty years ago—we find out we're not as enlightened as we'd like to be. We're still swimming in the Mulligan stew, aren't we? No matter how many colors and flavors, it always seems to boil down to black and white. If you don't believe me, ask Amory Justice's campaign staff. They're doing a great job of keeping the stew on boil."

"I want to know what came between Walk and Lister James, Ty. It's important that I do. It's for Faye's daughter's sake."

"You mean Dixie?" He exhaled loudly. "Dixie is what came between Walk and Lister. That's the best way I can put it."

"You're going to have to explain. Like I said, it's important."

He looked around to make sure no one had crept out the back of the El.

"About a year ago Dixie told Walk some very disturbing things about her grandfather. *About him and her.* Nothing graphic, mind you. Apparently Lister's pastimes didn't stop at rubber suits and leashes. He was into photography, too. Now Dixie didn't accuse Lister of anything criminal—not directly, anyway. If you know about her then you know that Dixie is . . . *simple.* She doesn't have a filter. She'll tell you anything about herself without hesitation, totally innocent. The one time I met her she asked me if I could help her learn to fly—and I don't mean airplanes. I mean fly as in superhero flying. Because, to her, Faye was Supergirl, you see, and Supergirl could fly. . . . Well, one day Walk was visiting the Jameses, and it just so happened that he and Dixie were in the kitchen by themselves, and she started talking about how her grandfather had been posing her for pictures."

"Porn pictures?"

My mind had gone right to the crotch shots C had shown me. Ty shook his head.

"Dixie would no more know to say 'porn' than she would 'exploitation.' Like I said, she's simple—she can't comprehend bigger concepts of what's right and wrong. All she told Walk was that her grandfather had been taking pictures of her in her pajamas and then gave her a nightie to put on. Now that in and of itself might not normally have caused much concern if not for what Dixie said next."

"Which was what?"

"She told Walk that Lister was her daddy."

I didn't know what to say. That left Ty staring into the shock on my face.

"You mean *literally* her daddy? As in incest?"

Ty shrugged. "Who knows? That's what I mean about Dixie not being able to distinguish between the literal and the metaphorical. Did Faye ever say anything to you about Lister pulling any funny stuff with her? It would explain why she was so estranged from the family."

"I told you, Faye never talked about her parents, other than to say they were dead."

"Well, if not Lister himself, who would you pin as Dixie's dad?"

I almost started to say High C, but I stopped. I didn't want Ty thinking I knew anything about the baby-making history of Montgomery's most notorious methmaker-turned-publishing-magnate.

Bad idea. That left Ty to misinterpret my silence.

"So you're the father, huh, Ennis?"

I laughed. "Not hardly, friend. There are a lot of things I can be blamed for, but that's not one of them. I didn't even meet Faye until after Dixie was born. Not that she ever told me about the kid. . . . What did Walk do when Dixie told him Lister was her old man?"

"He did what anyone would do at the first hint of incest. He went right to Lister and said he wanted Dixie out of the house and into a place of her own immediately."

"And what did Lister say?"

"What could he say? He denied it. The perverts always do.

But he did exactly as Walk told him. He moved Dixie into her own apartment the next day. It shot Brenda into the stratosphere. She was protective of that girl—at least, she thought she had protected her. Lister put his foot down, though. Did Brenda know why? I can't say. All I know is that Lister had to move Dixie out, or Walk would have laid the hammer to him."

"Why didn't Walk do that anyway? Why didn't he report what Dixie said to the police—both about the pics and the daddy business?"

Suddenly, my old teammate wasn't so talkative.

"Let me guess: the election is coming up. Walk couldn't declare his candidacy if his 'close associate' was being investigated for siring his own granddaughter—never mind popping snapper shots of her. Walk has to maintain his 'political viability,' I'm sure."

Ty stiffened at the implication. "If Dixie had said something specific about Lister abusing her, you can bet Walk would have reported it. He has always treated the kid like she was his own. He treated Faye like she was his, too—at least until the meth got the best of her and she fell in with the wrong crowd."

He looked at me, embarrassed.

"It's okay," I told him. "I *was* part of that bad crowd. I'm trying to make amends for it."

"By the time Dixie told Walk about Lister, Faye was long dead. There's no way short of a DNA test to know what she meant about Lister being her daddy. And nobody has ever found any pics of Dixie—"

I flinched, thinking of the images I had seen at C's. Apparently Ty had yet to go on the Internet. Nor did he seem to notice my buttoned lip, which was good.

"—Walk was doing what he could without the story leaking to the public. The Justice campaign would have gone great white on the rumors. Getting the girl into her own place was the best solution at the time, until the story could be sorted out."

"I'm guessing the events of today have made the sorting all that more difficult. . . . What's Walk doing about Dixie being missing?"

I regretted saying it; I hadn't meant to let Dixie's disappearance slip.

"Dixie is missing? Since when? Walk told me he just talked to her last Friday."

"I better get back inside." I didn't want to talk to Ty anymore. "I'm still on the clock."

He wasn't going to let me go until he knew he had sold me on his candidate.

"He's a good man, Ennis. And it's important for Montgomery for him to win. You understand that, right? We're the last city in the South with a quarter-million population never to have elected a black mayor. It's time that happened."

"I hope it does, for your sake and the Gump's. Just watch your back on the Justice crowd. I'm telling you, they're going to make hay of Walk's not being there for Mrs. James in her moment of need. As bad as it looks to have cops Tasering a black woman, it looks just as bad to have her crying out for a spokesman who isn't there to speak for his people."

"Don't worry about Amory Justice. We've got the grip on him."

"What's that supposed to mean?"

"I can't tell you, but buy a paper on Saturday. It'll be front-page news."

There were so many things swirling in my head I couldn't keep them straight.

"I need your help, Ty. I need you to tell me everything. I'm trying to find Dixie. I owe it to her because of Faye. From the sound of it, Walk owes her as well. So let's come clean and stop speaking to each other in riddles. I've got a bit of information that might be of interest to you concerning the Justice people—Reese Justice in particular. But in exchange for that, you have to tell me what's happening Saturday. I've had too many surprises in the past twenty-four hours to let another biggie sneak up on me."

Ty licked his lips. I could tell that despite that shiny suit he wasn't too good to handle any dirt I might have dug up.

"Okay . . . rumors about Saturday will start making the rounds, anyway. It'll be news soon enough. But you have to go first. Tell me what you know about Reese Justice."

I shrugged. "Maybe it's not a big deal, maybe it is. I just happened to see her this morning at Dirk's Filet and Vine with a guy I know has some . . . criminal associations, shall we say. I don't know the guy's name, but his face is hard to miss. It's flat as a paper plate. He looks like a truck ran it over. He answers to Treadface—at least, he answers to that with me."

"And what 'criminal associations' does he have?"

"This Treadface is muscle for a drug cook I used to know. Goes by the name of High C. Now High C claims to have gone legit, but the glimpse I got of the business he's in these days looks pretty shady to me."

Ty snapped his fingers. "Anarchy Ahoy! The minute you said drug cook I knew who you were talking about. That outlaw son of a bitch tried to contribute $10,000 to Walk's campaign. He's exactly why we need limits in Alabama—there aren't any on individuals, and barely any on corporations. We investigate any incoming monies, so of course we rejected his. Maybe his money wasn't too dirty for Amory Justice. You know why this High C character is trying to buy some influence, don't you? He's afraid the city will run him out of business. And Walk *will*, too—by hook or by crook. It's embarrassing to have a publishing house selling garbage like that in Montgomery."

"Tell me what's happening Saturday, Ty. I gave you my news."

He didn't want to, but he damn well knew he couldn't stiff me now.

"Last week we were approached by an anonymous source wanting to sell us a picture."

"More pictures? You'd think people would learn leave their kinks off camera."

"This isn't that kind of picture. It's even more incriminating than the ones Lister took. It's a picture of Amory Justice from fifty years ago, during the Montgomery bus boycott."

If that was supposed to be a grenade, the grenade was a dud. I told Ty I didn't get the point.

"There's not a politician in the South above the age of fifty who doesn't have to account for where he was during the Civil Rights Movement," he explained. "Not every white kid was Scout Finch back then, you know. Take Trent Lott. It's well known that Mississippi's former senior senator was president of Sigma Nu at Ole Miss when James Meredith tried to desegregate the campus in 1962. Don't think he hasn't had a lot of explaining to do over the years. It's the same with Amory Justice. He likes to claim blacks are better off since he came into office. But what if somebody turned up a picture of him, say, at fifteen or sixteen, showing his true feelings about colored folks?"

"Showing them how?"

My mind flashed to pictures I had seen of Montgomery in 1956: wild-eyed white men screaming and cursing at blacks, taunting them, trying to provoke them to violence.

"Showing them with a baseball bat, maybe?"

"Showing them with something equally violent," Ty said. "A middle finger."

"You're shitting me."

"Nope. According to our anonymous source, this picture shows our current mayor flipping the bird to 'coloreds' breaking Jim Crow's back."

"Kind of convenient that a picture like that would only turn up now, five decades after the fact."

"You can blame Amory for that. His current TV commercials are montages of pictures from childhood on, so he invited folks to ask what he was up to during the Movement. Like I said, it's time for Montgomery to have a black mayor. And this picture is going to make it happen."

"Just out of curiosity, how much money will it take for this picture to pass into the right hands? I'm assuming your source wants some cake. Something tells me that not even a Democrat would donate a shot of Amory Justice hoisting a high one."

"The source wants $25,000."

I whistled.

Before Ty could answer, the back door snapped open, and a drop-dead brunette in a black skirt waltzed out. "There you are!" she said, before planting a wet one on Ty's lips. I would like to say it was her beauty that had me blinking at my shoes, but I would be a liar. It was her color. She was white as *queso blanco.*

"This is my wife, Sonja," Ty said. The brunette and I shook hands before Ty sent her inside with a promise to join her shortly.

When she was gone his eyes tightened on my face like a vise.

"You know how I'll know things have really changed in Montgomery between black and white, Ennis?"

"I think I have a feeling."

Ty went ahead and answered his own question anyway.

"It will be the day I can introduce my wife to someone and not have to see the look of surprise you just gave me. Take care, QB. I hope you can keep your nose clean—really, I do."

CHAPTER NINE

I managed to keep it clean until my shift ended at eleven. It had been a twelve-hour workday, but there was no way I was going to be too tired to walk Red to the Fitzgerald house. As I clocked out, I took two shots of Jägermeister. Bubba agreed to deduct them from my paycheck since I was light on cash. Then I reminded Wookie to bring his scrapbooks the next day.

As Red and I walked up Boultier, I enjoyed the night smell of jasmine and crepe myrtle. Every few paces she brushed into me, and I would revel in a whiff of something even more powerful—her. I wanted like hell to put my arm around her and pull her close, but I was afraid to. Twice while we worked I had caught her on her cell phone looking flustered. Even with the phone's ringer turned to off, Eric the ex wasn't going away anytime soon.

The first thing I noticed when we walked into her apartment was a sheet thrown over the mirror.

"I didn't want you worrying about seeing your own kisser," she said with a grin. "You're not quite up there with the Elephant Man, but I understand. Honestly, it's kind of a relief. Eric couldn't take two steps without stopping to admire his own reflection."

On her roof she spread out a down comforter and we stretched across the shingles, a few inches of safety between us. The shingles were still hot, but I didn't care. Especially not when Red cracked her copy of *Save Me the Waltz* open and started reading from another tipped-in half-sheet of stationery.

"Along the staircases of dark streets, men wandered in search of girls, searching with nothing to navigate them but tenuous wisps of jasmine that taunted them with their ephemeral tracings. . . . The men peeked for them behind boxwoods and while tiptoeing through unbroken and untrammeled beds of corydalis and cowslip, never thinking that these sad, playful sprites of femininity know that a man's craving is incommensurate with his nurturing and that therefore a woman's best option is to remain a corona of his desire. . . . So the men were doomed to shadow the future of their own failure, wanting but incapable of truly having because truly having is truly giving, never realizing that the susurrations that said to them 'If you can only find you are free to take' mocked them with the lure of appetence. . . ."

That did it for me. I rolled over onto Red and kissed her, hard. I don't think she was expecting it. At first she wedged the book against my shoulder and started to push me away. Only it didn't seem like she really wanted me to stop, so I didn't. Then a crazy thing happened. She tucked an arm around the back of my neck and instead of pushing she pulled my mouth to hers.

It was a real gum-cruncher of a kiss. I felt my tongue in her mouth and hers in mine. Then she did this wild thing with her teeth. She sunk them lightly into the thick part of my tongue, the back part, and slid them down the length of it. Over and over again. Her mouth closed tightly around my tongue, and she just kept going back and forth until I thought the electric tickle the move gave off would blow out my whole circuitry.

Goddamn she tasted good.

Just as suddenly she stopped. She put her hand over my mouth and whispered, her voice a feather in the heat.

"You understand that I can't go any farther than this tonight, don't you? You understand why, too, right?"

Sure, I understood. Why wouldn't I? I was an ex-con. She had an ex-boyfriend. One more X in the equation and this game of ours was over.

I rolled onto my back, staring at the sequined stars.

"I just broke my cardinal rule," I confessed. "I waited ten years to practice it: 'Do No Bad.' I'm sorry I pressured you, Red. St. Dominic needs to get on the case to make me a better choirboy."

She propped herself on her side, above me, so her hair hung down onto my throat.

"Don't be too good of a choirboy, Hardboil. Just remember: you've got to sin to get saved."

"You smell so damn good. You know what you smell like? You smell like freedom."

"Dominic and that other saint of yours—Jude—they're looking out for our best interests, aren't they?"

"If they're not, they're out of a job. Bubba isn't the only one who can fire someo—"

I didn't finish because she had pressed the curve of her neck into my face just as she had at El Rey the day before. If I didn't have a single more minute to live, I wouldn't have cared. I would have died a happy bastard.

Of course, nobody really dies of happiness. If you don't learn to live with the modest moments of it that come your way, you're more likely to die from greed. I planned on a long life. I kissed Red on the forehead, shimmied down her roof, and left her and her Zelda to the shelter of velvet shadows.

It would have been a nice end to a dirty day, but dirty days rarely ever end nicely. I was swinging around the corner of Boultier and Westmoreland on my way to Dad's house when the headlights nailed me. Damn near blasted me out of my socks. I couldn't see a thing but the silhouette of an SUV. I didn't need to see more to guess it was red enough to look like a fat strawberry.

"Ennis, Ennis, Ennis," C said, motioning me to the back window. "Here my baby girl has gone missing, and what are you doing all day? Making burritos for Walk Compson and sniffing some waitress's taco."

"Keep it up, cretin, and you'll be eating that beard off your own chin."

That cracked up Treadface and Twitchy, who were stationed in the front seats. C smirked and kicked the passenger door open. When he stepped into the night, starlight sparked off the rhinestones on his leather vest.

"Maybe I didn't make myself clear. Finding Dixie isn't your part-time job. If you're going to put in overtime, it better be for me and not for El Rey."

"The El pays better."

C tugged his beard. "The hardest part of being a parent is patience. And Ennis Skinner is making me very impatient."

"Let me ask you a question, C: how do you know for sure you're Dixie's dad? What if Faye was bullshitting you? Neither of us would put it past her, would we? Faye was a scammer. I bet she had you paying child support right up to the day she died. She probably threatened to go to the cops if you didn't pay and rat you out over every meth recipe you ever cooked up. But what if it was all a con, and you aren't the jit donor? What if you've been a sucker for nineteen years?"

"You going to tell me Dixie sprung from *your* Crimson Tide loins?"

I laughed. "You're the third person to ask me that today. Maybe I should've been the kid's father. Maybe things would have been better for Dixie and me both if I had been."

"Sure, Ennis. You would have made a great dad. You know

how I know that? *Because you've been such a great son."*

He tugged his beard for a few more seconds so the insult could sink in.

"Boys, I'm walking down to Sinclair's to hear a pitch from a potential writer. Putting up with pitches is what a publisher has to do for a free beer, you know. This one's cheesier than most I hear. Some Confederate-loving bastard has written a book about Nathan Bedford Forrest. I'm sure Quentin taught you who he was, right, Ennis? Civil War general best known for introducing guerilla tactics into modern warfare. Later the Klan claimed him as its honorary Grand Wizard. Now you might think that this pitch is for a biography of old Forrest, but it's not. It's for a book about *management.* I shit you not. The lessons that modern businessmen can learn from the General's writings and speeches. Total rip-off of *Sun Tzu's Strategy for Managers.* Is that not the craziest fucking idea for a book you've ever heard? But like I said, it's what a publisher has to put up with for a free beer."

He patted the open window next to Twitchy with an open palm.

"While I'm having my quaff, boys, remind this quiff of the terms of our contract. Maybe I didn't articulate them clearly enough yesterday."

And with that he swaggered down Boultier, down toward the intersection with Felder Avenue where Sinclair's sat, two doors east of the El. Treadface and Twitchy slithered out of the SUV, their slamming doors snapping like gunfire. I backed a step away, but I didn't run. There was nowhere to run to. What the hell, I figured. I could always crazy glue my bottom plate back together a second time.

I turned to Treadface.

"How's the blond from Dirk's this morning? Whisper in her ear lately?"

If his association with Reese Justice was supposed to be a secret, my knowing it didn't faze him. Treadface just plopped his hands to his hips and smiled broadly. And with a face as flat as that sumbitch's, broad meant broad as a beam.

"How's the hot red up on the roof?" he fired back. "I bet she tastes just like a Red Hot, doesn't she?"

That made me madder than the fist he flew into my gut.

★ ★ ★ ★ ★

WEDNESDAY

★ ★ ★ ★ ★

CHAPTER TEN

By morning the bruises had turned purple, so my torso looked like chipped beef. The upside was they didn't lay into my face. The downside was I was pretty sure they had cracked a rib.

It hurt like fuck to breathe, so I didn't sleep much. I probably should've gone to a doctor but I was too mad. I wanted to keep the blade of pain sharp so I wouldn't walk it off. One way or another that was the last time those two futs would use me for a punching bag.

I rummaged the closet in Dad's bathroom and found some four-inch elastic bandage wrap. By the time I tucked the tail end under the last layer I was cinched tighter than Tutankhamen from belly button to armpit.

And still it hurt like fuck to breathe.

It was barely dawn, and I could hear Dad sawing logs in his bedroom, which didn't do much to ease my discomfort. I clicked on the television, curious how the local affiliates were framing the James story. According to a late-night press conference, the cops who Tasered Mrs. James had been suspended pending an investigation. There was a catch, though: they had been suspended with pay. I knew enough about politics to know that meant any investigation the mayor's office conducted would clear them.

Sure enough, Amory Justice stared down the cameras and assured Montgomery that the incident, however unfortunate, was not racially motivated.

"What we're investigating is whether the officers were justified in feeling that their safety was at risk." He announced this with a face straighter than a plumb-bob. "You have to remember what the police found when they entered the James residence. There was a dead body on the scene—*a dead body in unusual circumstances that none of our men had ever encountered before.* Suddenly, you insert an out-of-control woman into such a situation and the police don't know exactly what they're dealing with. It's the police's job to contain the scene. That's what they thought they were doing by attempting to remove this woman to the other side of the police line. Mrs. James has a civic responsibility to respect police procedure, and she wasn't respecting it. Now I understand she was upset. *I would be too if I saw my spouse in the state she had just seen hers.* But just because she claims her husband was 'best friends' with Walk Compson doesn't give her the right to disrespect the police the way rabble rousers like Mr. Compson have made a career of doing. There has to be the rule of law, *especially in such a peculiar situation.* Otherwise, the city will decay into chaos."

I had to hand it to the mayor. Short of pantomiming Lister James's "inclinations," he couldn't have reminded viewers more of their kinky nature. What a guy, that Amory Justice. He probably had an assistant send a back-channel flower arrangement to the funeral home before he went on-air to convey his condolences. That and cover his ass with black Montgomery.

I was about to flick the TV off when I caught a glimpse of the daughter in the background. Something told me Reese Justice was the architect behind her father's statement. She probably had a sample audience wired up in some consultant's studio to gauge whether the public had bought her bull. Knowing Montgomery, namedropping Walk probably did accomplish a lot of containing—in the white parts of the city, anyway.

The more I looked at her sharp face, the sorer I got. The fist prints I was sporting had some connection to her, and I wanted to know what it was. I decided I would give Reese Justice a little visit and let her see Treadface's handiwork. Why not? The only clue I had to tracking down Dixie was a name on a refrigerator, and figuring out who "Gilbert" was wouldn't be easy if C's goons planned to dance on my ribcage every night.

At the very least, playing the Kudzu Ann Coulter card would buy me some breathing room—literally.

So as Dad snored away, I slipped out of the house and borrowed his truck to head downtown. I didn't know exactly where the Justice campaign was headquartered, but I had a good idea it wouldn't be too far from City Hall. I was so anxious I skipped the crooked grid of streets that connected the boho to the city's commercial center and hopped on I-85 south, taking the last exit onto South Perry Street before the highway dead-ended.

A westward turn on Washington Avenue took me into the historical district. On my left I passed the First White House of the Confederacy, where Jefferson Davis lived during the few short months in 1861 when Montgomery was the capital of the South. A block farther up on my right was the Southern Poverty Law Center, which monitored skinheads and surviving remnants of the Klan. Across from the SPLC sat its Civil Rights Memorial, a huge granite obelisk carved with the names of forty men and women murdered during the Movement.

I thought about the White House and the memorial sitting only two blocks apart. That is the blood knot that binds Montgomery together: its dual identity as the Cradle of the Confederacy and the Birthplace of Civil Rights. You don't see Rosa Parks here without Jeff Davis lurking nearby. No MLK without Robert E. Lee. I drove past the historical marker on Dexter Avenue commemorating the old telegraph station where news from Fort Sumter first came across the wire. A hundred yards behind me, the street ended at the steps of the state capitol. I saw the building gleam in my rearview, and I imagined Davis standing in the front balcony as he was inaugurated as the president of the confederacy on February 18, 1861: *"We have entered upon the career of independence, and it must be inflexibly pursued. Through many years of controversy with our late associates, the Northern States, we have vainly endeavored to secure tranquility, and to obtain respect for the rights to which we were entitled. As a necessity, not a choice, we have resorted to the remedy of separation . . ."*

Then my imagination leaped forward one hundred years to March 24, 1965, when Dr. King stood on the steps below that same balcony after the Selma to Montgomery march to deliver his "How Long, Not Long" speech: *"Once more the method of nonviolent resistance was unsheathed from its scabbard, and once again an entire community was mobilized to confront the adversary. And again the brutality of a dying order shrieks across the land. Yet, Selma, Alabama, became a shining moment in the conscience of man. If the worst in American life lurked in its dark street, the best of American instincts arose passionately from across the nation to overcome it . . ."*

I thought again of Faye and how not a single feature hinted of mixed parentage. From what I had seen of Dixie, nobody would ever guess her ethnicity, either. I couldn't decide if the absence of color was a sign of assimilation or suppression. I suddenly wanted Walk Compson to win Tuesday's election, if only so his dark, undeniable face would force my city to confront the riddle of race—not with the upheaval it went through forty and fifty years ago, and not with defensiveness or the taint of politics or some melodramatic insistence that the South was doomed to suffer for the sins of its segregationist fathers . . . I just wanted somebody to talk about it, straight up, in words that cut through the confusion with such clarity that they sounded as if they had been unsheathed from that scabbard Dr. King spoke of.

The Justice campaign was headquartered on Montgomery Street, on the ground floor of an aging skyscraper—what passes for a skyscraper in Montgomery—called the Bell Building. Just a block away was the city's old centerpiece, a fountain that sprang from an artesian well that had been bubbling since the first streets here were mapped in the 1820s. I parked and peeked into the Bell's street-level windows, but there were no dagger-legged blonds to be found—just a gaggle of retirement-age volunteers stuffing envelopes. Every single one of them wore an oversized white T-shirt that said AMORY JUSTICE: A MAN WHO LIVES UP TO HIS NAME.

I watched and waited. Minutes later a slicker crossed the street waltzing in my direction. I knew it was one of the mayor's assistants because the guy was in a navy suit with a white shirt and a red tie. Same helmet hair even. I met him at the door.

"I don't suppose you could tell me where to find Reese Justice."

I tried to sound polite. Apparently, I didn't.

"Who's asking?"

"You talk to all your constituents like that?"

I doubted I was Amory Justice's ideal constituent. The slicker was looking at my St. Jude tattoo, which I hadn't covered. Why would I? It was 96 degrees, and I was sweating. The slicker wasn't. I decided to take another tack.

"I'm from Kinko's. Miss Justice has an order I need to deliver."

"Is it an invisible order?" Then he eased off the smart aleck. "You can give me the package. I'll make sure she gets it."

"No can do, I'm afraid. She slipped me a fifty to deliver it to her—*personally.* See, we don't normally make deliveries at Kinko's, but for an extra fifty, I'm happy to give a customer the personal touch. She might even ask for that fifty back if I don't follow her instructions to the T."

The slicker jerked a thumb toward the glass-fronted diner next to the Bell Building. "She's probably in there, working. That's her unofficial office." He headed into the campaign HQ. "Enjoy your fifty, friend. I'm sure you earned it."

I peeked between the stenciled letters that spelled ZELDA'S CAFÉ. They probably had a breakfast special called Save Me the Waffles—it looked like that cheesy of a place. Among the prim ivory tablecloths and mahogany chairs I spotted Reese Justice sitting by herself, the blades of her fingernails clattering at her laptop. Some detective I was. If not for the slicker, I wouldn't have thought to look into the restaurant.

"Do I know you?" she asked when I dropped into the empty chair across from her.

"Do you talk to all your constituents like that?"

It was becoming my favorite line. I might make it my motto.

"Only to jokers who sit down uninvited. Take a hike, Romeo. I'm not looking for a husband."

"What's the matter? I'm not your type?"

"Probably not. My kind of man knows when he's not wanted. Go find yourself a hobby before I call the manager over."

I had to hand it to her: she was good-looking. A real alabaster statue type. Most Southern women like her lay the makeup on thick as batter, but Reese Justice's skin was pure milk. I leaned forward on my elbows. She screwed her eyes so tight trying to figure my game that her sockets went to slots. I could've fed quarters into them, but I doubted I would pull Lucky 7s.

"You don't want to treat me like a dog," I told her. "You already have a friend who treats me like one, and this dog is tired of getting kicked."

I pulled my shirt up and showed her my chipped-beef torso.

Of course, the bandages spared her all that ugly purple, but they made my point. They made it even better by making her imagine what was underneath the wrapping.

"I can't say I've ever been flashed at breakfast." Her eyebrows rose and sharpened into overturned Vs. "If you want to show off your armor you better know I keep the mace handy. You can't be too careful in downtown Montgomery."

"You're real funny. I'd be interested to see how hard your daddy would laugh to know who you associate with. I saw you yesterday at Dirk's. Tell the tubby butter with the dishpan face you were talking to there to lay off me."

She was surprised, I could tell.

"Francis did that to you?"

I smiled. *Francis.* Some name for a guy with a treadface.

"Sure. Old Francis gets a little punch-happy when he's not toting your water. I figure you're the one to snap the leash. If not you, who? Your daddy? I doubt it. The way he smoked Brenda James on TV this morning, he probably wouldn't care about Francis's hobbies either. So if neither of you do anything, I'll have nobody to complain to but the *Advertiser.* I might even indulge in a little conjecture while I'm filling in the details. Conjecture like if the mayor's daughter's muscle can polka-dot my chest like this, maybe he can rope up an advisor for the mayor's opponent and make it look like autoerotic asphyxiation."

She didn't take kindly to the threat.

"I should've known that leash-and-collar business would come around to Lister James. You mind telling me your connection to Francis? I like to know what I'm dealing with."

I was having so much fun egging her on I decided to egg harder. I wanted to embellish those eggs like it was the night before Easter.

"Maybe the connection with the James family isn't as

farfetched as you think. Franny boy has it in for me. He has the hots for the James's granddaughter, a kid named Dixie. I'm a close family friend, though, and I told Lister and Brenda that Fran has a bad backstory. Your man didn't take it too well when the Jameses sang, *Look away, look away* because of me. He thought he was headed for the land of cotton with the kid, and the grandparents didn't want him trying to take a stand—you know—*way down South in Dixieland.*"

Treadface's reputation must have preceded him. The Kudzu Ann Coulter didn't seem at all surprised to learn that her Francis would have the hots for somebody's nineteen-year-old granddaughter.

"Do you ever read the paper, Mr. Whoever-you-are? Or are you too busy making idle threats to keep on top of the news?"

"I saw the news this morning. Spin it as you might, it didn't look good for your camp. Hard to overcome video of a black woman getting Tasered. Especially a black woman who lives in the east-side suburbs."

"Funny thing about the news: it never gets old. Something new is always breaking. Buy a paper tomorrow, friend. The autopsy report on Lister James will be released to the public. Then we can talk about what can and can't be overcome."

I didn't have a comeback. My silence disappointed her.

"What's the matter? Cat got your tongue? Maybe I should give you a little preview of tomorrow's news." She tapped a button on her laptop. "Now the *Advertiser* can't publish *all* of the details—it's a family rag, after all. But they can give out a URL to the website where it'll be posted. You might want to stay off the Internet tomorrow; the lines will be busy."

Then she read to me:

The decedent is clothed in a diving wetsuit with a face mask that has a single vent for breathing. There are numerous straps and cords restraining the decedent. Ligatures tie the feet to the hands. A single plastic cord extends from the feet to a leather belt about the midriff to the head and lower neck. There is a dildo in the anus covered with a condom.

"That's not the best part, though," she said, looking up with malicious glee. "There's a section called 'Personal Effects.' Let me quote it in its entirety: *Personal Effects: One platinum wedding band on left ring finger, one dildo.*"

She clapped the lid of her laptop down.

"Now tell me, friend, which will be more vivid in the minds of voters next Tuesday as they enter the polls? The Taser or the dildo?"

I sat back, still silent. So silent I could hear her chuckle rattle in her own throat.

"Like I said," I told her. "Tell Francis to leave me alone. That's the only reason I'm here. I don't care about the rest."

I left. I was in Dad's truck and turning off Montgomery Street before I thought of a good comeback. Of course, I couldn't have popped it on Reese Justice even if I had thought of it in Zelda's Café. I couldn't because I had been sworn to secrecy by Tyler Petco. That didn't mean I couldn't drop the bomb about the picture of the mayor in my imagination, though. All the way to the boho I replayed the scene as I wished it might have happened.

"Which will be more vivid in the minds of voters next Tuesday as they enter the polls? The Taser or the dildo?"

Every single time I gave the same reply:

"Your daddy's middle finger."

CHAPTER ELEVEN

I returned Dad's truck to Westmoreland and then walked down to the El. Bubba was surprised to see me when I rapped at the window; I wasn't due to clock in until after lunch. I told him I would help with the morning's prep work. Off the clock even. I didn't want to be alone. "If I'm alone," I told him, "all I'll do is think, and I've got too many things to think about. I can't keep it all straight."

"Well, here's one more thing to ponder: there's going to be a big protest march down Felder at noon. It's all over the news. Just about every civic group in town that leans Democratic is coming out to protest Brenda James's Tasering. The march ends at Huntingdon College. You know what that means—we're going to be swamped for lunch."

"I wonder if my Dad knows about it. It's been twenty years since he marched for anything. Maybe I should call and roust him out of the sack."

Bubba could tell there was more on my mind than local politics. He thought it had to do with Red.

"You overstepped last night, didn't you?" He shook his head as he chopped pineapple for today's sangria. "I know you don't have much patience after ten years in jail, but Lexi's no Easy-Bake Oven. You don't think every guy in the boho has taken a shot with her? Taken a shot and gotten shot down, Ennis. If you want quick cooking, go down to the Wrangler. That's where the Easy-Bake Ovens hang, not here."

126

I thought about the kiss on Zelda Fitzgerald's rooftop. I was pretty sure from the little dance Red did on my tongue that I wasn't the one who went too far. I was also sure I still wasn't ready to hear her real name spoken out loud, certainly not in the same sentence as "Easy-Bake Oven."

"Just because I don't want to be alone doesn't mean I much feel like talking, either," I decided. "How about putting me to work? I'm happy to do it for free so long as I don't have to talk."

I suppose I owed him a friendlier response considering how he had put me on the payroll, but with the bandages still constricting my breathing, I wasn't feeling all that genial. Bubba pointed me to a bucket and broom and told me to wash down the back patio. I grabbed a bottle of dishwashing soap on my way out the door and squirted down the concrete. The first blast of water from the garden hose whipped up a tornado of foam and bubbles. I entertained myself creating all kinds of natural disasters with hurricanes and tsunamis and avalanches of suds. I even took out a bed of fire ants. The hose turned their sand castle to muck. The maze-like orderliness of the colony collapsed into chaos and the buggers started clambering over each other, gasping for air.

I watched for a while before I started wondering what the hell was so entertaining about wiping out insects. I must be in sore need of a diversion if this was my idea of a good time. Pests or no, massacring fire ants was a long way from "Do No Bad."

I turned off the water and used the broom as a squeegee so the patio could dry. I had the slab sparkling like a china plate when the screen door flew open and the Wookie stuck his big grizzly head into the humidity.

"Hey man, I brought my scrapbooks like you asked. Get in here and see if you can find your old man in any of these pics."

On the bar were four huge binders stuffed to the gills with newspaper clippings, wrinkly handbills and fliers, diary entries. Wookie had an original copy of the Montgomery Improvement Association's first call to organize the bus boycott. It was dated December 1, 1955. I remembered the story from Dad: Joanne Robinson had mimeographed the note on the sly at Alabama State University just hours after Rosa Parks's arrest.

"This has got to be worth some cake, Wook. You shouldn't have it Scotch-taped onto plain old construction paper."

"Pretty soon it'll need Scotch tape to hold itself together. Don't get your paw prints on it, either. The oils on your skin can stain the paper."

"My point exactly. If you don't want the paper to fade, you should store it in plastic so oils can't get to it. You know that—you're a historian. Seriously, I bet a library or research center would pay top dollar for something like this. It belongs there or in a museum. The Smithsonian even."

"No, I would never sell any of my collection. Never donate any of it either. I keep thinking somewhere in it all I've got a book. That's about the only ambition left from my so-called academic career: I'd like to see a book with my name on it."

"I can't imagine you couldn't squeeze at least one from this stuff. Nobody has ever printed these pics."

"Publishing is a crazy business, dude. I've tried and tried to get somebody interested. A couple of weeks ago I thought I had a surefire in. The kid Bubba's about to ax, Elroy, he knows some guys who work for a publisher. Only the publisher wasn't interested. There have already been too many books about the bus boycott."

The talk seemed to sadden him, so I shut up and skipped ahead in the pictures.

There were hundreds of black and whites held in place with those little black-matte photo corners. Almost all of the shots were amateur candids, mostly of street scenes. In the foreground of one series smartly dressed African American men helped older women with heads bound in scarves into sedans and station wagons. These were the carpools that carried the black community to work during the 381 days of the boycott. You didn't need a college degree to figure out what was going on. There was almost always an empty bus lurking in the background, the driver scowling out the window.

Another group documented the rallies at Holt Street Baptist Church where protest leaders kept spirits high with sermons and songs. Then there were the more disturbing images: a single young man, bullied to a crouch by a mob. The only thing whiter than the mob's faces were the knuckles of their clenched fists. I thought of the rumored picture of Amory Justice, and I wondered if I looked hard I would find him in this shot.

If not, maybe the next. In this one a white crowd taunted a procession of elderly black women marching down a street. At least half of the crowd looked to be teenagers, some as young as twelve or thirteen. It made me wonder how many of them still called Montgomery home, if they ever feared seeing an image of themselves in a textbook or a documentary, heckling equality from the wrong side of history.

I had barely finished the first of the scrapbooks when Red strolled in. Today she wore camo shorts with Doc Martins and a tight black tank top. What got me most was the choker—just a band of ribbon around her throat with a little amulet dangling from it. Something about the contrast between the black fabric, her freckled skin, and that red mane made her seem like she had been born on a Botticelli canvas. Christ, she was gorgeous.

"If Quentin is in any of these," the Wookie said, blocking my view as he plopped the fattest of the scrapbooks in front of me. "It'll be this one. Lots of Robert Graetz shots in here."

The truth was my eyes were getting blurry. My mind was

wandering, too. I could smell Red's perfume as she circled the tables, lighting candles and refilling the condiment dispensers. The Wook jabbed at a contact sheet with a meaty finger.

"I should get this one scanned in so the individual exposures are clearer. You can't make out many faces on a contact sheet. But I know exactly what it is. Reverend Graetz . . ."

"No, you can't see squat." I slipped the sheet out of the photo corners and held it under the desk lamp that Bubba kept near the cash register. There were twenty-four individual frames on the sheet, a whole roll of a single car passing through a throng.

"If we had a magnifying glass, I might be able to read the license plate. Whoever took this seems to have been obsessed with license plates—"

The front door creaked open before I could plant a period on that sentence. Red must have forgotten to lock it back up when Bubba let her in. I was about to turn and tell whoever the early bird was that we weren't yet seating—only this was no early bird. It was two guys in ski masks. They caught me so by surprise I honestly asked myself why anybody would sport a ski mask during the hottest and longest heat wave in Montgomery history.

Dumb thought, I know.

The reason is self-evident, especially when the ski masks come accessorized with Ruger semi-automatics.

One of the robbers shook his 9 mm so wildly it went off. A bottle of amaretto exploded, sending a tangerine-colored shower raining down the wall behind the bar. Both guys starting yelling, but I couldn't make out a single word. They were shooting louder than they were screaming.

Wookie yanked me off my stool. I fell backwards on top of him as Tabasco, sweet tea, and salt streamed over the bar top onto us. Together we rolled to our stomachs, but there was nowhere to scramble. The glass wall cooler a foot from our faces shattered, and six shelves of import beer burst into a torrent of fizz that hit us like the goddamn Johnstown flood.

I craned my neck past the bottom edge of the bar and saw Bubba's feet disappear into the kitchen. I couldn't tell if he was hit or not. Then something hit me—not a bullet, but a thought. Where was Red?

I looked to my left. She was still standing behind a semicircular booth. Still holding her tray of table candles, grill lighter still in her hand. She was frozen in shock.

"Get down!" I screamed, but she didn't budge. I hopped into crouch and leaped like a panther over the booth, tackling her. Clumps of vinyl and foam upholstery erupted at my feet as shots ripped the back cushions into smithereens. When I landed I thought I was hit, but it was the pain of my bruised ribs. I buried Red under the weight of my body until the shooters turned their attention to the windows and mirrors surrounding us. As ricochets and plywood splinters whirled around us I tried to find something—anything—to use as a weapon. I needed one. All the shooters had to do was peek over the booth, and Red and I would be lying there like we planned to welcome the bullet holes with open arms.

I spotted a bottle of Bacardi 151 on what was left of the bottom shelf of the mangled cooler. Two feet, I reckoned. As I plunged my tattooed forearm toward it, I hoped St. Jude had enough juice that he could protect himself from a shot to the face—he sure hadn't done much for me lately.

My first try was unsuccessful; I was too cowed by the gunfire. Then I realized bullets weren't whizzing at us anymore—the shooters were having too much fun blasting bottles off the bar. I could hear the caterwaul of broken glass, whiskey gurgling out of decanters, whistling CO_2 from the severed keg taps. I took a deep breath and dove for the Bacardi. When I nabbed it I crawled backwards behind the booth, stripping the cap off with my left hand and thumbing the safety on Red's grill lighter with my right.

"You're crazy," Red whispered.

"Better crazy than dead," I told her. I dipped the lighter tip into the neck. One click and the rum ignited into a blue surge of flame.

With the glass growing hot in my palm, I hunched up high enough to peek toward the bar. One shooter was stuffing his pockets from the open register; the other was behind the bar, taking out rows of Grey Goose and Captain Morgan. He only stopped long enough to clean out Bubba's tip jar with his free hand.

"Hey!" I yelled. I hadn't thrown a football in nearly twenty years, but my aim was still good. The bottle rocketed across the restaurant and caught the one rifling the register square in his chest. The flame seemed to clutch him by the throat and choke the surprise out of him. I figured that ski mask was fireproof, but there's not much that won't burn after a douse of 151. Before I knew it the shooter looked like he had sprouted a blue beard. The bottle clattered to the floor. Rum gurgled over the shooter's tennis shoes, trapping him in a tight circle of flame that threatened to toast him like Joan of Arc.

It was all the diversion I needed. I darted across the hardwood, grabbed him by the scruff, and rammed his head into the cash register.

Coins went careening everywhere. The other shooter spun around, but he couldn't pull his trigger because I had his buddy in a headlock shielding me. I saw from his eyes he was weighing his options. He would never get by me to the door, so he took off the opposite direction through the kitchen.

He hadn't disappeared behind the swinging doors two seconds before I heard a single clank followed by a horrible scream. The second shooter staggered backwards out into the seating area, stumbling over his feet. He was sopping wet and seemed to be melting—his whole head and torso were covered with what looked like little shriveled bits of flayed skin. Then I realized that wasn't skin at all.

It was kernels of rice, fresh from a boiling bath of water.

Bubba kicked the doors open. Gripped in his fists was a thick copper skillet that he swung like a Louisville slugger. A single whap to the face and the second shooter crumpled into his own shoes.

"Nobody steals my tips," Bubba snarled at the steaming lump of unconsciousness. For an exclamation point, he drove his boot toe into the shooter's spine.

Now it was my turn to get caught by surprise. I still had the first shooter in a headlock, but he jerked back and slammed me into the paneled wall. I felt my ribs crunch and a flash of agony shot through my insides. I thought I was being Tasered. The shooter broke from my grasp, but instead of cutting for the exit, he did something completely crazy. He jumped forward and swiped one of Wookie's scrapbooks off the bar—the same one I was looking at when the gunfire erupted. Then he dashed out the door.

"Let the police get him," Bubba said, flipping open his phone and dialing 911. "Anybody hit?"

Wookie staggered to his feet, dazed but unharmed. I rushed to Red, who was curled in the fetal position, shaking. I took her in my arms and told her everything was all right.

"You know the worst of this?" Bubba grumbled. "The cops are going to shut down Felder now. That means no protest march. There goes our lunch rush."

He didn't seem to realize it would be a while before El Rey served anything again. There wasn't a strip of wood in the joint that wasn't damaged.

"Son of a bitch!"

The Wook was fishing his scrapbooks from the offal of salsa, guacamole, and hot sauce covering the bullet-riddled bar. He didn't seem to notice he was splattered with the same gunk. So was I for that matter.

"There's one scrapbook missing! Where the hell is it?"

"The one that got away," I said. "He took it. I tried to stop him."

I expected Wookie to ask what a masked gunman would want with a book of Civil Rights memorabilia, but he didn't. He just sank onto a barstool, his face white as the sugar and rock salt scattered all around him.

"Let's see if we know this bastard," Bubba said, stuffing his phone back in his pocket.

It wasn't a mystery to me. I had a good idea who the shooters were. The only question in my mind was whether Treadface or Twitchy was the one who took the skillet in the beaker.

Turns out my good idea wasn't all that good.

"Holy shit," the Wook said peering over the bar. Red and I raced over. The face was redder than El Rey's own salsa. The shooter's skin looked ready to blister from the boiling water. I didn't recognize him, but everybody else did.

"That's His Boy Elroy!" Red gasped.

Bubba shook his head in disbelief, his eyes wide as the cork coasters he stuck under every beer bottle he served.

"Remind me to think twice before I fire somebody again." He looked to me and Red. "You two better get out of here before the cops roll in. They don't need to know you were here, Ennis. I doubt that would sit well with your probation."

"Are you sure?"

He nodded at Red. "She needs you more than the police do."

I went to embrace Red again, but I noticed a scrap of paper on the floor near where Wookie and I had huddled.

"Well, Wook," I said, scooping it up. "At least something of your collection survived. Look—it's the contact sheet we were looking at, almost undamaged."

Only as I went to hand the print to the Wookie, something on its back caught my eye. An ink-stamped name and address. The address didn't mean anything, but the name sure struck a chord. I couldn't believe it. The spray of letters made my heart pump as hard as the spray of bullets had:

PROPERTY OF GILBERT'S PHOTOGRAPHY
JAMES A. GILBERT, PROPRIETOR
1437 HIGHLAND AVENUE
PROUDLY SERVING MONTGOMERY SINCE 1950

CHAPTER TWELVE

Once upon a time Highland Avenue was the main artery feeding the heart of black Montgomery. It was never rich but never poor either. It was home to many of the working-class men and women who risked their jobs in white kitchens and liveries when they refused to ride the buses in 1956. In its heyday Highland Avenue hosted black-owned groceries, gas stations, insurance agencies, tailors, and seamstresses. Churches and juke joints sat side-by-side, gritty blues and grimy jazz mingling with Baptist hymns.

Once upon a time this boulevard throbbed with hope and promise. Some of those hopes and promises had been realized. A lot of them hadn't. As the bigger dreams of justice and equality were deferred and politicians learned to play prejudices and ride the racial divide through code words instead of taking stands in schoolhouse doors, much of the vibrancy of Highland Avenue faded. Now it was a scorched stripe of keeling brick, rotting porch rails and Queen Anne spindlework, fenced-off plots of burnt grass and sand, with only a handful of geriatric businesses clinging on out of pride and spite.

I hoped Gilbert's Photography was one of those dogged ones, but I knew better.

I hustled Red to the Fitzgerald House and made sure her nerves were settled before borrowing her Volkswagen. On Highland I counted down the addresses until I came to the 1400 block, which was anchored on one end by an abandoned convenience store and by a head shop on the other. Between them was a single squat structure that looked to house four or five different storefronts. Number 1437 sat square in the middle.

At least, I assumed it was 1437.

Except for 1439 two doors down, there were no numbers on the doors. Most of them didn't look like they could carry the weight of their paint without bringing the whole rattletrap down. From what I could see the only storefronts open for business were the head shop and 1439—a shoesmith's.

I rapped on the door of 1437 anyway. Even if by some miracle it opened I doubted I would be able to get inside. The threshold was boarded up with two planks nailed in the shape of a cross. Some joker had graffitied the planks: WILL BE CRUCIFIED FOR FOOD. The windows were covered over with plywood. The wood was spraypainted, too, except for a spot where some other joker had slapped a row of Walk Compson campaign stickers. I figured nobody but the rats were home to hear me, but for whatever reason I kept rapping anyway. I rapped until I thought my knuckles would peel.

"You don't take no for an answer, do you?"

A withered old man in a denim apron stood outside the shoe-smith's, smoking. He held his arm straight out from his body and flicked his ash. He did it that way so the ash wouldn't catch in the cuffs of his jeans, which were turned up a good four inches from his feet.

"I need to talk to Mr. Gilbert. This was where he ran his photography shop, right? 1437?"

"You want to talk to ole Gil you better get yourself a time machine. He passed a good thirty years ago. Closed up his shop long time 'fore that. You want to talk to him about taking your portrait, you better set the dials on your time machine for 1958 or so. I reckon those were his salad days."

"You were here in 1958?"

"Friend, I been here since 1948. Right after I got out of the Army."

"So you were here during the bus boycott?"

"I was here, but I didn't pay it much mind. Now ole Gil, he damn near went out of business he got so caught up in all that. He would be out snapping pictures of folks waiting in line for a car ride while customers in his shop waited in line for their sitting. That's no way to run a business."

"You don't happen to know what he did with his stock, do you? I'm trying to find the person he may have given his negatives to. One of his children, maybe—an heir."

The old man shrugged. "Couldn't tell you 'bout that. Lotsa people have come and gone from this building since him. Now you want to talk to Miss Betty 'bout the watch shop she used to run in there back in the seventies, I can take you right to her doorstep. She's in an old folks' home up on the Atlanta Highway."

I shook the makeshift crucifix blocking the door. It didn't budge.

"I need to get inside."

"Now you should'a told me that," the shoesmith said. "These storefronts got 'em a common hallway in back. Used to have to share a bathroom in the way back when. Ole Gil, I used to have to get on him 'cause he would always want to stack boxes of chemicals for his darkroom along the walls. We couldn't have that. No sir, that would'a been a fire hazard."

He motioned me into his store, which was about as big as my cell at Kilby. The place smelled of leather and rubber from floor-to-ceiling rows of wingtips, loafers, and sandals lining the east wall. Along the west one was a wooden platform outfitted with five chairs and footrests. Five seemed pretty optimistic. I doubted the old man had entertained five customers at once since my own baby boots had gone to bronzer.

As he led me toward the rear hall, I damn near toppled over the shoetrees and brushes littering the floor. I saw a yellow sign above a register that wouldn't have looked out of place in Wookie's stolen scrapbook: YOUR FEET DESERVE A TREAT. VISIT URELEE HOOVER. Next to it was a framed picture that nearly tripped me.

"That's you, isn't it?" I asked, pointing to a boy-faced, smock-suited young man with a pencil-thin mustache. The kid was shaking the hand of another handsome man with a well-manicured mustache. Only this one belonged to Martin Luther King, Jr. "You really met Dr. King?"

"Well, that picture ain't dummied, so I sure must'a." Urelee folded his arms and nodded proudly. "I met him many a time. Ole Gil took that photo, too."

"But you said you weren't involved in the boycott . . ."

"I wasn't, but that don't mean I didn't know folks who were. The main players even. People think all colored Montgomery took a year off work to protest. That wasn't the case. Ev'rybody worked double because we were all raising money to keep the Movement going. Now Dr. King himself was a snappy dresser. That bothered the racists as much as anything. They tried to start rumors that all the money raised for the Movement was going straight into his suits. We knew better, of course. Colored folk know how to dress snappy on a dime. Now Dr. King liked a good shine, too. He knew where he could get the best one in town. A shine cost a man $1.50 in 1956, but Dr. King always paid a two-dollar tip. He came in twice a week back then. Seven dollars a week on shoes was a lot of money. Yes, sir—the man was a tipper."

Urelee tapped at his own image on the wall. "I never heard him preach. Ain't never been a churchgoer. But I sure heard about it when he mentioned me in one of his sermons. Not by name, mind you. He gave a speech about the dignity of the common man, and the 'shoeshine boy' was his prime example. You know what I told him the next time he came to see me?"

" 'Thank you'?"

"Nope. Not at all. I said, 'Dr. King, it was mighty kind of you to remember me, but the next time you go to put me in your preaching I want you to remember one thing: I'm not the 'shoeshine boy,' sir. I'm your 'shoeshine *man*.' "

With that he led me past a frayed sheet that curtained off his back office. The back door in the office led to a gray, fetid hallway littered with shattered glass—the windows were handy targets, I guessed, for neighborhood kids with nothing better to do than chuck rocks. Urelee motioned me into the hall. "Now if this glass slices up your soles too bad," he said, "you know who to come see. I'm gonna take it personally if you let some other smith fix them tenny-boppers."

I didn't tell him he was the first shoesmith I had ever met. I didn't have time. Before we even made it to the back door of what had once been Gilbert's Photography Urelee was scratching his head and pursing his lips.

"Now this is peculiar . . . I don't come back here much no more. No reason to since the toilets stopped working. Last time was probably a year ago. The new landlord brought me back here with all kinds of promises for how he was going to fix this place up. He was worried about the liability. What if kids broke in and one stepped on a nail or some of these here ceiling tiles caved in on them? He didn't want to be responsible, so he tarped over this door. I watched his people tape it up myself. No tarp on this door now. In fact, this here's a brand new door." He tried the knob, which was locked stiff. "I guess landlord was telling the truth when he said he planned on fixing up this ole lean-to."

I tried the knob, too. It didn't budge for me either.

"Does your new landlord have a name?" I asked.

"Sure. Got him a famous name. It'll be even more famous if he gets himself elected mayor . . . Landlord's name is Walk Compson."

"Christ," I mumbled. "This just gets better and better."

"S'cuse me?"

"Nothing . . . I guess I know now who stuck the Vote for Walk stickers to your storefront."

I looked around my feet. With the plot twists piling up at my ankles I guessed it was too much to ask for a crowbar to magically appear. When one didn't, I did the next best thing. I went down the hall to where a stack of spanking new two-by-fours blocked the entry to the toilets that no longer worked.

"What's this lumber here for?"

Urelee was surprised. "I don't know . . . I guess that's more proof that Mr. Walk was serious about putting some polish on this place. Those are studs. Looks like he's aiming to shore these sagging walls."

I grabbed one of the studs and hoisted it on my shoulder.

"The next time you see Mr. Walk, you tell him I owe him a two-by-four." I drove the stud into the door, just above the lock. The force seared my ribs, but they would have to take the pain and then some. The wood partition cracked, but it didn't splinter enough to knock the bolt out of the catch. I had to smash at the lock several more times before it gave way. The battered door creaked back on its hinges.

"You must really be wanting something of ole Gil's," Urelee whistled.

"This might be the point you want to head back to your shop. I'd hate for you to miss a customer because you're back here with me." I lifted a foot. "I'll bring these down tomorrow for you to fix. You're right—they're nicked up pretty bad."

Urelee knew as well as I did that my soles weren't damaged. For a second I thought he was insulted, but then he tipped his chin and gave me a nod.

"Just remember, friend: I'm the shoeshine *man*, not boy."

I waited until he disappeared back into his own shop before I slipped through the entryway of 1437. The layout was the same as Urelee's, only double in size. That meant it was luxury digs for the cockroaches and spiders, whose cobwebs stretched silkily and intricate as Chinese fans from the ceiling beams to the walls.

I doubted any business had been run out of here for a good fifteen years—any legal business, that is. Somebody had been up to something lately. The desk in the office was the one object among the clutter of wobbly chairs and tray tables not covered in dust. It was clean as a whistle and even smelled like it had enjoyed a fresh rubdown of Pledge. I checked the drawers but they were empty. The ledgers on the shelves had nothing to do with J. A. Gilbert; 1437's last occupant, it seemed, had been an electronics repairman. I clapped the dust chaff off my hands and sneezed. For once, my allergies did something good for me.

"Yancey?" a voice said. "Yancey come to play?"

I jumped back, startled. I couldn't tell where the voice came from. I thought maybe I was hearing things, but then it came at me again, full of yearning: "Yancey boy." It was all sing-songy, like a five-year-old reciting a nursery rhyme.

I spotted a ceiling vent at the top of the wall and imagined the line the duct work likely followed. It led me around a corner where three steps rose into the main showroom of the shop. What I supposed were the original display cases sat covered in sheets, looking like hovering ghosts.

I put my weight on the first step. It creaked.

"Yannn-ceyyyy," the voice sang again. "Yancey don't run away . . . Yancey come to play . . ."

It seeped from behind the wall on my left. I followed the bend into the showroom until I reached a large cabinet blocking the wainscot. I could tell the cabinet had been moved recently. There were several thumbprints on its trim, suggesting someone had repeatedly cupped his hand around the frame of the top drawer, pressing his thumb into the edge for leverage. I did the same.

The cabinet was heavy as hell, but I was able to swing it out far enough to spot a door that didn't look wide enough to squeeze a pair of shoulders through. "Yancey," the voice sang again. At least I wouldn't have to bust open this door: the padlock was unclasped. I slipped it out of the latch and threw open the flimsy louvered partition.

The cubby must have been J. A. Gilbert's darkroom. The floor was concrete and the air smelled, even all these years later, of chemicals. Just enough daylight leaked from the storeroom to silhouette the thin string of a pull cord dangling from the ceiling. I tugged it, and the room went soupy yellow. The flickering illumination was okay, though. I could see as much as I wanted to.

A clothes rack with bras and garter belts and stockings draped over its steel bar, a camera on a tripod, an old-fashioned soft-box cocked on a lightstand. On the floor, discarded cartons from McDonald's and Wendy's. In the corner, a black futon mattress with what looked like a mismatched green duvet.

And on that duvet, pale and seemingly as insubstantial as the yellow flicker dancing on her skin . . . a naked girl. Stretched out on her chest, legs in the air, her dirty feet kicking playfully at the backs of her thighs.

"Yancey come to play?" she said to my shadow. I stepped into the light, afraid to startle her. As it turned out, I was the startled one. Turns out the green duvet wasn't a duvet at all. It was money. Hundreds of $100 bills spread out like a blanket. The girl was rolling in it. Literally.

The fact I was a stranger didn't change her expression. The

way she grinned at me, I might as well have been Yancey—whoever the hell Yancey was. Yes, sir. What they said about the kid was true. She was simple. So simple she didn't scare.

"Playtime is over, Dixie. Let's put your clothes on."

Saturday, 2:43 A.M.

"That's the point when a smarter man might have realized he was being set up," C said. "I mean—c'mon, Ennis—you didn't stop to think the coincidences were stacking up just a bit too neatly?"

"Maybe so, but before you go insulting my intelligence, you should remember one very important detail."

"And what's that?" he gasped with impatience.

"The message at Dixie's—the GILBERT hidden among those refrigerator magnets—that was never meant for *me* to discover. After all, I'd never met Dixie before; I doubt she had ever heard of me, either. I'm guessing it was *you* that was supposed to be rifling her apartment for clues. Dixie didn't know you're too good to get your own hands dirty."

He nodded toward the body by the bookcase.

"I think my hands are pretty dirty at this point."

"That's your own hotheadedness. If there's one thing that ten years in the clink taught me, it's that 'shoot first and ask questions later' is never a good motto."

C went to mop the sweat off his pinched forehead, but all he succeeded in doing was leaving a smutch of red there. His hands were indeed dirty—with his own blood.

"I would say 'live and learn,' " he tried to smile, "but that seems pretty irrelevant at this point."

I didn't answer. I was eager for him to die. It was taking

longer than I expected.

"I keep waiting for my Maria Callas. C'mon, Ennis. You're a generous Joe. A little *Tosca*. You wouldn't have ended up the patsy in this mess if you weren't."

"You'll be hearing angels soon enough. Let them sing you into the afterlife."

He couldn't argue. The blood continued to pump slowly but surely from the bullet hole. C's entire stomach was a sticky crimson diamond now. But just because he couldn't argue his mortality didn't mean he wasn't willing to debate other fine points of the mess we were in.

"There's a couple of major flaws in your thinking. First, you're assuming Dixie knows I'm her daddy. That's not the case; Faye never told her a lick about her old man. I know that for a fact. How? Simple: Faye begged me not to tell her, no matter what. Said it would be better for her if she stayed in the dark. Second, there's no way Dixie hid that name for anybody to find. Not me, not you. She's dumb as Cracker Jack, remember? There she was, locked up for hours, never once thinking it might not be on the up-and-up for Yancey to leave her there, naked as a jaybird. What did she say she was doing? Playing hide and seek? Shit. . . . Dixie's such a shortbus she makes Forrest Gump look like Stephen Hawking."

Before I knew it, I had cocked my gun and drawn a bead on his forehead.

"I thought I told you not to talk about her that way."

C didn't scare. He just laughed.

"What are you going to do, kill me again? Don't—it would be redundant."

"You're wrong, anyway." I lowered the gun. "Dixie isn't dumb; she's just naive. She thought of hiding the name as a big game, you see. She likes games. She told me she and her grandmother played word games with refrigerator magnets long before she got her own place on Audubon Drive."

"I suppose rolling naked in $100,000 is a game, too, huh? I wonder who taught her how to do that."

"My guess? Lister. The grandfather."

"So you think Faye's old man really was a perv?"

"People keep telling me that you can't trust what Dixie says. That she can't distinguish reality and fantasy. The things she told me and Red about Lister these past two days—the way he touched her, took her picture . . . well, let's just say that I don't believe a kid as simple as her conjures stuff like that out of pure imagination."

"You think ole Lister diddled Faye, too?"

I thought of the story that Tyler Petco shared with me in back of the El, how Dixie had told Walk Compson that Lister wasn't just her granddad but her dad. I wanted to believe that story would draw as much blood from C as much as my bullet had, but I had my doubts. He had only ever been in this sweepstakes for the money. Dixie was nothing but a means to it.

"I don't think a perv waits until he has a granddaughter to get pervy. I suspect Lister did abuse Faye. It would explain the drugs—not to mention why she had such bad taste in men."

"Don't be so hard on yourself, QB. You won't see me getting guilty over Faye. She got what she wanted out of men, didn't she? She got me gutted like a deer and got you sent away. It's not like she shed a tear for either of us. But back to Lister James: I take it from your repeated references to him as 'perverted' that you think he really did die of autoerotic asphyxiation."

"I didn't say that. I'm pretty sure he was murdered. I don't care how Harry Houdini a man is: you can't tie yourself up all contorted like he was and manage to stuff a rubber stopper up your rump. I wouldn't be surprised to find out that was done to him postmortem."

"So who killed Lister James?"

Now it was my turn to smile. "You did," I said.

C shook his head. "Christ, you're going to besmirch me after I'm gone, aren't you? Like I said: the coincidences leading you to that conclusion stack up just a little too neatly."

"Let me tell you a story about coincidences."

"Better make it a *short* story, killer. I would hate to bleed out halfway through and miss your point."

"When I played football I didn't believe in coincidences. I believed in *circumstances*. Those are different things. Back then I believed if you were strong and you had willpower, you created your own circumstances. By calling a play, I set into motion a sequence of actions that had been so plotted and practiced they seemed almost predestined. If things didn't come off right, it wasn't because of any flaw in the planning—it was human weakness. And you know how you deal with weakness when you believe the world is a circumstance of your own making? You stamp it out."

"That's straight out of *Mein Kampf*. 'Heil Hitler' and 'Hut one' to you, Snake Stabler."

"Suddenly, a few years later, my world has gone phooey. I'm a methhead, reduced to shaking down lowlifes for drug money, stealing from my old man, so junked up I have needle tracks all over me. What was screwing me up even worse than the meth was self-pity. Nothing was my fault, you see. I no longer created my conditions. I saw myself as a victim of circumstances."

"Your circumstances had a name: Faye. Blame it on that train wreck. If it weren't for her, you never would have tried to kill me."

"If I believed that then I would still be a victim. That's not the case. You know why? At the height of my self-pity I went and got this." I showed him my St. Jude tattoo. "I told the guy who inked it that I wanted this saint with me at all times because

148

he's the patron of lost causes, and goddamn if in most folks' eyes I wasn't the most lost of lost causes. Ennis Skinner: big football star turned loser junkie. You don't get more lost than that, do you?"

"I guess not," C replied, distracted by a wince of pain.

"You know what the tatt man said, though? He said, 'Dude, you've got St. Jude all wrong. He's not about desperate or lost causes—those are faulty translations. He's about *forgotten cases.*' Did you know that St. Jude is called 'the Forgotten Saint'? No? You probably don't know why then either, do you? He's the 'Forgotten Saint' because, as the tatt man taught me, his real name wasn't Jude at all—it was *Judas.* Judas Thaddeus."

"Wrap it up, Ennis. I don't have long."

"It was this apostle's misfortune, by some fluke of co-incidence, to share the same name as the most loathed man in the New Testament. Don't think people didn't confuse him for Iscariot the betrayer just because Judas hung himself, either. Now St. Jude certainly didn't create that circumstance, but he didn't let it crack him up either. He could have—he sat up there in heaven with nothing to do for a good 1,800 years. That's how long it took for Christians to realize he wasn't *that* Judas and to start petitioning him for favors. You know how he survived in the meantime? He survived by *adapting* to the situation. He made his own name by serving people like himself—the forgot-ten."

C's eyebrows were high on his forehead. "I'm supposed to stay alive for this bullshit? Keep the rah-rah to yourself, Tony Robbins. It's time to shuffle off my mortal coil."

"What I'm saying is that everything that has happened this week started because you were convinced you were the victim of a circumstance: somebody had something of yours. The dead are on your shoulders, C. They're your fault. Nobody was the mastermind here. This has all just been a bad collision of coincidences that you've let pile up to high heaven. You don't believe me?"

I rose and kicked the pile of books off the face of the dead body.

"If you don't believe in coincidences, tell me what he was doing here."

I looked down into the vacant eyes of Amory Justice. When I couldn't take the dead stare any longer I leaned over and closed the lids.

"You killed the mayor of Montgomery, C. That doesn't bode well for your posthumous reputation."

C looked at the corpse, then at me. Then he chuckled until his breath failed him.

"Who knows?" he hacked. "The city may thank me. Think of the favor I've done them . . . now nobody has to go to the polls on Tuesday."

CHAPTER THIRTEEN

"You couldn't have put her in a different shirt?" Dad huffed.

We were in his house, watching Dixie from the kitchen as she sat on the couch, clutching a small purse and waiting for somebody to tell her what was happening. She was hunched forward so the design across her chest was hidden, which was fine with Dad. He had enough of an eyeful to make his eyes roll. The shirt was of a pit bull growling from the bed of a red truck, a Confederate flag spread out behind its raised hackles. REBEL BORN, REBEL BRED, it said. I'LL BE A REBEL TILL THE DAY I'M DEAD.

"It's not like I found her in the middle of Abercrombie & Fitch," I told him. "It was either that shirt or a bustier. Or would you rather have me bring her here in the buff?"

"I'd rather you hadn't brought her here at all. Or the money. I don't know what's going on, but I know they're both trouble—"

"Where's Yancey?" Dixie said without warning. "I need to go back to the fort! He'll be mad at me. . . . He told me to stay there until he came back for me!" She sounded as if she was going to cry.

I tried to soothe her, but all I could say was, "It's all right." I had no idea how to talk to someone mentally challenged. "Remember what I told you when I found you? I'm a friend of your family's. That means I'm your friend."

Dad cupped my elbow and pulled me into a huddle by the

refrigerator, out of Dixie's line of sight. On the kitchen counter was an old valise—Dad's from his teaching days, before Huntingdon College canned him for drinking. The valise bulged more today than it ever had when it was stuffed with textbooks and student papers. A valise will do that when it's crammed full of a thousand $100 bills.

"You were at El Rey this morning, weren't you?"

"No," I lied. I tried to make it convincing. "Why?"

My lie wasn't convincing.

"You know damn well what happened! The whole north side of Fairview Avenue is roped off, but the windows are shot out, so you can see straight inside from across the street. It looks like an explosion in a salsa factory. I walked down there to join a protest march for Brenda James, only to find out it was canceled. You want me to believe it's a coincidence that you're two days on the payroll and El Rey turns into the O.K. Corral?"

"So that's what you think of me, old man? Just because some burrito shack gets robbed, you *just know* your ex-junkie, ex-con son *must* be behind it?"

"What *I* think doesn't matter. It's what the police think that better be important to you! Do you honestly believe they'll take your word for it? The way they're being taken to task in the paper for Tasering Mrs. James, they're not inclined to give anyone the benefit of a doubt. They're not going to just accept it when you say you had the misfortune of being an innocent bystander!"

"They'll believe it when Bubba tells them the truth. He fired a kid nicknamed Elroy. The kid got pissed and decided to help himself to the register. Elroy got busted, the other guy got away. End of story. If my name does come up—and I'm pretty sure it won't—Bubba will tell them that the first time I even met His Boy Elroy was when Bubba was peeling a skillet off the twerp's face."

"So you were there!" Dad cried out.

"Are you listening to me? *I said it was some two-bit named Elroy!*"

"Elroy?" Dixie unexpectedly parroted. "I know Elroy! I even know his theme song!"

And goddamn if she didn't proceed to sing the whole thing. *Meet George Jetson, His Boy Elroy, daughter Judy, Jane his wife.* She took particular delight in the song's final line: *Jane, get me off this crazy thing . . .*

I rushed to the couch.

"Dixie, do you know a real-life person named Elroy, or you talking about the cartoon character?"

"I know somebody *and* I know the cartoon," she answered triumphantly. Christ, even when she smiled she looked displaced and distant, like she wasn't at home in her own head.

"*How* do you know him?"

"He's Yancey's friend."

Of course he was Yancey's friend.

Now I just needed to figure out who Yancey was.

"Dixie, how do you know Yancey and Elroy?"

The question was so obvious to her she thought it silly to have to explain it.

"Yancey comes to my church program. Every Wednesday night our church has a big dinner together and then we all go sit in a room with people our own age and we talk. We talk about everything. What's right and what's wrong."

Dad shook his head. "Did you miss the night they talked about what's wrong with letting somebody from your church lock you up naked in a dark room?"

"Quiet," I scowled.

Dixie answered anyway. "I like to have my picture taken. . . . It makes me feel pretty. Nobody ever tells me I'm pretty except when I have my picture taken."

I tried to smile, politely. Dixie had taken to curling her hair around an index finger, the way a little kid will do in her sleep. Between Lister and Yancey, it was hard to even imagine what the girl had been exposed to. Maybe it wasn't such a tragedy she was slow, I decided. It would've been more of a tragedy if she had known how she had been taken advantage of.

"Don't listen to Quentin, Dixie. He's a mean old man. He doesn't understand stuff like you and I do. You and Yancey were just playing a game, right? A simple game of dress-up. He told you what to wear, right? You put on the clothes he told you to and then he took your picture. I bet he promised you a picture for your purse even."

She beamed. "Yancey gave me my purse! He makes me feel pretty! Everybody always treats me funny because I'm slow. They talk super loud in my ear so they'll think I understand what they're saying. I'm not deaf, I tell them. I'm just not smart—that's what my momma always said before she left. Yancey is the only other person besides my momma that treated me like I was just not smart. That's why I love him."

"I want to share a secret with you, Dixie. I knew your momma. I was her boyfriend—just like I'm guessing you think of Yancey as *your* boyfriend."

"That's right! Yancey is my boyfriend, and I'm his girlfriend." She smiled sweetly. "I like love—it's fun."

"Sure, Dixie. Love's a blast. I loved your momma. Just so you know I'm not lying, I'll even tell you her name: Faye. But she had a secret name, too. A secret identity. You and I are the only two people who know it. Your momma was really Super-girl."

The kid's face lit up like a sparkler.

"You knew my momma! You knew how pretty and strong she was!"

"Yes, I knew both of those things—I knew them very well.

But now that I've told you what I know, you have to share something with me that I don't. So I'm sure you're not pulling my leg about you and Yancey, you have to tell me how Yancey and Elroy are friends."

Dixie frowned. "I don't know. . . . One day Yancey and I were playing at the fort and Elroy came."

"The fort?"

"You know the fort! You were in it! You came to play with me there."

"What is she talking about?" Dad demanded.

"The old store that used to be Gilbert's Photography, you call that your fort, right? I get it. It's dark and warm in that room where I found you, just like a fort. So when Elroy came, did he watch you and Yancey play your game?"

Shock seeped into her face. "I would never do that. . . . Only Yancey and I play the game. Love is only between two people, so only two people get to play. Me and Yancey, us two."

"There are different kinds of love, though. For example, your grandparents love you. They've taken care of you since your momma went away, right? I know your grandpa Lister loves you. Lister loves you so much that he asked you to play the game, didn't he?"

Her mood changed. She pulled her legs up to her chest and stared into her kneecaps, not saying a word.

"It's okay, Dixie. I know all about it. There's nothing to be embarrassed about. You did the right thing. You told Mr. Walk about Lister playing the game. He made your grandpa and grandma move you into your own apartment so you didn't have to worry about him doing anything to you, right?"

"You're asking leading questions," Dad growled. "All those 'right, Dixie?'s—you're telling her the answer you want to hear."

He snatched his phone off the counter and began dialing.

"Who are you calling?"

"Walk Compson. We need to get this girl back to her grandmother. Lister James is being buried tomorrow. Dixie should be there. And if she's somehow mixed up with what happened at El Rey this morning, the police will need to talk to her. Even if she's not, she shouldn't be in this house. We don't need to be involved—it's not our problem. Walk will know what to do."

It took me exactly two strides to reach him. I grabbed the phone out of his hand before it got anywhere near his ear.

"You mind telling me how we're going to explain a valise with $100,000? Or are we just going to ignore that part of the story?"

"I'll say it again: it's not our business."

"Not our business?" I tried to whisper so Dixie couldn't hear me, but I was so angry I was spitting fire. "I bet I know another son who heard those words from *his* father close to fifty years ago. As in, 'You don't need to get on that Greyhound bus and get yourself beaten up, Quentin. Civil Rights aren't our business.' You used to tell me how it broke your heart to hear that from your old man. Imagine what it does to me. I never thought I'd hear the great Quentin Skinner say we don't need to stand up for somebody needing help."

"I haven't done anything great since 1961. That was almost fifty years ago. I was fighting for a cause. You're caught up with this girl and whatever else is going on out of guilt."

I planted my hand on his chest and backed him up.

"I have amends to make. If I had met Faye a few years earlier, Dixie could have been my daughter. From what I see, nobody has done her right yet in her life. I won't let another person do her wrong. I want you to take her to a motel and stay there with her until I can get this mess sorted out. Whoever Yancey is, he's not going to be happy to find out that both her and his stash have been stolen. I don't want anyone knowing where we are—

156

not even Walk Compson."

"And what are you going to be doing while I'm in a motel room with a mentally challenged nineteen-year-old?"

It was a good question. I didn't have a clue. Or, rather, I had *too many* clues. I had C, Lister James and Walk Compson, Reese Justice and Treadface/Francis, Elroy and El Rey, and now somebody named Yancey to sort out. I had smutty pictures and rumors of incest, a handicapped kid, a mayor's race, and a shot-to-smithereens burrito lounge. Somehow they were all related.

Somehow.

I looked at my dad, who expected a better answer than the blank slate of my face.

"Whatever I'll be doing, I won't be saying it's not my problem. This girl is my cause."

I jabbed a thumb toward Dixie, who clutched the purse Twitchy had given her to her chest as she rocked Indian-style.

"She's fond of that thing all right," Dad sighed.

The girl watched us with big, beseeching eyes. REBEL BORN, REBEL BRED, the legend emblazoned across her chest said. I'LL BE A REBEL TILL THE DAY I'M DEAD.

"Can you at least get her into a different shirt?" he begged.

CHAPTER FOURTEEN

Of course, there was another girl who needed taking care of.

After I packed Dad and Dixie into his truck I started off to Red's apartment. I was halfway out the door when I realized I was still salsa- and guacamole-riddled from the rampage at the El. I doubted Red would appreciate me smelling like day-old appetizer, so I went back to the bathroom and stripped down. I undid the Ace bandages from around my ribs and noticed a declivity just under my right breast. I had been goddamn dented, all right. I couldn't even enjoy the shower because the blast of the head felt like a fresh pummeling.

I re-dressed and hoofed it to the Fitzgerald House. Some tourist group was gathered in the yard, not far from the drape of the magnolia tree, snapping pictures next to a big, bricked-off sign that said THEY BELONG TO THE WORLD.

Every other word out of the crowd's mouth was *Gatsby*. *Gatsby* this, *Gatsby* that. When I shot past them a little too rudely I heard somebody say, "Must be a Faulkner fan," and they all cracked up laughing. Funny people, tourists.

I knocked twice on Red's door. When she opened it I stepped past the threshold and took her in a wordless embrace. She was upset. I could tell because she didn't hug back. I pulled away and asked what was wrong. It was a stupid question considering that, not two hours ago, we were dodging Rugers.

Only bullets weren't what bothered her now. At least not the ones that had torn up El Rey. Red nodded toward the one chair in her apartment, the recliner by the window.

"Hello, Ennis," High C said, a copy of *Vanity Fair* propped open on the tops of his knees. There couldn't have been a bigger contrast between the smirk crowning his long beard and the pout of the glamour puss staring from the cover.

"Glad to see you didn't catch a stray this morning. No cuts or wounds? Not even a nick of tortilla shrapnel from an exploding chip?"

When I stepped toward him I discovered why he was reading the rag—or pretending to. He pulled a pistol from between the glossy pages and aimed it at me.

"Let's try to make this a pleasant visit," he smiled.

"Does Miss Manners say there's a polite way to shoot a Joe?"

As I spoke I reached behind me and grabbed Red by the wrist to shield her. C would have to shoot through me to get to her. My chivalry made him shake his head, amused. He tossed the *Vanity Fair* to the floor.

"You overreact—has anybody ever told you that? I'm not going to shoot you. I can't. I need your help."

I scanned the room. Something was indeed up. Twitchy and Treadface were nowhere to be found.

"Very observant," he said. "No, they're not here. I don't expect them back, either. I've been set up. Betrayed. Suckered, if you like. The boys slipped a Ruphie into my sweet tea and cleaned out my safe. As of today I'm a pauper. My whole cash flow for Anarchy Ahoy is gone. If I don't get my money back, I'll be out of the bookmaking business."

"Somehow I doubt the publishing industry will suffer in your absence. Just out of curiosity, how much cash was in your cash flow?"

"$100,000."

Well, that answered one question. I whistled and tried to act surprised.

He scowled. "No girl yet?"

"No girl yet," I lied.

"Well, then, I have a lead for you. My boys, they have Dixie. I suspect they're the ones who posted those porn pics of her on the Internet. Hell, they might have even taken the pics, not Lister James. Who the fuck knows? Only one thing's clear right now: I'm as big a moron as Dixie. I should have known those no-count bastards would have no loyalty."

"What's the skinny one's name? The big boy with the radial face is Francis. I know that much. But Twitchy, what's his name?"

C didn't hesitate. "Yancey—his name is Yancey Peters."

Well, that answered *two* questions. This time I didn't bother acting surprised.

"What about this Francis? What's he to Yancey? Brother? Cousin?"

"Uncle. That's what I picked up, anyway. I overheard the two of them arguing one day. Francis didn't like the way Yancey had been talking to his momma lately. He told Yancey he'd be up for a bruising if he didn't start showing respect."

"Knowing personally what a good bruising Francis can give, I'm sure Yancey did exactly as told. Did either of them ever talk about somebody named Elroy?"

"Elroy? Are you fucking with me? Are you going to ask next if they talked about Pebbles and Bam-Bam?"

"Any friend—did they ever mention any friend to you?"

He thought for a moment.

"They never mentioned any names, but they pitched a book to me once. It wasn't for one of their friends, though. Some friend of a friend of a friend. One of those deals. It was a Civil Rights book. The bus boycott. Supposed to be a new take. I said no. There are no new takes on Martin Luther King and Rosa Parks. Do you know how many books are out there on

Montgomery in 1955–56? It tells you something that this friend of theirs would come to Anarchy Ahoy. It means he struck out with three or four dozen—"

He almost said *reputable*, but he caught himself.

"More *appropriate* publishers."

Something else clicked, but I knew better than to share it with C. I felt Red tug on my arm, as if she was signaling me to make a break for it. We could have. We were only two steps from the door. Ten steps down the stairs to the vestibule and we could bolt across the yard. I wasn't going to risk it, though. C could pot us from the window, easy. With my luck he would take out a Fitzgerald tourist and I would be blamed. Some joker would say it was my fault because I'm a Faulkner guy.

"Your girl is shy," C observed. "I was here a good hour before you decided to show up, Ennis, and she hardly said a peep. I had to read a magazine to entertain myself."

He stood and walked over to a draped canvas on an easel.

"She's so shy I bet she hasn't even talked to you about her latest masterpiece. I had to ask her what her influences are. Are you more Picasso than Grant Wood, sweetie? More Andrew Wylie than John Singer Sargent? I don't know. What do you think?"

With his left hand he whipped the drape off the canvas. The portrait wasn't finished, but you could see where she was going with the strokes of green, gold, and brown. The face was tight and sad. Full of regret. Disappointment. Maybe even a little self-loathing. No, make that *a lot* of self-loathing. The saddest face in the world. It took me a second to recognize it.

It was my face.

"Move away from the door," C ordered us. "Best if you shut it, too."

"I can't shut the door after I've moved away from it."

"Sticklers die young, Ennis. Don't get bogged down in the details."

We were sidling along the wall, the door closed now, Red still behind me. My eyes were so glued to C I damn near tripped over a coffee can stocked with art supplies—pens, colored pencils, scissors, a roll of twine.

"I'm afraid I'm going to have to ask you to step away from the girl, too. No offense, but your ugly mug is no match for hers. She's quite the looker."

"Get out, or my face won't be the only thing that gets ugly here."

He chortled and stepped behind the recliner, slapping its back rest with his free hand.

"This is how this is going to work. I'm not going to ask twice. Ennis, you sit here. Your girlfriend is going to take that twine from that can there and tie your ankles to these chair legs. Then she's going to tie your wrists to your belt loops."

"No," I said.

He pulled a switchblade from his pocket and snapped it erect, resting the blade's tip against my portrait, right on the acrylic strokes shading the lines of my forehead. "Don't make me lobotomize you, Ennis."

"Do what he says," Red whispered.

So I did. I sat, and Red lashed me down. She was careful to leave slack in the twine. A few twists of my wrists and I was pretty sure I could Houdini my way out of the flimsy knot. Unfortunately, C was careful, too. He was watching Red's every move.

"Pull it tight, honey. Hog tight. I want to see his wrists go blue."

"Just like you pulled them blue on Lister James?" I asked. "Was it your idea to slip him a phony pickle, or was that your boys' work?"

"I don't know what you're babbling about," he replied with mock innocence.

When Red was done tying, she stepped away from the chair.

"Good," C smiled. He looked at Red. "Now take off your clothes."

"No!" I bucked in the seat, but Red had followed orders too well. I was tied too tight. Before I could jerk to my feet, C was behind me. He pressed the gun to the tip of my temple, and slid the switchblade along my jugular. The blade pushed deep enough into the skin that if I so much as swallowed I would slit my own gizzard.

"There was no question mark on the end of my sentence. 'Take off your clothes'—grammatically speaking, that's the imperative voice. See how much grammar I've learned publishing books? Now go ahead and drop those Daisy Dukes, Daisy Fay. If you don't, I'll make sure your canvas there gets the Jackson Pollock treatment—with Ennis's blood."

I couldn't look her in the eyes. I was staring at my feet. I felt weak, beaten. I couldn't escape my peripheral vision, though. I saw the blur that was Red tug her T-shirt from around her shoulders. Then she unsnapped her cut-off jeans and slid them down her thighs.

"Don't be a toenail gazer, Ennis." C jerked my chin up with a pop of his wrist. I had no choice. My eyes were on her.

Red kicked the cutoffs from her ankles and caught them in her fist. Instead of dropping them to the ground she threw them at C. The shorts whapped him in the face before flopping onto the lounger at my shoulder. Far from angry, C laughed.

"Feel free to do that with those panties, too."

She didn't. When she pulled them off she dangled them tauntingly from her index finger and then dropped the sliver of elastic to her toes. I was trying not to gape, but I couldn't help myself. A pair of tattoos in the shape of pythons curled sinuously from her inner thighs, winding around a diamond of auburn pubic hair to tangle three times between her bellybutton and sternum. From there they shot out and encircled her breasts, the snarling jaws of each beast positioned just above her areolae, thirsty to sink fang into flesh.

"Holy Paradise Lost," C whistled. "You're Eve and the Eden snake all in one."

Red's reaction was to uncoil the middle finger of each hand. The gesture was as venomous as the twin designs decorating her.

"You sure know how to pick them, Ennis. I love a girl with spunk."

"Shut up," I hissed through my clenched teeth. "Shut your goddamn mouth."

The blade fell away from my neck as he circled around the chair.

"You shouldn't begrudge me. You want to know something funny? Well, it's really not funny—it's sad. Tragic even. That shot I took from you ten years ago? It wasn't just a hunk of intestine you blew out of my belly. You took out a whole mess of circuitry, too. Thanks to you, I've been as limp as macaroni ever since. I suppose I should be grateful you didn't put me in adult diapers for the rest of my life, but still, you can understand my resentment."

He stood behind Red and dropped his nose into the curve of her neck, inhaling so deeply I half-expected her whole body to disappear into his nostrils.

"You know who she reminds me of, Ennis? *Faye*. You would disagree, no doubt, but I'm talking the Faye of way back when before she was pocked and stank of ammonia. The innocent Faye. Before she met you, in other words."

He sniffed again and put his lips to Red's ear.

"Can you imagine what it's like, honey, to feel the same lust that every man feels and yet lack the machinery to relieve it? It's enough to drive a man insane. To make him mean even."

He closed his eyes, enjoying her scent with exaggerated delight. I would have rather he stabbed me in the neck.

"Touch me and you die," Red said without emotion.

"Touch me and *he* dies," C snapped back.

Then his eyes popped open.

"You know what, though? *Touch him and you both live.*"

When she didn't move, he nudged her in the spine with the gun.

"Why so shy, buttercup? I just told you my sad condition. That should reassure you I'm not trying to start a *ménage a trois* here. Go ahead. Go sit on Ennis's lap. I want to see you kiss him. I want to see *him* kiss *you*."

Again, she didn't move. Flustered, C slapped a hand to her back and shoved her at me. She stumbled and fell at my feet, her head at my lap. Red spun into a crouch, ready to leap. She didn't, though, because the pistol was aimed straight at her forehead.

"A kiss, snakebite, just a simple kiss. Or maybe you don't think there's such a thing as a simple kiss. Frankly, I could give a fuck what you think. Kiss him and kiss him now—and with tongue, please."

I was staring into space. Red rose and sat on my lap. She did as told. I felt her tongue slip into my mouth. Then I put mine in hers. It was nothing like the previous night on her roof. I closed my eyes so I didn't have to see C's grinning monkey face. I couldn't help but hear his moaning, though. With my hands tied, I couldn't stick my fingers in my ears.

"She's a great piece of ass, Ennis. Try to not ruin her the way you ruined Faye. Oh—and keep something in mind: until you bring me Francis and Yancey's heads on a platter, and until I get my $100k back, there's nothing to prevent me from coming back and making this gal put on another show. Only next time kissing may not whet my appetite."

"You're forgetting something, aren't you?"

He thought for a moment.

"You're right. I am. How silly of me . . . I want my money *and* Dixie. Happy now?"

He didn't wait for a reply. He yanked open the door and ducked down the stairs. As soon as he disappeared Red flew off me and threw the deadbolt. I was straining so hard against the twine that my wrists were raw. "Let me get my scissors," Red yelled as she kicked through the piles of her paint supplies with her bare feet. "Where are they? Where are they?"

"Get dressed. Just get yourself dressed."

I managed to wrench my right wrist enough to curl my fingers into my palm and jerk my hand free. I untied my legs in time for Red to collapse in my embrace. She was still naked, so my bloody wrists stained the fluttering white sheet of her body.

"I won't let anybo—"

Before I could get the words out her cell burst into song: Tom Petty, "Don't Do Me Like That." She screamed as she fell away from me and lurched for her purse. "Leave me alone, Eric!" she shouted into the phone. "I said we're over, dammit! Leave me alone!"

Then she dissolved into sobs. I scooped her back into my arms.

"Nobody's going to hurt you. I won't let that happen. I'll get you to a safe place until I can take care of C. My Dad's staying at a motel up on Madison Avenue with Dixie until this ends. I'll get you a room there. C won't bother us or anybody after I get through with him. Please, trust me."

"There's something you need to know," she cried into my shoulder.

My mind reeled. I felt like I knew too much already. "What? What?"

"My name . . . my real name . . . it's Lexi."

"I didn't know that," I lied. "You won't regret sharing it with me. I promise you that, too."

★ ★ ★ ★ ★

THURSDAY

★ ★ ★ ★ ★

CHAPTER FIFTEEN

Tyler Petco entered the coffee shop and walked to the farthest seat in the back, exactly as the voice on the phone had instructed him to do. This was his first time in Café Voltaire and from the looks of it he wouldn't be back any time soon.

Nothing against the establishment itself. It seemed a decent enough muffin shack, although if he were honest Ty would have to admit he wasn't too keen on all the androgynous white kids. That was who mainly staffed Voltaire's, and every last one was pierced and tattooed and began every sentence with a bemused *um*. Who mainly frequented the shop were blue hairs with nothing to do all day but walk their Labrador retrievers and slurp lattes as they wondered who in Montgomery, Alabama, had ever been named Voltaire. Some of the blue hairs weren't necessarily keen on Tyler Petco. Ty could see it in their faces. He was the only black man in the bakery.

Ty sat for several uncomfortable minutes before the bell on the door rang, and a stranger walked in. The stranger didn't look like he belonged in Voltaire's either, although he wasn't black. This guy was too nervous for such a low-key café. He kept looking right and left as he passed the counter where an espresso jockey said, "Um, you want something, man?" The stranger ignored the kid and sat down instead across from Ty.

"You're him?" the stranger asked.

"You see anybody else here who might be me?" Ty replied.

"What I want to see is the check."

Ty stared at him for a hard second or two before withdrawing an envelope from the breast pocket of his spiffy cobalt-blue suit. The stranger peeked in the envelope and whistled. "I guess this means the first round's on me," he smiled.

"Before you cash that and open a tab, I'd appreciate it if you handed over your part of this little exchange. That $25,000 isn't a charitable donation."

"Of course it's not," the stranger answered. "It's not charity because I don't take charity."

He reached to his back pocket and threw his own envelope onto the table. His was bigger—a 4 × 5″ as opposed to a standard letter size. Without taking his eyes off the stranger, Ty emptied the envelope's contents next to the napkin dispenser.

"So this is Amory Justice," he said, studying a single wrinkled photograph.

"You can tell it's him because of the long jaw. Amory has always had a Leno face. He had a Leno face before Jay Leno grew his."

"I'm not looking at his face. I'm looking at the obscenity flying off his finger. The racist son of a . . . He's flipping off a little old lady!"

"Yes, sir. If a picture speaks a thousand words then I'd say you've got your very own *All the King's Men* condensed into a single snapshot. The election's a wrap now, huh? Only I hope you're not counting on my vote." The stranger snapped the cashier's check between two proud fingers. "I'm on permanent vacation. As of right this nanosecond."

Unfortunately for the stranger, right this nanosecond was also when Red and I slipped from the nearby supply closet from which we eavesdropped.

"I hope you haven't booked your tickets yet, Wook."

We pulled a chair to either side of him and sat down. The Wookie was sure surprised. He was blinking so fast his eyelids looked like he was tapping out a Morse code mayday.

"Ennis . . . Lexi . . . what are you guys doing here? What's this all about?" He squinted at Ty. "This deal was supposed to be between the two of us. What are you doing yakking to my co-workers?"

"You mean the co-workers you almost got killed yesterday?" Red asked. "Tell me you weren't in on the shootout, Wook. Bubba's been good to you. So has El Rey. Everybody there has been, especially me. I was your friend, not just your co-worker."

"In on it?" His back stiffened, indignant. "Are you kidding? Those cruts could have killed me! For all I know they were trying to. You saw them, Ennis. They nabbed my scrapbook. That's what they were after: that picture right there, dude, not the till. Don't you think they're wishing they were sitting here with this cashier's check instead of me? They would be, too, if I'd been dumb enough to keep that pic with the others . . ."

I plucked the photograph from Ty's hand. I had imagined it for so long now that to see it finally was damn near disappointing. One black woman, one white man, one violent, ugly gesture. The only thing that surprised me was how easily identifiable the mayor of Montgomery was. Add a wattle and a little wear and tear and the features were exactly what stared down at the city from Justice campaign billboards. Too bad for Amory that fifty years hadn't changed him enough that he could do what politicians are supposed to be good at: plausible deniability.

I looked at the back side of the picture. No surprise here, either. J.A. GILBERT, it said. SERVING MONTGOMERY SINCE . . .

"Let me guess," I said to the Wook. "Somebody in J.A. Gilbert's family gave you his Civil Rights cache back before you gave up working on your dissertation. The family never knew what a gem it had hiding among all his old mementoes. Mr. Gilbert has been gone for almost thirty years, but Amory's only been mayor for twenty-five, so why would anyone even think to look for him in all these old pics? I bet Mr. Gilbert didn't even know back then this kid was named Amory Justice; he just took the shot and stuck it away. . . . I'm only curious, Wook, how long you had Gilbert's portfolio in your collection before you realized you had hit the jackpot."

"Years," he answered. You could hear those years in his voice: he sounded tired. "Probably ten of them. Gilbert had hundreds of pictures from the bus boycott. The guy must have been out snapping all damn day long. I never catalogued them because it was too much work for one person. From time to time I would open a box and sift. The box this particular one was in—I just chose it by accident one day about a month ago. I could've chosen one of a dozen different boxes and none of us would ever be the wiser."

"Why tell Elroy, though?" Red demanded. "That kid wouldn't know his Civil Rights from his civil lefts."

"We were just gabbing one day back in the kitchen. I told him my biggest disappointment in life was that I had never published a book. I could give a shit about the Ph.D., but it was the book that bummed me. . . . Elroy said he knew these guys who worked for a local publisher. He told me they were on the 'distribution' side, and then he busted out laughing. He said he would tell his buds that I had some never-before-seen stuff from 1956 that might move a couple thousand volumes. He was surprised as I was when the guys came back from their boss saying never-before-seen doesn't necessarily mean needs-to-be-seen. If I wanted a book, the boss said, I needed a new spin on the subject."

"And so when you found Amory's picture you told Elroy you'd found that spin."

Wookie shrugged. "I told him I had something so new that it would make *heads* spin. I asked him to ask his buds to set up a meeting so I could convince them to pitch the project again to their boss."

Ty spoke up. "I don't understand. . . . You wanted to print the picture in a book *and* sell it to Walk Compson? How were you going to manage that?"

The Wookie's eyes dropped to his fingernails. When he didn't speak, I picked up the 4 × 5″. I blew into the envelope, and then tapped the open edge on the tabletop. Nothing but air spilled out.

"There's something missing here. The first person who guesses what that something is wins a slice of coffee cake— courtesy of Wookie here."

"The negative!" Red said with a jolt.

Ty stammered. "I—I didn't think to ask. . . . I'm so used to thinking of *digital* pictures anymore, I—I'm not sure I've even seen a negative in six or seven years."

"If $25,000 only buys the original print," I asked Wookie, "how much for the negative? Or was it even up for sale?"

The Wook sighed heavily. "The negative's not important. The newspaper could scan this in. At 300 dpi, a scan is as good as a negative. These days, negatives are—you know—obsolete. Unnecessary."

"I don't doubt it." I set his envelope down and put out my palm. "Let me see your cell phone, Wook."

"What? What for?"

"Just let me see it."

He shivered as he handed me the phone. I flipped it open and scrolled through the list of numbers recently dialed. "This is interesting. . . . Here's a 241- prefix. That's a downtown number. Who downtown might you have called not five minutes before you waltzed into Café Voltaire? Let's find out."

I no sooner pressed the send key than Wook's paw gripped

mine. "Don't," he pleaded. "You already know, goddamn it. Don't."

"Who?" Ty asked. "Who are you talking about?"

"Your opponent," I informed him.

"You were double-dipping!" Red realized. "You sell the Compson campaign the picture and the Justice campaign the negative, and by the time the one realizes it's been double-crossed by the other, you're long gone!"

"How much were you asking from the Justice people?" Ty demanded.

"The same. $25,000, not a penny more. I was treating you equally."

"You've got some sense of equality," I told the Wook. "You were ripping them off equally."

"I—I need the money, Ennis. I've got student loans, credit cards, hospital bills. I'm hourly at the El. I don't get medical, and I've got a lot of medical problems. Just last week I had to—"

"I don't care about your medical problems. I want Francis and Yancey."

His face wrinkled. "Who?"

"Elroy's friends. I want to know where to find them. I'm guessing from the second shooter's build that it was Francis I had in the headlock yesterday."

"Jesus—why would you think I knew where those guys were? I didn't even know their names until you just said them. I only ever met them once, and they wouldn't even roll their windows down more than halfway. I damn near combusted from standing in the parking lot waiting for them to show up it was so hot. What kind of business guys make you meet them in a parking lot in this kind of heat?"

"What parking lot? Was it on Highland Avenue, over by J. A. Gilbert's old photography shop?"

Wook shook his head. "No, no—it was out in east Montgomery. Off Ray Thorington Road."

Ty and I locked eyes. "Are you thinking what I'm thinking?" Ty asked me.

"What?" Red wanted to know. I ignored her. It was hard because she was so gorgeous, but I had more pressing things on my mind.

"I'm going to take a wild guess. I'm going to guess this meeting took place two mornings ago, on Tuesday. Am I right?"

Wookie's eyes nearly crossed. "How did you know that?"

"Think about it. What's right off Ray Thorington Road? Hallwood Lane. What happened on Hallwood Lane Tuesday morning? You should know, Wook. You and I were watching the news reports. Not three hours after you met with those guys, it was all over the news . . ."

Red spoke when the Wookie couldn't. He was too busy choking on the implications.

"Lister James . . . Tuesday was the morning they found him. The morning Mrs. James was Tasered."

"Oh, God . . . Jesus, no. You think those two bozos had something to do with that?" The Wook was incredulous. "Surely not . . . I mean . . . the James guy, he just lost control of his kink and choked himself to death, right? That's what they said on the news. His autopsy is in the paper this morning. The guy had a dil—" He looked to Red, embarrassed. "—a *Steely Dan* in him. He died sitting on his own light saber . . ."

"Give the check back," Red said sternly.

"What? No way . . . I mean, c'mon, guys—I've got bills . . ."

"You heard her," I told him. "You're going to give the check back. Consider it a campaign contribution."

The Wook couldn't have deflated more than if you'd popped his balloon body with a safety pin. He stared at those three zeros after the 25, his eyes almost watery, and then pushed it across the table to Ty, who slipped it back into his cobalt suit.

I leaned into Wookie's ear. "Now you're going to tell us where and when you're meeting Reese Justice. I know she was on the other end of that 241- number—she has to be. She wouldn't dare trust word of this photograph to any peon in the Justice camp. Something tells me she'll know where we can find Francis and Yancey."

Wook's head shot up hopeful. He couldn't have looked more like he was praying than if he had clapped his hands together and started petitioning saints.

"Will you at least let me keep *her* $25,000? You don't understand, Ennis. *I got bills . . .*"

CHAPTER SIXTEEN

We didn't have to wait long for the rendezvous with the mayor's daughter. Eager to get out of Montgomery with his money, the Wook had booked his extortion drops back to back. Only this second meeting wasn't scheduled in a muffin shack like Café Volatire; that would be just a little too public for the Kudzu Ann Coulter.

She and Wookie were set to meet north of downtown on a stretch of Lafayette Street, a winding two-lane that was the former main drag in an old industrial park abandoned when Amtrak left town. I had a vague memory of the geography, having countless times during my party days driven the road up to Captain Pat's Marina Grill on the other side of the Alabama River. Faye and I used to go this route because there was less chance of getting pulled over when we were methed up. The police weren't real keen on patrolling Lafayette Street. It was too dark and deserted.

"You should go back to the motel and stay with Dad and Dixie," I whispered to Red on the way. We were squeezed tight on the back floorboard of Wookie's Tercel, afraid someone might spot us. Mayor Justice had a lot of constituents, after all.

"I want these yea-bobs as bad as you do," she said. Her breath smelled like grape gum and was hot in my face. It was taking all I had not to kiss her deeply. "Once we get them, we're going back for that pig who busted into my apartment yesterday."

I stroked her hair. "You'll have to tell me the story about the

179

snakes. If C didn't have a gun in his hand, those tattoos would have intimidated the bejeezus out of him."

"I didn't want you to see those. Not like that. I don't want to scare off St. Jude." She drew a finger along the face on my forearm.

"Patron saints don't scare easy. What's a little snakebite, anyway? That's why they make antivenin."

She spread my fingers out between her hands as she kissed my palm. Without warning she bit lightly into the web of muscle between my thumb and forefinger. "Here's hoping I don't have to find you antivenin for a bullet," she said.

Wook pulled his Tercel up to a hangar. I had him roll down his window and describe what he saw. Off to the right were three abandoned boxcars, shedding so many rust strips in the humidity that they looked like metal slats of Swiss cheese. Twenty feet away, kitty-corner, sat an old wooden water tower. A thick lock hung on the hangar door.

"Find us a spot," I ordered him. "We can't stay back here. We'll never get the jump on her lying down like this."

"The middle car—the door is open about a foot and a half. That's the best I can do."

I told him to scan the horizon for silhouettes and shadows. When I felt reasonably sure we weren't being watched Red and I crawled out the back passenger door and bolted between the boxcars. The door on the middle one was off its track and wouldn't budge, so we had to wedge our way inside shoulder first. I made a point to shoot Wookie a look and let him know his sense of measurement was screwy. The opening was barely a foot wide. It squeezed the hell out of my bruised ribs. "Watch out," Red whispered, pointing to a sledgehammer that sat upright on its mallet next to a pail of abandoned screwdrivers and drills. "Here—over here." She found a rotted crack in the wall that looked straight out onto the Tercel. As we huddled around the hole together, Wookie got out and paced hood to trunk. His jaw was moving the whole time, and every few steps he'd stare straight at the boxcar, throwing up his hands as if to say, "What do you want me to do?"

"He might as well point straight to us," Red said, exasperated. "She's going to know he didn't come here alone."

"He's wishing he hadn't found that picture of the mayor. He realizes now he's out of his league."

"Are you?"

"Ask me that in about fifteen minutes and I might have an answer. I appreciate you saying 'Are you?', though. You could have said, 'Don't you?' As in, '*Don't you* realize you're also out of your league?' "

We waited like that for a good thirty minutes, whispering about how Wookie's pace was getting jitterier and jitterier. Finally, a black BMW convertible pulled up, its bumper as short and turned-up as a snooty nose. Reese Justice slid out of the driver's seat. The wind whipped hair across her mouth so she looked like she had covered her face with a handkerchief. She looked every inch the blond bandita.

"Took you long enough," the Wook growled as he pulled his second envelope of the morning from his pocket. When he shoved it toward her, the mayor's daughter pulled an identical one from her purse.

"A 'thank you' would be nice," she said as the envelopes were traded. She pulled the negative out and held it a few inches from her face, checking out the image. "You sure no prints are floating around? I'd hate to have to file a complaint with the blackmail wing of the Better Business Bureau to get my money back."

"No prints as far as I ever found." His lie wasn't very convincing. "What are you going to do with it?" he asked quickly.

"I'm going to donate it to a Civil Rights museum. What the hell do you think I'm going to do with it?"

She stuffed the negative back in its envelope and then stuffed it in her purse.

"A little advice, Pooh Bear. Don't let the money go to your head. It hardens people who're not used to having it. I'd hate to think I corrupted a pup like you."

"You're not as hot as you think you are. You got ugly in you that's as obvious as the mean streak you like to think you're famous for." The Wook smiled. "How's that for harmless?"

It was a good comeback. Maybe a little labored, like he had been mulling variations of it the whole time we'd been waiting.

If that was the case, then it was a lot of work for little payoff. The Wook wouldn't get the chance to savor his own wit. Before he could tuck this check safely away, there was a loud thunder-crack. For a second I thought the Kudzu Ann Coulter was look-ing at her shoes to make a joke about scraping Wookie off their soles. Then I realized the shot hit her crown so forcefully that it snapped her head straight down. She seemed to hit the ground faster than the chunks of brain matter that leaped off her skull.

Red gasped. I clapped my palm to her mouth, but my heart was beating so hard I was sure the echo was as audible as a clang from the unused sledgehammer next to us.

"Oh, Jesus! Jesus! God!"

The Wookie looked at the dead body and then at our boxcar.

"What do I do?" he screamed. "What do I do?"

It was a question he didn't need to worry about answering. A second thundercrack sounded. Unlike Reese Justice, the Wook didn't go down immediately. He staggered a half-step, slipping up against his Tercel. It was just enough to tip his balance the opposite direction and land him prostrate instead of prone.

Instinctively, I pulled Red away from the peephole. She was struggling to break my grasp to get out the door. "They've already killed two," I panted sternly. "Two more aren't going to bother them at this point."

She went limp except for the heaving of her fear. As I struggled to hold her up, I kept my eye to the hole. Across the road two silhouettes shimmied down the ladder of the water tower and came jogging across Lafayette Street. It was Treadface and Twitchy all right. Twitchy's .30-06 was slung across his back. Treadface was sweating heavily, but not enough to wash out the letters blaring across his chest: B-A-M-A.

The younger one bent over the Wookie's corpse and dug the check from his back pocket. "Thanks for not bleeding on our money. One speck and we'd a'been shit out of good fortune, huh?" Then he leered over Reese Justice. "Hate to ruin such a pretty face," he sneered sarcastically.

Treadface dumped the contents of her purse on the roadway and scooped up the Wook's negative. "She ain't gonna fuck you dead any more than she would've alive, moron. Let's get out of here."

"What do you want that for?" Twitchy nodded at the negative. "Ain't like the mayor gonna pay to get it back now."

"So you're in charge of strategy all of a sudden? That's great. Fantastic even. Maybe you can hook up with another melonhead and let her run off with this money, too."

"I ain't gonna tell you again: Dixie didn't snook us. She ain't got the brains."

"She's gone and $100,000 is gone. Add it up, dumb ass—oh wait, I forgot: *you* ain't got the brains."

Treadface's eyes rode up and down Lafayette Street. Then he twisted and let his gaze fall on our boxcar. I could see him clear as a moonbeam. Then I realized he could probably see my eyeballs staring right back. I ducked back to the wall behind me, but in taking the step I forgot completely about the sledgehammer, and I set the handle wobbling. I couldn't steady it without dropping Red to her knees. The handle seemed to take a lifetime to tip. When it finally did, the thud sent a jolt of vibrations swimming through my soles.

"Over there!" I heard Treadface yell.

I shoved Red across the boxcar and sprang to the open door. As footsteps smashed the gravel I grabbed the sledgehammer and swung it above my head. When the barrel of the .30-06 poked through the door's opening I let the mallet arc forward, hoping I kept it high enough not to scrape the floor. Not to worry: the flat steel head connected with the muzzle and drove it backwards into the open air.

A tortured scream seemed to shred the rivets around me. There was no time to see how far into Twitchy's eye socket I had driven the gun sight; still holding the hammer I bolted to the far end of the car and took three swings at the rusting wall. I knocked a hole round enough to push Red through. Then I dropped to the ground behind her, the gravel slicing into my bare kneecaps.

I grabbed Red's wrist and we tore across Lafayette Street toward a ratty guard shack. Running was a crazy, futile gesture; it was a good mile and a half back to downtown Montgomery, and north of us was nothing but a series of dead ends that anyone with a car could trap us in.

As we dove behind the guard shack I looked back. Twitchy was on all fours, one hand over his bloody eye. Treadface had the .30-06 aimed our direction. Shingles and bits of cedar siding began popping off the flimsy shack. A few short rounds and we'd have nothing but toothpicks to hide behind. Red pointed ten yards behind us to the Alabama River.

"I hope you know the patron saint of swimmers," she said, scampering toward the bluff.

I didn't, but if I was going to drown, I would rather do it in water than my own blood.

We didn't leap together, Butch and Sundance–like, into the river. It was more like a lunge. We spilled over the edge and dropped fifteen feet, far enough that the impact of the belly-smacker hit like a punch. I was sure my fake teeth had been knocked loose. The current flipped me onto my back, sucking me under and filling my nose. I thrashed and lost hold of Red. I couldn't find her or the surface. I opened my eyes, desperate for air. Everything was brown—muck and murk.

The more I thrashed the faster the colors faded until nothing was brown, just black.

All black.

CHAPTER SEVENTEEN

I awoke to a kiss. Of course, it wasn't really a kiss. It was Red breathing the life back into me. The feel of her lips on mine was so much sweeter than the rocks grinding at my back, however, that I combed a hand through her dripping hair and tried to pull her on top of me with the other. I didn't understand why she resisted until both the dreaminess and the water drained from the stupor of my near drowning, and I remembered with cold clarity that two goobers had just tried to kill us.

"Let's save that for a time when we're not picking weeds from our teeth," Red said, patting my chest.

"Where are we?" I asked, rolling onto my side.

"The amphitheater." She pointed up the bank toward a stage that sat in a deep bowl of a field. "The current carried us all the way downtown. I thought you were done for—you went under instantly. I tried diving for you, but you were gone. I couldn't even cut across to a shore; the rapids were that quick. I knew if I could keep my head up until I got down here I'd find my footing. Everybody knows how the river shallows out here. What I wasn't sure I'd find is you. That fallen trunk there caught you by the armpit. Lucky for you it twisted you around so you were floating backwards. Otherwise you would have drowned, facedown."

"You saved my life?"

"Don't I owe you? You've saved mine twice in two days. No offense, but I'm ready to not need a hero. Getting shot at is getting tedious."

"I wonder how Reese Justice feels about that tedium." I sprang to my feet and pulled Red to hers. "We need to get back to the motel, back to Dad and Dixie. I need some time to figure out how to handle this. We can't just call the police and tell them that the mayor's daughter was murdered by her own goon squad—not until we know who else is in on this."

"Those bodies back there aren't going to wait for you to make a decision. Don't you think it would be better if we went to the police right now? We're witnesses, for God's sake, not prime suspects."

"I'm an ex-con. That means I'll never not be a prime suspect."

I led her across the rocks to the slope of the bank. There a dirt path carried us along a weed-strewn trail to an underground tunnel, which emptied onto a brick plaza on Commerce Street next to the old train station. The tunnel used to be a hangout for skateboarders and rollerskaters, but now it was chockablock with families. I didn't understand what a crowd like this was doing downtown. In my day, downtown Montgomery might as well have been downtown Kabul.

"There must be a baseball game," Red said. She pointed two blocks west where a stadium rose from the clutter of what had once been a crumbling block of shuttered cotton warehouses, fruit stands, and liveries. Sure enough, a throng swarmed the streets, kids and parents in identical blue caps and jerseys, everyone perspiring as if we lived in a suburb of the sun.

"When the hell did baseball come to this town?" I said. I was staring at that stadium like I had stumbled upon an unexpected Sphinx.

"Four years ago. We've won the Southern League championship for the last two."

I thought I had wandered into a parallel universe. This wasn't the grubby town I had grown up in—it was Disneyland. Then I saw something else that stopped me cold in the crosswalk connecting Commerce and Tallapoosa streets. Directly ahead of us, stationed under a street sign, three bike-patrol cops stared at a tottering drunk.

I was painfully aware of the squish of my tennis shoes as we strode to the far side of Tallapoosa, opposite the cops. The closer we came to the stadium, the thicker the smell of beer, chili sauce, and cheese. People around us began to slur. The tottering drunk had tottered over to a thin, black-haired man with silver-framed glasses.

"This sumbitch here is named Warren Higgins! And this is Warren Higgins's ninety-ninth straight home game! And you know what? 'Less he drops dead in the next twenty-four hours tomorrow is gonna be his one-hundredth straight one! Now *that*'s a fan, you fair-weather bastards!"

The black-haired man looked about as happy as if he were hanging out with in-laws.

"Tomorrow old Warren here is throwing out the first pitch!" the drunk hollered. "Last year they let him lob the opener and the sumbitch couldn't make it over home plate. Don't embarrass us again, you catfish sniffer! Don't embarrass us!"

"I've been practicing," the black-haired man said through his gritted teeth. "Like a damn first-chair clarinet—I've been practicing, already."

"Suddenly inconspicuous doesn't seem so challenging," I told Red.

It didn't, anyway, until a bicycle cop crept up on us.

"You folks okay?"

"Okay how?" I said. All I knew to do was play dumb like the tottering drunk.

"You're soaked, bud—that's how."

"Oh, that. The wife and I here were sunning ourselves down by the amphitheater and somebody turned the sprinklers on.

The last sprinkler I ran through was thirty years ago. It made our day."

"I felt like a kid all over again," Red added, clutching my hand. "We just got married four months ago. We had more fun by the amphitheater than we did on the honeymoon!"

The cop seemed to buy it. For a second, anyway.

"You're not wearing a ring," he observed.

Red was quick on her feet. "I wouldn't wear a quarter-carat Princess cut in downtown Montgomery! I might lose a ring *and* a finger."

"Downtown has changed. That's why Amory Justice will be reelected on Tuesday. You folks got any ID on you?"

I gave him a grim smile. "Those sprinklers didn't ask for ID when they came on. They just took my word for it that all we were after was a good time."

The cop raised his sunglasses to his forehead. "I'm just curious about your name. You look familiar to me. Like I know you."

"You a football fan?"

"Sure. Bama all the way. Bama since I was a kid."

"Then you do know me. I quarterbacked up at the university. It's been a while, but if you're the fan you say you are, you may just have my autograph socked away somewhere."

"I very well might. Quarterback, huh? What did you say your name was again?"

I gave him the biggest inebriated smile I could fake.

"Joe Namath."

The cop didn't smile. I started to worry I had gone too far when a shout sliced the air. "Bobby!" one of the other bicycle cops yelled. "Get over here." The two other officers had dropped their bikes to surround the drunk, who was getting belligerent.

"What did I do?" the totterer said, staggering in a circle. "I'm only having fun! No need to get your Tasers out, boys!"

That did it. All three cops swooped in at once and took the drunk to the ground. The crowd began to boo and jeer. "He wasn't hurting anybody!" somebody screamed. "Jackboots!" somebody else yelled.

"Let's go," I told Red. "I can't watch this—not again."

As we hustled off, Red wiped the sweat from her forehead. "You like playing Russian roulette? That Namath crack was a bit gratuitous."

"Something I learned a long time ago: threaten a cop and he'll take you down. Annoy the hell out of him and he'll let you go. Because if he doesn't, he has to put up with your bullshit."

"That's a nice theory, but it doesn't seem to apply to Montgomery anymore. That drunk they're making eat gravel wasn't threatening them." I felt her look at me. "We're lucky those cops aren't real observant. You know why?"

"Tell me."

"The sprinklers at the amphitheater—they weren't on. Thanks to this heatwave, there's a water shortage. The city has banned lawn watering until we're back below 100 degrees."

We hoofed it past the baseball stadium, shoes still squeaking. As we turned south onto Court Street we were met with an oddly plangent sound, like a low wind whistling off a sloping porch. Only it wasn't wind—it was singing. We'd barely made it three steps when a column of marchers came around the corner at us. A hundred of them. Some with arms locked, some waving placards, others holding banners, nearly all black. Feet gliding forward to the same soft but unswayable rhythm: *"I shall not be moved. Just like a tree that's planted by the waters, I shall not be moved."*

Lister James Was Murdered, a bobbing placard read.

Mayor Justice: Afraid to Investigate, said another.

And a third: Afraid of What He Might Find.

"Jesus is my savior, I shall not be moved. In his love and favor, I

shall not be moved."

Red and I respectfully stepped aside as the column passed. "They're going to the baseball stadium," she shouted in my ear. "That's Amory Justice's crown jewel, the biggest accomplishment of this last term. . . . He'll go bat shit if they protest outside of it."

"That's exactly what they want. Walk Compson has planned this to a T. He's even got the crowd singing a song straight out of the Civil Rights marches. I know that song—my old man used to sing it to me when I was a kid."

"There's only one problem with that theory," Red said, nodding at the marchers. "There's no Walk Compson anywhere in sight. Not even your friend Tyler. You know why, right?"

I didn't wait for her to tell me. I knew why like I knew the next verse of the spiritual swirling around us.

"There's an election on Tuesday. He can't afford to alienate the white vote."

"Not even if what the signs say is true?"

"Not even *when* what they say is true. You notice anybody else missing?"

When Red didn't answer I told her: "Brenda James. She's Lister's wife and Dixie's grandmother."

"It seems a little crazy that a widow would be a no-show to her own murdered husband's protest march. Where else would she be?"

It was a good question. It took me a second to remember.

"Burying Lister," I said. "Come on."

I pulled her off the curb and we cut diagonally through the last of the protestors. When Court Street intersected Madison Avenue, the main downtown drag, we went left, hugging close to the refurbished office buildings until they gave way to little bric-a-brac shops and then to fast-food joints. It was a mile up to the Capitol Plaza Lodge where we had stayed the night before, Dad and I in one room, Dixie and Red in the other.

Back in its glory days, the Capitol Plaza Lodge was where state legislators stowed their whores. Now it was little more than a fleabag for rubber tramps vagabonding through the Southeast, which is exactly why I chose it: anonymity. Halfway there, Red and I finally dried off from our ride in the river.

By the time we pounded on Dad's door, we were wet all over again from sweat.

Dad didn't answer; Dixie did. I only had to peek over her shoulder to know why. Dad was snoring away on one of the lumpy twin beds, passed out in the fetal.

Not two inches from his head, on the nightstand, was a bottle of Conecuh Ridge.

"Get her next door," I barked to Red as I pushed my way inside. It was a good thing it took her a second to guide Dixie off; I wanted to throttle my old man so badly I had to ball my fists and calm myself. When I was finally able to shake him awake, all he could say was, "Poor kid . . . Poor little kid . . . She's got nobody . . . Nobody but you and me, Ennis . . ."

I shook the Conecuh Ridge under his nose. "Where did this bottle come from?"

"Where do you think it came from? It came from the goddamn ABC store. . . . Because you can't buy a damn drop of liquor in this monkey-hole without going to the government . . ."

"I told you not to leave this room! Don't you understand what's going on here? People are getting killed left and right, and the two dumb asses doing the killing won't stop until they get Dixie and that $100,000 back. Then they'll keep one and get rid of the other. The dumb asses aren't so dumb as to get rid of a hundred grand, either!"

Dad threw his legs to the floor, sitting up. As violently as he wagged his finger at me I thought the motion would tilt him face-first onto the floor. "All I did was stop at a damn ABC store. . . . If that's such a sin to you, get the hell out of here. I couldn't help needing a drink . . . I was so damned depressed for that little girl . . . especially after the way the grandmother treated her . . ."

"What are you talking about? What grandmother?"

"Dixie's grandmother! What she said to Dixie at the church. She wouldn't let her own granddaughter into the funeral . . ."

"You took Dixie to Lister James's funeral? What's gotten into you? We're supposed to be *hiding* the kid—*for her own good!*"

Dad's finger was still wagging.

"They raised this girl, son . . . I told you yesterday I wasn't getting between this family. . . . The girl has every right to say goodbye to her grandfather."

"Even when the grandfather likely abused her?"

"I did what any moral man would: I took Dixie to see the closest thing she's had to a father for one last time. It made me so sad, Ennis. . . . It made me wish Dixie was *your* daughter. You and I could have raised her. We would have protected her. It's too bad you and Faye never had a baby. . . . You'd have been a good father, son . . ."

"Jesus, you must be close to ninety proof to be saying that."

"You don't understand! Mrs. James wouldn't let Dixie into the funeral! If you'd seen it, Ennis—if you'd seen the confused look on the kid's face . . . why, you'd have wanted *to be* her daddy, just like it made me wish I were her granddaddy. . . . It would have made you wish you had a drink, too . . ."

I tossed the bottle onto the spare bed and sank in the chair next to the room's junky TV.

"You're not making any sense. What exactly did Brenda James say? *Her* exact words—not yours. Yours are slurred."

He scowled at me before deigning to answer.

"I took Dixie to the church. I waltzed her right through the front door and into the nave. I had every intention of delivering her into her grandmother's arms and coming straight back here. Only we didn't make it to the sanctuary doors before an usher said it was a *private* service. For family only. I said, 'This girl is family! She's the poor man's granddaughter!' That caught somebody's ear, and one of the ushers went running to the preacher's office for Mrs. James.

"I expected her to come burning into the hall arms wide open to greet the girl. Well, she came burning all right. Only she was burning like the Tennessee defensive line used to burn after you. She was screaming at Dixie. 'I don't ever want to see you again! Never again! This is your fault! Your grandfather would be alive if you hadn't lied about him! You lied! You lied!' "

Again, I remembered what Tyler Petco said behind El Rey. Lister took porn pics of the granddaughter he had raised as a daughter. Lister had fathered that granddaughter with his own daughter.

"That wasn't the craziest thing, though," Dad babbled on. "Mrs. James is screaming at Dixie. She says, 'You lied about your grandfather just like your mother lied about him! Your mother stole every bit of money we ever had from him, too! Is that what's next, Dixie? Are you here to steal his money? Because you're too late—there is none! Your mother stole it all!' "

"What money?"

Dad look offended. "How should I know?"

I looked at the battered valise that was tucked between the bed and the nightstand. I thought of the $100,000 inside and of the two cashier's checks for $25,000 each. That was just what this situation needed—more money. More money likely meant more dying.

"What did Dixie do when Mrs. James said all this?"

"What do you think she did? The kid broke down and started bawling. She didn't understand what her grandmother was telling her. 'I'm not a liar!' she said. 'The doctor told me I couldn't lie even if I wanted to! And I don't want to!' The ushers didn't know how to handle the situation. One of the security men came up to me and said it was best if we left. So we did. And as we did I did what Mrs. James wouldn't do. I put my arm around Dixie and showed her that somebody gives a good goddamn about her. . . . I thought her poor little eyeballs would wash straight out of her head she was so sad. I've never seen anything like it. So on the way back here when we passed the ABC store—well, I was so rattled I couldn't help myself. I needed a jigger."

I held up the Conecuh Ridge. "You've got a generous idea of what a jigger is."

He wanted to come at me, I could tell. He probably would have if he had been able. He stood, but he was too woozy to keep upright, and it made him sad. He crashed backwards onto the bed, crying.

"She's just a poor kid. . . . Got nobody but us. . . . Nobody but a junkie and a drunk . . ."

I grit my fake teeth. "I'm not a junkie anymore. How many times do I have to tell you that before you bother to believe it?"

"She's got nobody but a drunk and a con," Dad corrected himself. This time I didn't argue. I sat and watched his body shake from sobbing. It made me sick. Then a siren outside whizzed by. I remembered the Wookie and the mayor's daughter lying in a dead pile up on Lafayette Street, and I felt even sicker.

"Where are you going?" Dad asked. I was halfway out the door before he noticed. He had started to pass out again.

"I've got exactly one card in this game that hasn't gone phooey on me. Keep an eye on Dixie and Red. I'll be back as soon as I talk to Walk Compson."

CHAPTER EIGHTEEN

The story was that Walk Compson had sold out.

Whoever set that story circulating sure seemed onto something.

As recently as the 1980s when he and my dad were still actively fighting for civil rights, Walk was celebrated for residing in the same two-room rattletrap on Fifth Street he had been born in—the same Fifth Street whose proximity to Recipe Row Reese Justice would be making political hay out of if her cranium weren't dotting another rundown street in another rundown part of Montgomery.

Once Walk abandoned the movement to open a Lexus dealership, though, he felt no ethical obligation to keep his vow of poverty. He took the hefty advance that a New York publisher paid for his autobiography and bought the biggest, most baronial manor he could find—on the east side of town, of course. Thanks to a little reconnaissance, I discovered that the house anchored a gated oasis called THE DOWNS.

It wasn't the pretentious name that made me laugh—it was the community. The next subdivision over was THE WOODS. That meant Walk Compson and High C were practically neighbors.

To even get near the house I had to leave Dad's truck at a CVS drug store, hike a half-mile down a freshly blacktopped lane, and cut through a pasture of grazing cows that backed up to THE DOWNS. And all that was before the eight-foot brick wall I had to scale. Still, I figured the roundabout was easier than getting past the front gate. It was manned by a security guard who looked like his job was to sniff your wallet to ensure that your cash had the right nosegay to get in.

As it turned out, the subdivision's back lots were wide and woodsy, so I didn't have a problem keeping out of residents' sight. I found Walk's place and managed to get over the privacy fence by climbing a pear tree and worming it to the end of a dangling branch. From there I squatted among the lantana in the rose garden that overlooked a whirling pool with a rock waterfall. I had to wait for hours. So long, in fact, that eventually I fell asleep.

When I woke up it was early evening. The house still seemed empty until a light in what looked like a downstairs study clicked on. As I stole up to the French doors I could see Walk's thick neck and broad shoulders over the back of his chair. He was still a mountain of a man. The mountain didn't budge as the door hinges creaked open. I didn't congratulate myself for being so stealthy. I wasn't dumb enough to think he hadn't heard me.

"You should lock your doors. A man of your stature has to be careful."

"Locks aren't always the deterrent they're made out to be," he said, calmly twisting toward me. "I've found this is a better alternative."

He leveled the .38 straight at my ribcage.

"You weren't packing that forty years ago when you and Dr. King marched over from Selma, were you? I seem to remember him preaching something about nonviolent resistance."

"I used to tell Martin he needed one of these. Who knows? If he had protected himself, things might have turned out differently at the Lorraine Motel, don't you think?"

"I think Dr. King has been better off than the rest of us for a long time now."

"Then you have something in common with him. You have a death wish, too."

"You'll want to know that I'm not armed. I wouldn't make for much of a martyr, but I'd hate for you to shoot a constituent so close to the election. It could cost you more than just my endorsement."

"It seems the constituents have lately taken to shooting the candidates—or their families, anyway. Don't you follow the news? Somebody murdered the mayor's daughter today. Shot her dead up on the road to Captain Pat's Marina."

"Are you worried people will pull the lever for her father out of sympathy?"

"I'm worried about people who break into my house." He let the gun fall. Now it was only aimed at my liver. "You haven't told me who you are or why you're here."

"I'm here because of Dixie James."

His thick brows rose, though not from surprise. More from resignation, it seemed.

"Then that makes you Quentin Skinner's son. The mysterious acquaintance Tyler has been telling me about for the past few days. I understand I owe you my thanks. You saved me $25,000 by convincing your fellow mystery man to donate that unflattering picture of Amory."

"The money is pretty irrelevant at this point. It wouldn't have done my friend much good even if he'd kept it. If you know what happened to the mayor's daughter, then you know what happened to my friend on Lafayette Street, too."

"What's worrisome is that *you* know what happened up there."

"Like I said, I'm here because of Dixie. She fell in with a bad crowd. The crowd is responsible for all this mayhem. I can't go to the cops. They won't believe me that Reese Justice was murdered by her own goobers."

I watched his eyes wander to the windows behind me. He looked like he was off in another world. Then he set the gun on his desk. He didn't put it away, mind you. It was still right there in easy reach.

"What is it you think I can do for the girl?"

"You've got a funny way of putting things, sir. It's very simple. I think you can keep her from becoming the next Reese Justice."

"And how am I supposed to do that?"

"No offense, but you haven't gotten this far in life asking questions like that. It won't be long before this bad crowd comes looking for her. She's got a lot of money of theirs that they won't walk away from. It's a lot more money than they killed Reese over."

"Don't you mean *you* have this money of theirs that they'll kill for? Dixie isn't anybody's idea of a mastermind. She could no more steal anybody's money than she could shoot them dead with this gun."

"I don't expect you to care about me. I'm not the granddaughter of your chief legal advisor—the chief legal advisor who also happens to be dead."

Now his eyes fell to my shoes. He looked at them for what seemed like forever. Without a peep. "The knots in my laces aren't that interesting," I assured him.

He answered very slowly.

"There was a time when if Amory Justice's daughter was murdered my first instinct would've been to pick up the telephone to personally offer my condolences. No intermediaries, no backchannel, no public statements, just man to man—the way it ought to be. I don't doubt the mayor would tell you the same thing. For all the years he and I have been political enemies, we've always had a grudging respect for each other—if only because we had something in common. We were both survivors."

Walk's eyes darted back up, and he blinked hard and with recrimination. For whom I wasn't sure.

"Amory is cut straight from George Wallace cloth, you know. The governor was his mentor way back when Amory first ran for city council in 1970. He was even there in Laurel, Maryland, in 1972 when George was shot. Toward the end of the governor's life you could find the two of them eating lunch together at Martin's, a couple of good ole boys. Amory always used to tell a famous story about George Wallace, about how when George was nothing but a podunk county judge in the forties, he always addressed black plaintiffs in his courtroom as 'sir.' Of course, that was long before he had his tail whipped in the 1958 election and swore he'd never be 'out-niggered' again. See, to men like George and Amory, the racism was never personal. It was what you had to do to get elected. It was always 'just politics.' I can't tell you how many times over the past twenty-five years the mayor of Montgomery, Alabama, has said that to me."

"The racism in that picture from 1956 looks pretty personal to me. I'm no politician, but a middle finger has never struck me as 'just politics.' "

"Amory Justice was fourteen years old when that old photo caught him in the act. I don't doubt that the memory of it has been in the back of his mind for fifty years. His fear of airing his ignorance so blatantly is probably what motivated him to become such an astute politician."

"I can't believe you're defending him."

"I'm not. I'm *explaining* him. There's a difference, son. Men of my generation—black and white—had to be astute to survive. After Dr. King's assassination, we either reinvented ourselves, or we risked becoming relics. Your father, for example. He was a real leader. That picture of him beaten up at the Greyhound bus station was iconic. He could have parlayed his fame into real power, but instead he chose to teach history at Huntingdon College. I once asked him why. He said, 'Because it's easier to point minds toward good at twenty than it is at forty.' "

"It's been a while since Dad pointed anyone's mind anywhere—especially his own. Not many in Montgomery would consider him a survivor."

"There's something called the Great Man theory of history. Have you ever heard of it? The idea is very simple: 'The history of the world is but the biography of great men.' Thomas Carlyle wrote that. It's fallen out of fashion now, but I used to believe in it deeply. I believed that the direction of the world is determined by men of commitment, strength, charisma, moral surety—but most of all, vision. I don't hold to the theory anymore . . . mainly because I discovered that there's another quality that proponents of this idea never talk about: humility. It's a precious commodity, son. I learned that I certainly don't have it, which is one reason I got out of the civil-rights business."

"I always heard you got out to make money."

"I wasn't worthy of the movement, not after I realized that the truly Great Men know enough to debunk their own mythologies. Someday you'll understand that whatever your father has been going through these past twenty years, however destructive it's been for him, it's had the positive benefit of humbling him. I envy him his humility. I don't consider many men great; your father is one of the few."

"Theories are fine things, but they don't do much in the way of stopping bullets."

"Is that your way of saying you don't consider yourself a Great Man?"

"As I'm sure you know, I just spent ten years in prison. That's a lot of time for debunking. You'll forgive me if right now greatness and humility both seem like luxuries. Right now it's more

201

about survival."

"Ah, yes. Only four days into freedom, and here you are, knee-deep in shootouts and murders. That hardly seems like freedom."

I shrugged. "Whatever happens, I'll at least be able to say that I haven't done anything this week that didn't need doing. I had amends to make."

Walk smiled. Apparently I had just said the most naive thing in the world. Or maybe just the least humble.

"You *do* believe you're a Great Man then. That's your vanity speaking, Ennis. Just a little dash of cold water from the real world: at some point if you do get through this week unscathed, you're likely to wonder if there is any real difference between surviving and succumbing."

"Two other things that don't stop bullets: riddles and maxims."

"Of course. Let's get back to the matter at hand then. Do you know who I called when I heard about Reese Justice's murder? I called your friend and my advisor, Tyler Petco. I told him we couldn't possibly publish that picture of Amory right now. Not because it would be wrong to. I told Ty we couldn't put it out there because it would backfire on us. Exposing the mayor's childhood history of racism would seem like we were bashing him at his darkest hour, and that could conceivably do us more harm than good on Tuesday. I need the white swing vote, and the opportunism of the picture might turn that block away. Then I made another phone call. I called my pollster and said I wanted hard numbers on how Reese's death might change the margins. Before this morning I was ahead four points, but that's not counting the two-point margin of error."

"Is that why you didn't publicly defend Lister James? Because it might eat into your precious two-point lead?"

Walk sighed and seemed to drift off again. "Like I said, there was a time when I wouldn't have thought twice about picking up the phone. Either to call Amory or Brenda."

"And the rally at the baseball stadium? Tell me you at least helped put that together. There were signs saying Lister was murdered. They're true—he was. The same people who shot Reese killed Dixie's grandfather. I'm certain of it."

"I don't know anything about a rally. That's my official response to that question."

"And I don't deserve an unofficial response? I'm Quentin Skinner's son. Maybe you don't owe me from Adam, but you owe my father for his sacrifice."

"There's too much on the line until Tuesday. My people have fought too hard to get to this point. I let them down once by leaving the movement—I can't let them down again. Here's a pun for you: until Tuesday, Ennis, I can't do anything unpolitic."

It took me a minute to realize what he was saying.

"You're not going to help Dixie, are you?"

"I *can't* help her," he spat bitterly. "For reasons I just explained to you."

"Not even if I can deliver the guys responsible for all this mess?"

"*Especially* not if you can do that. I can't be involved in any of it."

"Maybe the Great Men should stick to selling cars instead of changing this city."

"That's a theory I can almost believe in: 'The history of the world is but the biography of car salesmen.' Call Thomas Carlyle."

I was getting hot. "I guess I would expect the first black mayor of Montgomery to have tougher skin."

"Despite what the papers say, this isn't about skin. It's *not* about black versus white anymore in Montgomery. It's too hard to tell the two apart nowadays. Dixie is proof of that, isn't she?

And I don't mean because of her grandparents' interracial marriage. There are other complicating factors involving her that you have no clue about."

"I know all about you making Lister and Brenda get the kid her own apartment. I know all about Lister supposedly taking pictures of her, and I know Dixie told you Lister was her father. I know how bad all those facts would look for your campaign. See how much I know? Doesn't seem there's much that has escaped me."

"You're wrong. I wish you weren't, but you are."

Walk looked at the gun. For a second I thought he was going to pick it up again, if only to shoo me away. Then, scarily, I had an image of him pointing it at himself.

It didn't happen. Instead, he leaned back in his chair and folded his hands over his belly, like a Buddha. "She used to talk about you," he said.

"Who? Dixie? How could she? I only met her yesterday."

"Not Dixie, Ennis. Her mother, Faye. She used to come here wanting money. Two or three times a month if not more. I knew it was for drugs. I tried to tell her to get clean, but she said she had a man in her life that would kill her and her daughter if she left him."

"She was talking about her dealer. A guy called High C."

Walk shook his head no, eyes hard as pebbles. I couldn't believe the implication.

"Faye said that *I* threatened her and Dixie? That's impossible! Not only had I never met the kid before yesterday—I didn't even know she existed until this past Monday! Faye never told me she had a daughter . . ."

"I don't doubt it. I believed what Faye said until I did a little checking. I found out this man was Quentin Skinner's son, the infamous flame-out football star, and I knew Faye had to be lying. It didn't matter if you were a methhead, Ennis. You were

Quentin's son, and I knew Quentin's heart. No son of Quentin's would threaten to kill somebody's daughter."

I leaned against the French doors, hurting for breath. I wasn't sure I wanted to know, but I asked anyway. I needed to hear what other lies Faye had spread about me. But Walk wasn't in a sharing mood.

"It's not the lies we have to fear in life—it's the truths. And the most hurtful truth is that I had a vested interest in getting Faye cleaned up. I knew her from the day she was born, and I saw how methamphetamine turned her into a devil. I wanted to save her as badly as you wish you could have right now. That was her greatest power over men. She knew how to make men want to save her. She used that power on you to try to kill a drug dealer for his stash. And she used it on me to get something of far greater leverage than that crumb's dirty dope money."

He leaned forward.

"You understand what I'm telling you, right? You understand that if this ever got out—no matter who in Montgomery is left living and who is dead—it would destroy my people's chances— *the movement's chances*—not only for Tuesday, but probably forever. Because of me, no black man might *ever* be mayor of Montgomery."

I didn't understand, and that fact appeared to cold-cock Walk. He resisted putting into words what he hinted at. Maybe this was the first time he'd had to say it out loud, and he was scared he didn't have what it would take to survive the confession.

"Dixie is mine, Ennis," he whispered heavily. "I'm that girl's father."

* * * * *

Nine Years, Six Months,
Eighteen Days
And Twenty-One Hours
Earlier

* * * * *

Faye naked on my bed was as irresistible as whipped cream on hot chocolate. The night I tried to kill High C, though, a queasiness was eating my stomach, and it had me hesitant to take my normal nibble. Not that Faye noticed, mind you.

"You know how I know we're right for each other?" she asked, eyes closed as she greedily awaited the rush of her high. "Because no other man would do what you do for me. Have you always been such a giver, sweet pea?"

I pulled the needle from the second of the two spots a sane person would never think to shoot into. She had been hiding the tracks since she conned Walk into believing she was clean. She even signed a cockamamie contract with him. As long as she stayed away from meth he gave her money and free use of a demo from his Lexus dealership. Only to collect the money she had to let him scour her for needle marks. Yeah, it sounded pervy to me, too, but you find you'll put up with a lot of perversion for a grand. Faye swore that all Walk did was rub down her forearms and peek into the webs of her toes. Somewhere along the way she had discovered that there are two primo places on the body where punctures are undetectable. The first is the tear ducts.

I'll leave the other to your imagination.

"Why are you still dressed, sweet pea? Get out of those clothes right now. Supergirl can't wait."

As the rush overtook her, Faye closed her eyes and started

rubbing the spot where I had slammed her—"slamming" being junkie lingo for shooting. She rubbed more and more vigorously until she finally looked like a carpenter trying to sand down a bump. Maybe that's what she was doing; the spot was engorged, after all. One peculiar side effect of meth is that it plumps up this particular part of the female anatomy. By this time in our lives Faye's particular part had taken so many direct hits that it bulged like a blueberry. As I watched, she bit her lip, arched her neck and trembled, all in one luscious gesture that spread her dark hair across the pillowcase like a halo of black sun fire. *"Sweet pea,"* she whispered. *"Sweet pea . . ."*

I stared at the hypodermic in my hand, a dab of her blood still on the tip. Between us we had only ever managed to muster a single prohibition—no needles—and it was months to the wayside. I could feel us building up to something that one or both of us wouldn't come back from. Yet each line we never thought we would cross was so quick to become part of the daily drudgery of procuring pseudoephedrine and phenyl acetone that waiting to hit our limits had become pretty boring business.

"Out of those clothes now!"

Faye sat up and yanked the old practice jersey I was wearing over my shoulders. She caught me so off-guard I almost repoked her with the needle. I tossed the hypodermic to the nightstand, not caring that the tip was exposed, and yanked off my jeans. We kissed, and a bit of acrid spittle passed from her mouth into mine. I attributed that taste to the lithium we stripped from batteries to cook our meth. We both stank of ammonia. Faye hopped off the bed to fetch another pencil—junkie slang for a needle. We got our pencils free from an anti-HIV program that was every day inspiring a rage of controversy in the newspaper. She filled another syringe from the fondue pot as I wrapped a tourniquet around the mound of my biceps.

"Please, sweet pea. You know where Supergirl wants to give it to you. Just once, let me. I promise it'll feel good."

"No way," I said. I tapped the crook of my arm where the cephalic and basilica veins meet. I told her it was here or my neck, nowhere else. She was always talking about the adventurous places we could slam—in a muscle, maybe, or under the skin. She even wanted us to booty bump each other. I'll leave that to your imagination, too.

"C'mon, scaredy cat," she would purr. *"If you let me do anything I want to you, you can do everything you want to me. Anything for everything. Isn't that what being man and woman together means? A woman will give anything so a man can feel he's everything. That's what love is all about, sweet pea . . ."*

"Lie down," she said, pushing me back onto the bed. "You're not hard yet."

As she straddled me, backwards, she set the pencil on the floor, the needle right there for anyone to step on. What did it matter? I was in her mouth. That was what mattered. I was in her mouth, and her musk flushed my nostrils as she slid her hindquarters up my chest until my lips were smeared with her juice. I playfully bit the backs of her thighs and buttocks. She wriggled. I sucked on that engorged blueberry. *"Oh, sweet pea."* I was grateful there was at least one part of her that still smelled natural, that didn't smell like phenyl acetone and lithium.

"Close your eyes," Faye whispered, stopping long enough to look over her tattooed shoulder. "I'm going to take you to a whole other world. We're going to take each other. Are your eyes closed, sweet pea?"

When I told her they were I felt the reassuring stroke of her tongue and the warmth of her breath as her lips closed around my shaft. I didn't need the meth, I thought. This was all the pleasure there could be in the world; anything more was inauthentic. I wanted only to be lost in Faye's glide, the tease of her teeth.

Suddenly I felt something stab into my groin, followed by a quick, chilly flush in my blood. I screamed and bucked, dumping Faye to the floor, where I almost stepped on her as I jumped up. She had gone and done it anyway.

She had injected me in the dorsal vein of my cock, right where for weeks I had been telling her I would never shoot.

I had heard horror stories about guys getting abscesses from slamming there. Urban legends about tweakers having to have their dicks amputated when they grew too pocked to even piss. Why sacrifice your manhood when a fuck was the only productive thing you could manage on meth?

"It's okay, sweet pea," Faye whispered. "It's just a little poke. Now you get to poke me back as hard and mean as you want. C'mon. That other world is waiting for us . . ."

The syringe was still dangling from my groin. I yanked it out and hurled it against the rotting drywall, where it stuck like an orphaned dart. Who cared? I didn't. I was flush with the rush, as we used to say. I grabbed Faye by the hair and threw her facedown on the bed. I shoved my way inside her. With one hand I pressed her head into the mattress. The other clasped her nape. My fingernails dug into her skin. It wasn't disfiguring her, I rationalized. She already had scabs all over her arms and chest from where she picked at herself when she was high. *"Oh, sweet pea . . ."* My heart pumped so loud I thought my eardrums would explode. I didn't just want to fuck. I wanted to kill.

It was the easy juxtaposition of those two desires, the easy bleeding of one instinct into another, that made me pull out. I backed away until I backed into the desk of bottles and cans, the gurgling fondue pot. With a sweep of my arm I sent all our supplies careening. I started throwing books, CDs, whatever I could get my hands on. What was in me wasn't love, and it certainly wasn't intimacy. It was the devil tap-dancing on the grave of my soul. If a knife had been handy I would have plunged it into my gut and pulled out my innards like a string of gooey sausage, just so I could get him out of me.

"Where's a blade!" I screamed. "A knife! Scissors! Machete! A fucking razor, for God's sake!"

I wanted to dig for the devil and choke that red-caped bastard until he went blue.

"It's okay, sweet pea, you're okay."

Faye scrambled to her feet and sat me down. She slipped behind me, holding me as we rocked. I felt her breasts on my back and her hair stream down my chest. She kissed my neck.

"We're out now—that was the last of our stash. We have no money, no nothing. It's not fair. We're only the most poetic lovers the world has ever known, and nobody will help us out. We can't just sit around waiting for somebody to throw us a bone. We're not dogs. We're Sweet Pea and Supergirl . . ."

"What are you talking about?"

I had my palms over my heart, trying to steady its rhythm.

"We'll run away. We can go and clean up for good, the two of us. I read about a beautiful place up in Michigan, between Petoskey and Traverse City. Do you know what Petoskey stones are? They're so smooth and beautiful and natural, Sweet Pea, just like you and me together. . . . We could go up there and make a baby. You and me, lover, we could make a beautiful baby together. Then we would be happy. All we need is money."

I was crying like a goddamned two-year-old. All I could think of was the people I had failed since I was twenty-one—my dad, my Alabama coaches and teammates, the city of fans who packed into Legion Field never suspecting that someone with the blessings I had had in life would waste it all and end up a methhead.

"I know where there's money," Faye whispered. Her hands

crept down from my chest to my stomach. "C's got a safe in the back of his closet. Bales of cash. Bricks of green. I know; I've seen them. Think, sweet pea, think how much fun we could have with that green."

"You want me to rob High C? Are you crazy? We'd have every chapter of the Outlaws after us! Even in Michigan. We'd be fish food for whatever kind of fish swarm around those Petoskey stones."

"All we have to do is scare him, and he'll cough it up. Deep down, he's a scaredy cat. You're more of a man than he'll ever be. Plus I've got a secret weapon."

Her hands now crept from my stomach to my cock. It was sore, and her grip on the spot on my dorsal vein where she had slammed me made me writhe. She shushed me but her stroke was so firm and steady I couldn't bring myself to stop her. My will was melting. Everything in me was dribbling away, the last slivers of conscience or resistance. I had said I would never shoot and here I was a slammer. I had said at least if I slammed I wouldn't do it in a crazy place, and here I was with a needle hole in my cock. There was no lower circle of hell to descend into. I had lost everything except the ability to come. That struck me as the last simple thing in the world. That's all living amounted to, anymore—a measly tug job's worth of jit.

I so only cared about coming that I was unaware where Faye's left hand had gone. I didn't even think about it until she put the object she snuck from under the pillow into my grip. It was a gun. She wrapped my finger around the trigger and we held it together straight out in front of us. All the while her right hand continued to work me.

"This is what will scare C into giving us that money. We'll take that cake and go to Michigan. We can be there by this time tomorrow night. You know what?"

Her left hand held steady even as her right tugged faster and faster.

"Promise me you'll shoot C between the eyes with this—" She waved the gun—"and you can shoot my face with this." She wiggled me. I had to grab her wrist because I was close, but I wasn't ready. I wanted my coming to last forever. Why not? It was the only pleasure left in life.

"You know you want to," Faye purred. "What man doesn't? All you have to do is tell me when you're ready to rocket, and I'll be there for you, baby. Pow, pow! My eyes, my cheek, my chin, wherever you want . . ."

She pretended to fire the gun into the wall. *Pow, pow!* she moaned.

"Tell me what Supergirl always says."

"Anything for everything," I gasped. "A man will give anything so a woman can have everything."

"No, it's a *woman* who will do anything for a man to feel like he's everything."

Whatever.

"Now," I groaned.

Faye kicked around, dropped to her knees in front of me, and presented her face just in the nick of time, just as she promised.

Later that night I kept my promise. Kept it as best as I could, anyway. As it turned out, my best wasn't all that great, but my junky ineptitude was the publishing world's gain, I guess. My bullet only tore up C's belly, not his face.

And all that talk about "anything for everything"?

Bullshit.

Faye and I had nothing.

Nada.

CHAPTER NINETEEN

The nothingness hit me anew as I watched Walk Compson break down and bawl. I felt it as freshly and intensely as I had the second I pulled the trigger that night and left High C with his guts looking like a blendered bowl of Spaghetti-Os. Only this time I wasn't reeling for my own sake. What did it matter if I had been rooked by a junkie? *I was a junkie.* A nobody. Walk Compson, on the other hand, was once a Great Man.

"That was why you quit the Movement twenty years ago, wasn't it?" I said. "Not because you were disillusioned, not because you wanted a quick payday, but for no other reason than you believed you had made a baby you couldn't cop to."

"Do you want to know the worst?" Walk gurgled through his tears. "The worst is that I wish I could tell you that I couldn't admit I fathered Dixie because of what it would do to the Movement. But it wouldn't have hindered what we'd fought for at all. The struggle for civil rights was always and *will* always be greater than any single man. . . . No, I couldn't 'cop to' the girl because it would ruin *my* career. I knew it as surely as I know this gun is loaded, Ennis Skinner. And the minute I knew it was the minute that I stopped believing in the Great Man theory of history."

I watched him cry for a while.

"How much did she take you for?"

"What?"

"You said you gave Faye money to keep clean. I knew it back then, believe it or not. She used to tell me how she was duping you. If my head had been clear at the time I would have known nobody was gullible enough to believe she was clean. You were paying her hush money. Maybe it was easier for you to think of it as child support—I won't try to guess your thinking. Faye's only been dead three years. Dixie is nineteen; that means Faye was into you for almost a decade and a half. You must've paid her a fortune."

"I paid her $5,000 a month."

It took me a couple of tries to do the math. "Jesus. That's $840,000."

"Yes, $840,000 over fifteen years . . . but that's not counting the last three."

"You've been paying hush money *since* Faye died? Who the hell have you been paying it to?"

He said a name like he was trying to spit a bad taste out of his mouth.

"Lister James."

I fell back against the wall, speechless.

"Right before Faye died," Walk explained, "Lister and Brenda made one last effort to get her into rehab. Dixie was always asking for her mother; she spent a day here and there with her, but Dixie was never more than a means to a scam's end for Faye. Even so, Dixie adored her. She called her momma 'Supergirl.' Isn't that the saddest goddamn thing you've ever heard? Lister and Brenda tracked Faye down on Recipe Row and pleaded with her to go clean. For Dixie's sake. Faye was furious. She was so furious she told them that I had seduced her when she was fifteen. That was a lie—Faye was twenty-two the first time I slept with her. And *she* seduced *me*. But Lister didn't believe that, of course. He didn't want to believe it, especially not when he realized how much money a year could be made off of me."

"But then Dixie told *you* that Lister was her daddy. She obviously didn't know you'd thought you were for all these years."

217

"Faye begged me not to tell her. She said Dixie would never understand. But I *am* that child's father, Ennis. I know it."

"She looks nothing like you. She doesn't look like she has a drop of black in her."

That chafed him. "What do you know about that? Faye didn't either. White drop, black drop—that's all irrelevant anymore. I don't care if Dixie is only as ginger as her mother; that girl and I have a connection. If you saw us together, you would see it, too—a real father/daughter connection. As best I could I've protected Dixie since the day she was born."

"As best you could without publicly admitting you had fathered her."

I felt bad for taking such a swipe; I still wanted to believe Walk Compson was a Great Man.

"Do you believe Lister abused Faye?" I asked.

"Lister was evil. Nobody should be lamenting his death, even if he was murdered. But did he abuse his daughter . . . ? Honestly, I don't know. I wouldn't be surprised if he and Faye did have an affair. But whether he seduced her or she seduced him. . . . You know as well as I do what Faye was capable of. I wouldn't put it past her to have slept with her own father, just to get the goods on him. She always got the goods on people. Because the goods always made for a good payday."

There was only one question left to ask: "Where's the money that you paid Lister?"

Walk wiped his eyes. "I don't know . . . I assume it's in a bank account somewhere, or maybe Lister hid it in that house on Hallwood Lane. I don't care a damn about the money. I don't want it back. I want it to go to Dixie. It's hers."

I thought of a beat-up valise stuffed between a bed and a nightstand in a room at the Capitol Plaza Lodge.

"She'll get at least some of it," I said. "If nothing else, I can guarantee you that."

It seemed disrespectful to stand there gawking further at Walk's humiliation. I left him to sob in solitude.

I was halfway out of the French doors when he stopped me.

"You believe that Dixie is mine, don't you, Ennis? I mean, you don't think she's yours, right? That's not why you're going out on such a limb for her, is it?"

I almost spilled the beans about High C believing *he* was Dixie's old man, but then I thought better of it. The last thing a Great Man needs is to wonder if he's really the great father that in his own mind he makes himself out to be.

"I have no doubt she's yours. Dixie may not have your color, but I can see the good in you in her. That's only one of two things I'm convinced of, though."

"What's the other?"

"I'm still convinced you'll make a great mayor."

Chapter Twenty

"Oh, my God," Red said when I made it back to the motel. "Do you think it's true? *He*'s Dixie's dad?"

"Maybe he is, maybe High C is . . . hell, maybe Lister James is—or was. I don't know. All I do know is that Treadface and Twitchy won't give us until after the election to wait for help from Walk. They know we know they killed the Wookie and Reese Justice, and they've probably guessed we have Dixie and the money. They're looking for us right now, I have no doubt."

I put my ear to the hotel wall and listened. I could hear the blare of the TV in Dad and Dixie's room. I assumed it was the TV, anyway, until I made out the words: *"Yannn-ceyyyy,"* a voice lolled. *"Don't go away . . . Yannnncey, won't ya come play . . ."*

"She sounds like a siren's song. If that doesn't summon those two goobers running right to our doorstep, I don't know what would."

"I feel so sorry for her," Red admitted. "Did she tell you what they did to her in that old photography studio?"

"She said they took pictures of her. She should've been used to that if what she told Walk about her grandfather was true."

"Ennis, they double-teamed her."

I stepped away from the wall. "What do you mean?"

"Come on, you weren't in Kilby that long. You know what I mean."

"She told you that Treadface and Twitchy did her at the same time?"

"Well, 'double-teamed' is my word for it, but basically, yes. The sad thing is Dixie doesn't have words for all the ways they worked her over. You should have heard her trying to describe what happened. 'They put it here, they put it there.' My heart broke."

"I asked her that same question and she said something completely different. She said it was never more than her and Twitchy. 'Love is only between two people, so only two people get to play'—those were her exact words."

"Maybe she was embarrassed to tell you the truth. She could admit what they did to me because I'm a woman. There aren't a lot of trustworthy men in her world, apparently."

"Everybody keeps saying she's too simple to lie, but the flip-side is that she's too simple to know when what she says is untrue. What Tyler Petco told me the other day is becoming painfully obvious. You never know what's real and what's imaginary with Dixie."

"Can you blame her? With the mother she had?" Red sat on the edge of the bed, smoothing the duvet with her palm. "Do you know what else the kid was telling me while you were off discovering who else thinks he's her father? I had to figure it out because half the stuff she says is so abstract and discon- nected it's a non sequitur, but basically . . . Have you ever heard of a boondoggle they used to have here in Alabama called a 'crazy check'?"

"Please tell me it's not some variation of double-teaming."

"The state health department used to have a program that paid $500 a month to women with disabled children. Only what counted as disabled was sketchy. Basically all you had to do was bring your kid into some supervisor's office for an interview—a supervisor who wasn't a doctor and who had, like, zippo experi- ence. The supervisor would decide if Jack or Jill seemed abnormal enough to deserve state support. I knew a girl in elementary school whose parents had her act the fool whenever it was time for her review. She wasn't the smartest but she wasn't *Flowers for Algernon,* either. People like her were ripping off the system left and right until the governor got wise and shut the program down."

"Dixie told you that Faye had her playing this scam?"

"Again, not in so many words. She could no more say 'scam' than 'double-team.' I was asking her about her mom. Can you blame me? Here I am getting shot at because I met a guy only days ago who has some mysterious connection to a dead woman. I like to know whose ghost I'm dealing with, especially when I may be heading to the otherworld myself because of her. Dixie's mom must have some power over you to make you risk so much."

"The power is diminishing daily, trust me. None of this is about Faye anymore. It's about Dixie. I can't walk away from her."

I nodded toward the next room. Red blinked at me, accusingly.

"That makes it about you *and* her then. Just tell me the truth, choirboy. Straight up."

It hit me what she meant. I laughed.

"No, no, no. Dixie's not mine. However many men Faye may have tricked into thinking the kid was theirs, I wasn't one of them. She couldn't have duped me—the math is off by about three years, I promise."

From the look on her face, Red didn't have much faith in my math skills.

"At one point while you were gone this afternoon Dixie stood up and peed herself, right in front of me. This was after I had asked her if she wanted me to run up the street and get her a hamburger. I couldn't believe what I was seeing—the dark spot on her shorts just got bigger and bigger while she grinned like a hyena at me. Pretty soon it was dripping on the floor, and still she didn't budge. When I asked what she thought she was doing, she said I had used 'the word.' Faye taught Dixie that no matter what, when she heard 'hamburger,' she was supposed to let her bladder go. That was Faye's scam to score a crazy check. She'd bring Dixie down to the state mental health people and say something like, 'She's so slow she can't eat a hamburger without help.' "

Red settled back against the headboard, her long legs aimed at me.

"Turns out state bureaucrats are only too happy to cut a crazy check if it keeps people from pissing on their carpet."

I sat on the warm edge of the mattress where she had been, staring at the red polish on her toes. Dixie's nursery rhyme still seeped from the next room.

"Maybe I should get her over here. With all the trouble she has distinguishing what's real and what's not, it's not safe for Dad to be alone with her. There's no telling what story she might come up with."

"Whatever it is, it'll have to involve snoring. That's about all your father's been capable of tonight."

I stroked Red's right foot. A thick cuff of a tattoo ringed the ankle. The design wasn't an image but a phrase: *Love First, Live Incidentally.*

"Let me guess," I smiled. "Inspired by Zelda Fitzgerald. *Save Me the Waltz.*"

"You're half right. Zelda said something very similar, but earlier in life, during the happier times. Promise me that if we make it out of this alive we can tip in some new passages into that book, together."

"How about I promise you that *and* that we'll make it out of this alive?"

"Don't make more promises than you can deliver, choirboy."

223

I started massaging her foot. I worked her arch and bridge before my fingers stretched past her ankle and pressed into the muscle of her calf. I had worked my way up her leg when her cell rang.

"Let me have another guess," I groaned. "Eric the ex."

She dug her phone from her purse and turned the ringer off.

"I haven't asked him to walk me home in four days now. It's driving him nuts. He's thinking I've met someone new. Either that or the Bicycle Rapist got me."

"Funny, I've been thinking you met someone new, too. Maybe you should answer one of those calls and let him know he's an ex-bodyguard as well as an ex-boyfriend."

"Maybe I should."

She seemed distracted. It didn't stop my massaging.

"You haven't told me the story behind the snakes. I've told you how St. Jude and I ended up together. Tell me about your tattoos."

Instead of speaking she tipped her chin back and closed her eyes. Her hair dripped over her shoulders, red on white. My eyes traced the overturned V of her jaw. She squirmed a bit as my kneading dug deeper and higher up her leg. She didn't stop me until I reached her thigh. Then she pushed my hands away, sat up straight, and pulled her shirt off, all in one sleek gesture.

"My father had a tattoo of a rattler on his biceps. A rattler coiled in a cotton plant with a Latin phrase: '*Noli me tangere.*' It means 'Don't touch me,' of course. It used to be the image on the Alabama state flag until the state government replaced it with something less defensive, something that didn't smack of what the Caucasoids around here politely call 'states' rights.' Do you know what that something was? They replaced the snake with a cross."

She laughed sharply until she saw that my gaze had fallen to her breasts. I couldn't take my eyes off the snake fangs hovering above each areola. For a second Red covered herself, teasingly, and then she broke into the biggest smile I've ever seen on a woman's face.

"I knew you were no choirboy, choirboy."

She lay back and slipped her shorts down her thighs. She was completely naked now, her body a lithe glide of tight flesh. She let me stare for a bit. "Don't be afraid," she said. "I don't bite. These, however—" She rolled her hands up the curling snakes—"I can't speak for them."

"It's not them. It's me. It's been a while."

"It could be worse, you know. If those goobers today knew how to shoot straight it might have been never."

She took my hands and pulled me forward so I was on my knees hunching over her. Then she laced her fingers within mine and pushed my thumbs erect. She guided each thumb to the spot on either side of her mons venus where the snakes first curled from between her legs, and she pressed them both deep into her flesh.

"I wanted to replace my father's tattoo with something less defensive, because I'm a daughter of the South but I'm tired of all the negative connotations associated with being both Southern and a woman. I'm tired of the defensiveness of Montgomery and of men like Amory Justice. I love this city. I believe that Montgomery's contribution to America lies in its complexity, the fact that this is the birthplace of *both* the Civil War and of Civil Rights. Everybody wants to resolve the opposing forces that those two things represent, but they can't be resolved, and they *shouldn't* be, because they're the yin and yang of America."

The whole time she spoke she drew each thumb up the inky outline of the snakes, stopping only to rub her hipbones.

"Somewhere along the way a yoga instructor of mine gave me this book called *The Serpent Power* by an Englishman named John Woodroffe. John Woodroffe was the first man in the Western world to popularize the Indian idea of the *kundalini*, the life force that leads us to maturity. You've seen its symbol: two snakes just like these on me, curled around a stick, almost like a caduceus, but not quite. . . . I decided the *kundalini* was the perfect symbol to replace my father's rattler because I want to believe that we Southerners are maturing out of our defensiveness. I want to believe that we're learning to live with the fact that our dual history can't be reconciled."

She slid my left thumb all the way up her abdomen to the base of her right breast. When I tried to touch her nipple, she curled her index finger around my knuckle and wrestled it down.

"This snake is the *ida* or yin, the negative energy. The other is the *pingala*, the positive yang. They coil around the *sushumna*, the spinal cord, and the tension between the two is what drives us to a union of *prana-kundalini* and *para-kundalini*, of knowledge and action into will . . ."

She pulled my other thumb to her other breast and circled her chest with both, moaning softly as she stared me dead in the eye. She was so beautiful I was afraid to blink. I was afraid she might disappear.

"The question I have for you, Ennis Skinner, son of the South, is what *your* will is. Do you want the union that these snakes represent, or are you willing to let your halves stay at war with each other? And if you do want *shakti-kundalini*—the name for the union of knowledge and action—can you accept that you're not dissolving each into the other, but allowing them to live in a tension that is the electricity of life? Show me . . ."

Without warning she stretched my fingers wide and pushed my palms onto the snakeheads circling her nipples, squeezing tight until she shivered.

"Show me what you want, Ennis Skinner," she said again.

So I did. I stood up and yanked her to her feet. I kissed her deep and hard and then I spun her so her back was to me and her shoulder blades pressed into my chest. I sank my lips into her neck and clutched her tight. I closed my eyes and when I opened them again all I could see was the red whirlwind of her hair. I didn't need eyes, only hands. I felt the energy emanating from those snakes scorch my palms. I wanted to take hold of them, to tame them.

Instead I took Red by her hipbones. We pushed against each other and then crashed backwards onto the bed, tangled in each other's legs. When I gripped her wrist in my fist, she took mine in hers. That was what she meant by the union of the *prana-kundalini* and *para-kundalini*. We were knowledge and will, two into one. That meant I could lose myself and all my regrets in her.

For that gift alone I owed Red.

I owed her big time.

CHAPTER TWENTY-ONE

Afterwards, she whispered in my ear: "There's one person who might help us that we haven't thought of. Do you know who I mean?"

I did, and the fact that I did convinced me that the love we had made was genuine. It meant we could read each other's minds.

"She's stopped finally," I said, sitting up. I nodded toward the next room. The siren's song no longer sounded.

"She stopped a long time ago," Red corrected me. "At first I thought it was because of us. These old motel beds can be creaky. That would seem a little self-important, though, wouldn't it? The world doesn't stop for two people to fuck."

" 'Fuck'? Is that what we just did?"

"You want euphemisms, honey, get me to Tuesday. I'm sure Dixie fell asleep, that's all."

I lay back down, Red snuggled to my shoulder. I didn't want to talk or think. I just wanted to enjoy feeling good for a few hours. It had been a while indeed.

Red knew what I needed. That was another sign that the love we made was genuine. She didn't fall asleep, but she didn't speak, either. Maybe she knew that I hadn't had silence in ten years. There wasn't a second's worth of it at Kilby—not a single second. So I held Red to reassure her that even if my yap was shut I was still one hundred percent with her, and I drank up the silence. I drank so much of it I almost fell asleep.

"Hey," she whispered at some point. "I hate to interrupt your meditating, Maharishi, but you got me starving over here. We probably need to get Dixie and your dad something to eat, too. They haven't all day."

I stood up and started dressing. "I don't think I've ever felt so hungry." I felt rested and alive, damn near giddy. "There used to be a great place up by the train station: Lek's Railroad Thai. Do you know if it's still there? I haven't had Thai food in ten years."

"Tonight seems to be your night for getting what you haven't had in ten years, huh?"

She sounded funny. Looked funny, too. She had the bedsheet tucked all around her, like she was shy all of a sudden. I sat down next to her.

"You regret what just happened here?"

"No regrets, choirboy. Aftermaths are just awkward. For a little while I forgot yea-bobs out there are trying to kill us. Now the funny feeling I've had in my gut since meeting you is back. It's not your fault. I'm just scared. I'll try to be a big girl about it. Let me know if you prefer weepy to crabby. Crabby is my preference—then I don't feel so goddamn weak."

I found my shirt in the clump of our clothing. "Well, if nothing else, I hope you trust me enough to pick something good off the menu."

It was a shitty thing say. I regretted it the minute I was out the motel door. I didn't go back, though. I don't know why. I guess words didn't seem likely to settle Red's fears. I slipped down the steps, keeping an eye on the cars in the parking lot. No strawberry red SUVs anywhere. Still, I stayed to the shadows as best I could, invisible except for the times that a headlight from a turning car swept over me. I walked all the way up past the new baseball stadium that was ghostly quiet now and to the tunnel we'd rushed through after Red fished me from the river.

Just past the tunnel was a rubicund brick structure, newly refurbished, where passengers once boarded and disembarked trains. Back in my day the trains still ran out of Montgomery, but it was clear that the station house hadn't seen one in years. Instead, it housed a Civil Rights museum and a restaurant, both built in hopes of drawing tourists to town via their own cars.

Montgomery had changed so much in my absence that I might as well have been a tourist.

The restaurant was cool and smelled rich and spicy. I ordered four meals and then shot a Jägermeister at the bar while the waitstaff boxed them up. The Jäger took the edge off Red's anxiety. I was tempted to buy a bottle for us both on the way home, but Quentin's example had taught me that getting drunk wasn't the answer. I had to show Red I could protect her. Making her forget the people I was trying to protect her from— whether by making love or through alcohol—wasn't enough.

I was out in the street with a plastic bag of take-home containers in each hand when the beam of the flashlight hit my eyes.

"I hope you got her steamed rice instead of fried. She hates fried rice."

Blinded, I couldn't see a face. I didn't recognize the voice, though. That meant it wasn't Treadface or Twitchy, so that was good. Maybe not better, just good.

"I've known all week she met somebody new. You can always feel when your girl meets someone new, you know? They start talking to you from the sides of their mouths."

"You must be Eric the ex."

That last bit slipped out. I didn't mean to say it. I tried to subtly pivot a few degrees to my right. A streetlight glowed off to my side, and I wanted to draw him into it. I needed to see if a gun accompanied that flashlight.

"You don't need to be moving. You break into a run, you'll

230

drop that food. Lexi isn't pleasant to deal with when she's hungry. High metabolism. The girl needs her grub."

"You've got me at a disadvantage. It's only fair to see what I'm dealing with if I have to set these bags down for us to go at it. If you stop burning my corneas, I promise not to run."

"I don't think you want to go at it with me, friend."

The light snapped off. The night grew so silent I almost believed I could hear him think. Slowly my eyes adjusted to the dark, and his features took shape. Old Eric had me beat in the handsome category, that was for sure. His eyes were as blue as Tyler Petco's cobalt suit. His skin was tan and his build athletic. With his blond hair trimmed close to his temples he appeared to have the square, muscular jaw of a Rock-Em, Sock-Em Robot.

That wasn't the detail I dwelled on, though.

The one that I did convinced me Eric was right when he said we wouldn't be going at it. I nodded at his uniform. "You're a cop. Red didn't tell me that."

"Red, huh? So you're one of those nickname guys. I bet she has a nickname for you. Apparently you two have a nickname for me. Eric the ex, is it? Well, I've got a message for you to give to Lexi. Tell her I'm happy to be her ex. I'll move on as soon as I get my ring back."

"Your ring?"

"We were supposed to get married in a month. Lexi didn't tell you that? She has a Princess-cut rock that cost me three months of overtime working the door at the Gypsy Wrangler. You need to know that about her—Lexi is as predictable as she is unfaithful. That's right: *she* cheated on *me*. I wouldn't be surprised to find out it was that damn bartender at El Rey. My whole family told me when I bought that rock that I would get ripped off, but I'll be damned if I let that happen. Tell Lexi to get it to me and I'll get out of her hair."

"I would think what with the bad week the police are having

you wouldn't have time to worry about a diamond ring. Tasers one day, shoot-outs the next, a dead mayor's daughter after that—the whole city seems to be falling apart."

He shrugged. "Once the blacks get settled after this election, things will get back to normal."

"The blacks, huh? Sure. They're the problem. How dare one of them run for mayor. I take it you're voting for Amory."

Eric stiffened. "I'd make you eat curb if I didn't feel so sorry for you. Trust me, Lexi will do to you worse than anything I could do to you. I'm not here for politics. Whoever wins Tuesday means nothing to me. I want my ring back. Tomorrow, or I'll be knocking on that motel door you're shacking up behind."

He started to leave. I stopped him.

"You mind telling me how you found out about the Capitol Plaza? We were trying to be discreet."

He grinned. Eric the ex had a shiteater of a grin. It was as broad as his shoulders.

"You're a bigger sap than you know, sap. Lexi called me this afternoon. I leave her umpteen messages, and today she finally decides to return one. All she can say is that she's scared. She sounds like she did every night she called when she got off work at that burrito shack, asking me to walk her home. Christ, the boho is the safest part of Montgomery, but she thinks she deserves a personal escort. She tells me she's scared, that she's stuck at a dive motel, that she's gotten into a mess that she can't get out of. Then the bitch hangs up. You think I care if she's scared? I want my ring, goddammit."

"She told you where we were?"

"Do you have fried rice stuffed in your ears? I just said she hung up before she could get to specifics. A funny thing about cell phones, though. When you use one it's just like a global positioning system. All I have to do is call the phone company, and they tell Officer Eric here anything he wants to know. It's one of the few benefits of being a cop."

He clicked his light back on and blinded me again.

"Take my advice, sap: don't trust her. She'll take you for everything you're worth."

I started to tell him that what I was worth wasn't much, but he was already gone.

At the Capitol Plaza Lodge I discovered that Red had gathered Dixie and Dad in our room. Dad was slouched in a chair, groggily flipping channels on the TV. Dixie sat Indian-style on the bed, giggling like a six-year-old as Red crouched behind her combing the kid's hair. It wasn't until Dixie jumped up to hug my chest and yelp "Ennis!" that I realized what a game of dress-up they had going. Dixie was in pigtails, denim shorts, and a sleeveless T-shirt, the only thing of hers on her that damn purse. She looked like Red's kid sister, right down to the knee-high socks.

"What the hell do you think you're doing?"

My anger caught Red off-guard.

"We're killing time, waiting for you . . ."

"She's not girling it up for tips at the El, dammit! Don't you get it? Every person in her life has exploited her by making her baby-girl it up—I won't let it happen anymore."

I threw the food down and grabbed Dixie hard by a pigtail. With my other hand I started digging at the rubber band that held the second tail in place, trying to snap it. "Get these out of your hair!"

The kid started bawling. That only made me angrier. I pushed Dixie face down onto the bed and yanked at the knee-highs. Red was behind me, struggling to wrap her arms around my elbows and pull me back. "Dixie asked me! *She* asked *me!* It was harmless!"

When I couldn't rip the sock I snapped her purse strap off

her shoulder and pitched it against the wall. That was when my old man got into the act. He leaped out of the chair and wedged himself between me and Dixie. "Get a hold of yourself," he grunted.

It wasn't what he said that made me stop. It was the whiskey he breathed into my face. I staggered back, nearly plowing Red down. I had torn a gash into one of the socks. Dixie rolled over and curled into Dad's embrace, howling as tears ran down her cheeks.

"Look what you made her do," Red whispered. A dark wet oval widened on the bedspread under Dixie. "C'mon, honey. Come into the bathroom with me. I'll help you clean up . . ."

She pulled Dixie to her feet and together they disappeared behind a slammed door. Dad and I stared at the wet oval on the bed, unable to look at each other.

"You're too angry. You're not angry at anybody but yourself, but it's the rest of us who're going to take the licking. You've got to get a grip, Ennis. You better get it quick, too."

He was right, of course. And that made it all the worse.

"Nice philosophy," I growled. "For an old drunk."

I went outside and sat in the stairwell.

I stayed there, just thinking, for pretty much the whole damn night. It was hours later when I heard the soles of Red's tennis shoes clapping on the concrete walkway. She stopped at the top stair.

"They said to thank you for dinner. They're asleep now. You need to come back and eat. There's a microwave in the room. I can warm your order up for you."

"You should've told me you didn't like fried rice."

"What?"

"I said I need to borrow your cell."

"What for?"

"Have you forgotten? You said it yourself. There's one person we haven't thought of who can help us out of this mess. We need to call him. The sooner the better."

I counted the number of steps she descended the stairwell: three. They weren't hard to follow. Each echoed like a ricocheting gunshot along the brick walls.

"I'm not sure we're talking about the same person, choirboy."

"Then maybe we should talk in specifics. We don't seem to have done that this week."

"Maybe you're right. Maybe I should call you 'Ennis' instead of 'choirboy.' And maybe you should use my real name instead of 'Red.' Seems like we're at that point, doesn't it?"

"So go get me your phone . . . *Lexi.*"

She didn't leave. "I'll do that, but you've got to promise me you won't get mad. I never said I was simple. If you wanted simple, Dixie should've been your girl, not me."

"Dixie is my daughter. When all of this is over, I'm going to adopt her. I'm going to make sure nobody messes with her ever again."

"If that's your plan, maybe you ought to buy her a new purse. You broke hers. I taped the strap up, but it looks like shit."

"I'll buy her a million new purses when all of this is over."

"That's admirable of you, but the operative word there is 'when.' It's not going to end on its own. I have an idea of how we can get out of it. I've been hashing a plan out in my head all night. Do you trust me enough to hear it?"

"Sure," I said.

The crazy part? I wasn't lying.

No matter what bug Eric the ex put in my ear, I trusted her. I wanted, too, anyway.

I rose and followed her back to the room. The whole time we walked the corridor, I resisted the temptation to check her ring finger for a tan line.

★ ★ ★ ★ ★

FRIDAY

★ ★ ★ ★ ★

CHAPTER TWENTY-TWO

It was so hot the next day that the city almost canceled the evening game at Riverwalk Stadium. At six P.M., the temperature gauges on the bank signs still said 111 degrees. As anybody you talked to giddily pointed out, though, the heat index was actually 115—a new record.

That left the air feeling like soup as I walked up Tallapoosa Street to the stadium's main gate. Volunteers handed out visors and bottled water to folks who couldn't be persuaded to go home and listen on the radio in the comfort of their air conditioning. I already had my hat—a souvenir from a gas-station gift shop near the Capitol Plaza Lodge—but I accepted the water and gulped it down in exactly four swallows. I was wearing a loose short-sleeve jersey over my T so nobody would notice the newfound bulkiness of my chest. I was taped up like a mummy, just like the morning I confronted Reese Justice. Only I was sweating such a cataract that the bandage tape wasn't sticking well to my skin. I had to clamp my upper arms tight to my sides and hope I could keep the ten bundles trussing me from slipping. It wouldn't be pretty if my contraband plopped to the ground at my feet. Especially not when security was out in force today.

"What's with all the blackshirts?" I overheard a hippie type ask.

"You don't know?" the lady in front of him at the WILL CALL window line replied. "Somebody made gumbo out of the mayor's daughter yesterday. It's been all over the news."

Nobody in Montgomery could get enough of talking about Reese Justice. Nobody seemed to remember or care that the Wookie was also dead.

Fortunately, the police weren't patting the line down. They didn't want to—not when the entire crowd was as wet as greased pigs. Not when word was out that Brenda James was filing a lawsuit over the Tasering incident.

I picked up the ticket I reserved by phone earlier that morning and let the turnstile keeper scan the UPC code on the back. The old guy had to run his scanner twice over the black bars because my fingers had stained the cardstock with oily streaks. That's how bad the sweat was gushing.

Once inside it was a bit cooler. There was shade and a breeze blew down the stairwells from the concourse above. I killed time with the trinketeers hawking stick flags and beer cozies, not wanting to get any more sun-blasted than I needed to. I considered buying Red a gift, but the souvenirs weren't too inspiring. I checked the digital clock on the wall and realized it was later than I thought. I mopped my forehead and ascended into what felt like a furnace.

The concourse ran 360° around the baseball field. Only about a third of it was shaded by a metal roof. That was the section that lodged the concession stands. I didn't envy the hourly folks having to work the Philly cheese-steak grills or the pizza ovens. The rumor was there wasn't a lick of air conditioning in the stadium anywhere but the luxury boxes. You could see the resentment on the servers' faces when the hoity-toits wandered down to the stands from their Plexiglas heavens, not a damp spot to disfigure them.

I bought myself a beer to steel my nerves. Then I stood at the railings by the seating bowl and tried to drink it. Despite the heat the game was a sell-out. Why not? The Montgomery

Biscuits—that was indeed the team's name—were going for
their third straight division championship. They were playing
the Carolina Mudcats, who had lived up to their moniker by
sinking to the bottom of the league's standings with a lousy
win/loss record of 56–78. Even though this was a meaningless
game, Montgomery was so proud of its champs that some of its
citizenry was even willing to camp out on the grass berm behind
centerfield and roast like hams in a smoker.

In the heat the beer tasted acrid, so I poured what I couldn't
finish into the trash and waited as a church choir gargled
through the national anthem. Like everybody else, I plucked off
my cap and slapped a hand to my heart. Unlike everybody else,
I was looking left to right for anyone I might recognize. They
were all rank strangers to me.

After the land of the free and the home of the brave was duly
extolled in four-part harmony I found my seat. It was dead
center in a middle aisle, which had its good and bad points. The
good was that nobody could get to me too easily. The bad was
that I couldn't get away from anyone easily.

I excused my way through a line of chubby families mowing
on greasy chicken and chili dogs and slid into my seat. It was
like sitting on a coal. I tried to readjust the bundles but the tape
was soaked clean through. The man on my right leaned over
and offered me a French fry. He looked like a lifelong French-
fry eater—pudgy, sweaty, jowly in a way that made the rest of
his features more porcine than he probably deserved. The fries
were in a little paper boat smothered under a glut of cheese that
gurgled like orange lava. My stomach already felt like a rock, so
I declined as politely as I could.

"You here alone?" the guy asked.

I closed my eyes, my skin hot as flame. "I'm here alone, but
that doesn't mean I'm looking to make friends."

I could feel the guy glare. He seemed harmless enough—just

a little snobby, the type who thinks by offering you a bite off his plate he's performing some kind of community service. You could tell he wasn't used to having his generosity rebuffed. "Jesus Christ," he burped. "I was only making conversation. You don't have to be a jackass about it."

I didn't answer. The bundles felt like pads of butter melting down my chest.

"*Ladies and gentlemen,*" a voice boomed over the PA system, saving me. "*Before we begin tonight's game, the Montgomery Biscuits ask you to join them in a moment of silence for a fallen member of our family, a friend and supporter without whom this beautiful facility would never have been built in Montgomery . . . the daughter of our favorite Montgomery mayor. . . . Ladies and gentlemen, let us take a moment to remember Miss Reese Justice . . .*"

I never heard silence so raucous. Boos poured onto the field as ugly as hurled litter. It caught the press box so off-guard the announcer forgot to turn his PA off. "*This isn't good,*" he mumbled absentmindedly. "*Don't let that go out over the radio, for God's sake . . .*"

I felt breath at my back.

"Not too many people mourning the Kudzu Ann Coulter," a voice whispered in my ear. "Can't figure out why . . ."

I made no effort to whisper. "It's enough to make you wonder if the person responsible for her demise could be sitting among us."

Treadface slipped his hand around the back of my neck. Under the guise of a friendly pat, he gave it a spine-crushing squeeze.

"Don't get so cocky, Gummy Bear. I would hate to see your fake teeth rounding third."

Twitchy leaned in from the other side. That meant his head was between me and the guy eager to share his food. I couldn't decide which was worse, the vinegary smell of cheap cologne or the greasy sizzle of the fries.

"I don't see no bookbag anywhere. I hope you didn't come here with nothing to your name but a foam finger."

"Nice patch," I said, nodding at the bandage that covered his right socket. "And they don't let you carry book bags into the ballpark, genius. You don't need to worry. I wouldn't have set this little shindig up if I weren't planning on coming through for you. I just want out of this. I didn't intend to haul off with your stash. The girl said it was hers."

"Dixie is part of the stash," the younger one insisted. "Unless you got her rolled up in your sock, I'm guessing you didn't bring her. She's part of the deal or there is no deal."

"You better quit nibbling at my earlobe then. No way would I ever throw a lamb like her back to a couple of lions like you two. I know what you did to Dixie at Gilbert's Photography. Two on one, huh? I saw that a lot at Kilby. I saw enough of it to know it's never about love but about brutality. Be happy you're getting your stash. The only reason is that I want my life back. And Dixie deserves hers—what's left of it, anyway."

"No two-on-one ever happened at that studio," Twitchy huffed.

I turned toward Treadface. "Is that your story, too, Unc?"

"The girl's not important," he harrumphed.

Twitchy's seat creaked as he reared back. "What?"

"I said the girl's not important. You can have the dummy, QB. You know what we want."

I knew what I didn't want, which was to attract attention. That was what we were doing, however. Mr. French Fry was eavesdropping. I could tell. I saw his eyes drift to the crinkled edges of his sockets, as if he were trying to find his peripheral vision. He was so caught up in what we were saying he didn't realize he wasn't munching his grease sticks anymore. The guy was nibbling his fingers.

"Did you hear what I said?" Treadface growled when I didn't answer.

"Sit back and shut up," I softly ordered him, staring straight ahead. Goddamn if the goober didn't do the exact opposite. Treadface leaned in closer.

"What did you say?"

I twisted suddenly in my seat, facing the two of them with as much irritation as I could fake. "I'm not going to tell you assholes again—I don't have a program for you to borrow! Go get your own already!"

Mr. French Fry couldn't help but gape. I gave him a commiserative look, as if to say, *Can you believe the shit we've got to put up with just to enjoy a good game of minor-league ball?* The busybody wiped a streak of salt from his fingers on his Biscuits T-shirt and locked his eyes on the green diamond in front of us. Hopefully, he would stick those fingers in his ears and mind his beeswax.

Out on the field, the home team's mascot—a Snuffleupagus-faced thing whose connection to biscuits seemed a bit ambiguous—jogged a skinny man in jeans to the pitcher's mound. *"Ladies and gentlemen . . ."* The announcer was trying to regain his game voice over the still-raining boos. *"We want to honor another milestone today. The Montgomery Biscuits love all their fans, but one Biscuit-head in particular has shown his team spirit like no other . . ."*

Mr. French Fry slowly set his snack box at his feet and hoisted himself upright. He kept blinking nervously at my kneecaps.

"Please give a hand to Mr. Warren Higgins. . . . Today's contest is Warren's 100th straight home game!"

"Excuse me," Mr. Fry said, pointing toward the aisle. "I've got a bladder the size of a penny pouch."

Instead of swinging my legs out of his way I pressed my foot to the seatback in front of me, blocking his path. "Are you sure you need to go? You're gonna miss ole Warren throwing out the first pitch. It's a historic occasion. The way the world's spinning, none of us may make it to one hundred straight."

"I'm pretty sure I've got to go," the guy mumbled.

How could I stop him? I swung my leg down and watched him nervously hike the stairs. Sure enough, only four steps up, he threw me a sweaty glance over his shoulder.

"You better get out of here," I told Treadface and Twitchy. "There's a parking garage down the street. Find the far-right corner facing Dexter Avenue and I'll try to be there in fifteen minutes. If I don't make it, leave my dad alone. If anything happens to him, I'll spill every bean I've got."

"What are you talking about?" Treadface muttered.

"Get out of here!"

The dumbasses jumped up and shuffled off. At least they were smart enough to head the opposite direction as Mr. French Fry. I settled back and watched Warren Higgins nervously palm the ball. The booing had become a thumping chant: *"War-ren! War-ren! War-ren!"* The Biscuits' No. 1 fan drew back and threw. He had been practicing, all right: his pitch was a driller. The ball cannonballed into the catcher's mitt, snapping so sharply you could imagine flakes showering off the leather palm. *"Holy Guacamole,"* the announcer's voice crackled. *"What size trousers do you wear, Warren? With a gunner like that, the Biscuits may just have a uniform with your name on it!"*

"Sir, would you mind coming with us?"

Two cops stood at the end of the aisle. Thank God neither was Eric the ex. Or the bike officer from the previous day. I knew my drunk act wouldn't fly twice. I decided to play dumb.

"Are you talking to me?"

"You see Robert DeNiro sitting in these stands?" the second one wisecracked. "If not, then, yeah: you, bud. Hop up, please."

"You mind telling me what for?"

"Let's get out of the heat," the first one smiled. "The shade's more conducive to conversation."

What choice did I have? I re-clamped my arms to my sides so the tape held, and I rose. They weren't taking any chances. One led, the other followed. I was sandwiched. Halfway up to the concourse we passed Mr. French Fry, who had the queasy look snitches always get. "Don't worry," I told him. "Next time you offer I'll lick your plate clean."

As we stepped onto the concourse I thought about bolting. The stairway to street level was only fifteen paces away. If I could make it outside I could dart across Tallapoosa and disappear into the crumbling blocks of old downtown. It was too risky, though. The concourse was still crowded with people not wanting to expose themselves to the sun until the game actually began. All I needed was for some hero to toss aside his four-dollar Bud Lite and tackle me in the name of civic duty. As I let the first cop lead me past the concessionaires, I floundered for a credible story. It was hard to come up with one when I was wondering how many paces I had to do my inventing.

They led me down a far stairwell and into a little room that served as the security lounge. At least it was the coolest place in the stadium. No less than six oscillating fans blew at us from shelves along the walls. It made me wonder how long sweat-soaked tape might take to dry. My biceps were starting to quiver from the strain of holding the ten bundles in place.

"You got some ID on you, DeNiro?" the second cop asked.

I didn't know what else to do. I dug into my back pocket and tossed my state-issued parole card onto the desk. "I didn't realize being rude to a Biscuit-head was a criminal offense," I shrugged.

They weren't listening. They were staring at the card. The first cop scooped it up and flipped it over, front to back and back to front, as if convinced it wasn't real.

"Looks like you have some experience with criminal offenses. How long you been out?"

"Since Monday."

"What are you doing here?"

"Where would I rather be on a 115-degree day? I love this stadium. It sort of reminds me of Kilby."

"What were you in for?"

"If you really want to know, call it in. You'll find out quick enough. I did my time and I'm clean. I came here today because nothing's cleaner than baseball. I don't know what that guy back there said about me, but—"

"He said you were acting funny," the first cop cut in.

"Really? I would've thought booing a dead woman would count as acting funny. You guys plan on grilling all seven thousand people out there?"

"Our boys were probably booing as loud as anybody," the second one admitted. "The police weren't too fond of Reese. Not to speak ill of the dead, but we had a nickname for her: The Daughtinator. We haven't had a cost-of-living raise in three years, and she'd put a bug in her daddy's ear about raising our health insurance."

"You should have Tasered her when you had the chance— you know, like you guys Tasered Brenda James the other day."

They blinked at me for a few beats. "You think that's funny?" the first one went. He was almost drowned out by a roar from the seats above us. The Biscuits had just scored the first out of the opening inning.

"What I think is that I'm missing a game I paid for. Go ahead, call in and see for yourself that my parole's in order. Either that, or let me get back to my seat."

They looked at each other, speaking telepathically like I suppose cops are able to after they've been partnered a while.

Finally, the second one handed me back my ID. "Enjoy the game," he chided as he let the fans whirr at his back. "It's supposed to be a scorcher."

I took my card and started out of the office. Two steps into my exit a question popped to mind.

"Either of you guys know a cop named Eric?"

"There are about five Erics who are cops. Maybe you want to ask if we know a Bob or a Bill while you're at it."

"This Eric works third shift."

They shared an *ah-hah!* moment. "Eric Stinson," the first cop nodded.

"He a friend of yours? You guys like ole Eric?"

"He's an idiot," the second officer spat.

"Even worse," the first one corrected him. "He's a liar. Can't tell you his driver's license number without gilding it. Why do you care?"

I was too busy laughing to explain. "You guys just made my day—maybe my week. And I bet y'all solve Reese Justice's murder by this afternoon. Something tells me you're on the verge of cracking that case."

I found the nearest men's room and locked myself in a stall, where I stripped off both shirts and peeled the bundles from my chest. They were wrapped in black plastic and held together with gaffers tape so they looked like a Kevlar vest. I hung the whole contraption over the hook on the steel door and turned my T inside out so I could wipe my chest and back down. The T was completely soaked through. I sat on the toilet for a second to let my nerves settle. Then I re-strapped the bundles across my torso. The bandage tape at the top and bottom of the truss was nearly useless now; I wish I had packed the roll before coming to the stadium. Then again, if the cops had asked me to empty my pockets, bandage tape would be tricky to explain. I pulled both shirts on and pinched my arms tight, once again.

Out of the stall, I went to the sink and turned the faucet as far to cold as it would go. I soaked my face in handful after handful of water until I couldn't take the sting anymore. Then, as I reached for a paper towel, I forgot all about avoiding the mirror, and I saw my face.

It was my first sight of it in years if you didn't count Red's painting. You *couldn't* count the painting—Red had been too generous. I looked nothing like her portrait of me.

My skin was prickled red from the dousing, but that wasn't what shocked me. It was how old I looked. My hair was gray, my cheeks craggy, my mouth sunken. I didn't feel like a dead man, but I sure resembled one. I wiped the paper towel across the mirror, hoping the burst pores and tear channels and hollow expression were optical illusions.

They weren't.

I left the bathroom and then the stadium itself. From the cheers and stomping that boiled out of the seating bowl the Biscuits appeared to have taken an early lead. Well, someday maybe Red and I would come back for a whole game. Maybe we would even offer our French fries to our neighbors. That was for the future. I looked up Tallapoosa Street and saw a comforting sight about four blocks ahead: a beat-up blue Saturn four-door. Well, at least something was going right today. I took out the cell phone Red lent me. As far as I knew she hadn't had time to erase her call history, but I wasn't going to snoop. I had to be better than that.

I had never heard of text messaging until this morning, so I fumbled clumsily to type a short message and hit SEND. I hoped I did it right. If I did, tonight would be the first night of the real rest of my life. If not, I was unlikely to see tomorrow.

I took a deep breath and walked toward the parking garage that sat roughly halfway between the stadium and the Saturn. I ducked past the guard station, which—thankfully—was empty. I made my way past an endless line of Explorers and Expeditions to the back left corner, where I found Treadface and Twitchy huddling next to a camouflage-topped Jeep that sat in the final slot of the last row.

"What did you tell those cops?" Twitchy snarled.

"I said I had a date with a couple of inbred knuckle-draggers."

They didn't appreciate the humor. "Fork it over," Treadface grunted, his eyes sweeping the rows of cars. I lifted my T and yanked my improvised vest loose. Neither goober knew what to make of the sweaty truss.

"Rip the plastic," I said, tossing the bundles to them. "Your money is inside, every single dollar. It took me all day to stack it. Even in hundreds, $100,000 adds up to a lot of bills. When I found Dixie, you know, she was rolling around in them like some kind of a pin-up queen. I'm sure you'll tell me you didn't teach her that, either."

"I don't let dummies touch my green," Treadface smirked. "That's called devaluing the dollar."

"*Your* green?" I smiled. "Funny, I could've sworn this was High C's money—money you cobbed from his publishing company. That's what C said, anyway. Of course, we all know where it really came from. This is the green that Walk Compson has paid Lister James since Faye died. You two took it from Lister after you killed him."

Treadface froze. "Pat him down," he told his nephew from the side of his mouth. "Make sure he's not wired."

I didn't object as Twitchy ran his hands up and down me. I even apologized. "I sweat like a hog," I said as Twitchy wiped his hands on his jeans.

His mind wasn't on my perspiration, however. "Stop calling Dixie 'dummy,'" he said belatedly. He wasn't talking to me.

Treadface ignored his nephew. Instead, he dug his thumbs

into the first of the bagged bricks. When he got it free the plastic vest dropped to his feet, but he didn't seem to care. He was too busy flipping through the bills to make sure I hadn't stacked his deck with filler paper.

"You plan on checking every single brick?" I asked, impatiently. All I needed was an unsuspecting security guard to come whistling along the bumpers. I was antsy.

"Damn straight I'm checking every one. Why? You got a date?"

"I just want to be left alone."

"Don't worry. We're out of Montgomery as soon as this little transaction is through."

He flipped through the second bundle. I took a step backwards, throwing my eyes to Twitchy to cover my feet.

"So you're taking off without your girlfriend? That's going to break Dixie's heart. You managed to make her fall hard for you. Of course, that wasn't too hard, was it? It's not like you have to be Don Juan to land a shortbus."

"Don't call her that. She ain't handicapped—she's just slow. And I'll be back for her."

"No, you won't," Treadface disagreed. Now he was on the third bundle. I was on my third step back. I had to walk a thin line between distracting him and distracting myself.

"Honestly, it's probably best you *don't* come back for Dixie. It's not like you guys didn't leave loose ends dangling everywhere; they might trip you up. There's one loose end in particular I don't get. I mean, I understand how you ended up at Gilbert's. You broke into that photography studio after getting the address from the stamp on the back of the Wookie's pictures. Highland Avenue made for a nice little lair. But how does His Boy Elroy fit into the picture? I figured tubby butter here was the other shooter at El Rey, but it's a big step from getting fired from a burrito joint to shooting it up. Aren't you worried that the kid will talk to the police? You left Elroy at the

El lying there scalded in hot rice."

"Elroy knows how to take his lumps like a man. I taught him well. I taught him something you've probably never heard of, Ennis Skinner—I taught him good sons are loyal to their daddies, no matter what."

It took a second to get his point. Then I whistled. "So Elroy's the fruit of your loins? Wow. At least one thing about Montgomery hasn't changed in my absence. The apple doesn't rot far from the tree."

"If you don't quit yapping you'll find out how fast something will rot in this hea—hey, wait a minute!"

The goober was halfway through the fourth brick when he realized the bills had indeed been replaced with paper—specifically, pages from a copy of Anarchy Ahoy's bestselling book, *Mysteries of Methamphetamine Manufacture: Exposed!* I had managed to find a secondhand copy of it that morning at the Trade 'n' Books on Madison Avenue, a couple of blocks from the Capitol Plaza Lodge. Treadface angrily yanked the next bundle from its plastic wrap. The only bills in this one were the first and last. The sixth didn't have any. I hadn't even bothered to bookend those pages with real Franklins.

"Son of a bitch!" Treadface threw the stack down and lunged at me. I was already pivoting toward the entry of the garage, however. I made it past the security gate and cut right onto Tallapoosa. Soles smacked the ground behind me. I had a hundred yards to the Saturn. I blasted through an intersection, a light pole to my left. I glanced to the sidewalk to make sure there was nothing to trip me. Then I twisted my head to calculate how many paces behind me the goobers were. *One, two, three, four, five—*

It felt like the longest count of my life, longer than the counts twenty years earlier before the football was snapped into my hands and it was up to me to make a play happen. I wanted to throw every ounce I had into my speed, but I couldn't. Maintaining the count was vital. When I finally came to the Saturn I felt like I had been running for an hour. I cut a hard right into the alleyway beside the car and counted out loud: "One, two, three, four, five—now!"

Twitchy came around the corner first, so he got it first. I saw his boots lift off the ground as the blow knocked him backwards onto the oily pavement. The baseball bat caught him across the clavicles, just under his throat. Treadface came around the corner just in time to see his nephew lying there, out cold. I dove into him. The momentum sent us stumbling backwards across the sidewalk into the Saturn, cracking the rear passenger window. I shook off my dizziness and spun him around, booting him back toward the alley. The bat crashed across the back of his skull and drove him facedown, fittingly, into a pile of garbage.

"I hope they've got money in their wallets," Bubba Burch said, taking a few unnecessary practice swings. "Somebody owes me a new window."

"There's a good twenty thousand back in that parking garage. You can buy yourself a whole new car if you want."

"If that money is dirty, I'll live with the cracked glass. Which one of these guys shot up my bar with His Boy Elroy?"

"The older one. He's Elroy's old man."

Bubba grabbed a fistful of hair and jerked Treadface out of the garbage and onto his back.

"I see the resemblance. Maybe I shouldn't have cracked him so hard. Then I might have been able to take two swings at him. Oh, well. We better get them tied up and into the car."

We stretched the goobers out back to back and tied their wrists and ankles together. Then we sat them upright and bound them to each other with at least a half roll of duct tape. Even if they tried to run away, the run would at best be a hobble, and they would look like Siamese twins doing it. It was a sight I'd almost pay to see.

We laid them back on their sides and then picked them up, Bubba at their shoulders, me at their legs. Lugging one sociopath is hard enough, I suspect, but two at the same time, especially when they're taped together, makes for clumsy work. We had them stuffed in the Saturn's backseat when cheers exploded from the baseball stadium. "The Biscuits are winning," Bubba said. "I'm thinking we will win that third straight championship easy."

We peeled back to the parking garage, where I ran in to retrieve the bundles. I left the pages from High C's bestseller fluttering against the mufflers and hubcaps. Bubba popped his trunk as I raced back. "Get the sign," he said through the open window. I did as told and jumped back into the passenger seat, cradling the cardboard between my knees as the bundles of cash spilled over my shoes.

"You're some artist," I said, reading the sign as we squealed off.

"That's your girlfriend's handiwork, not mine. *She's* some artist."

"She's a lot of things, all right. This is for you."

I passed him five one-hundred dollar bills.

"What's this for?"

"It's to repay the money I took from your tip jar ten years ago. I told you I would pay it back."

"You're repaying me out of somebody else's stolen stash?"

"As far as I'm concerned, the money is Dixie's inheritance. It's going to her, not back to High C. He owes it to her for what he did to her mother. I'm only taking my commission for getting her inheritance back, and I'm paying my debt to you out of that. So we're all square."

"I hope High C sees it so square."

"He won't have a choice."

Bubba laughed as he eyed the bills. "I'll tell you what: go ahead and give the kid that money. I don't need it. Besides, you're forgetting you already slipped a hundred in my tip jar on Monday. However guilty you might feel about what you've done in life, you don't want to overpay what you owe. That throws things out of balance, too."

I *had* forgotten I had already paid him off—at least, paid off a part of what I had stolen in my methhead days. The car turned off Ripley Street onto Upper Wetumpka Road. On our left was Oakwood Cemetery. Bubba cut into a turn lane to zip into one of the cemetery's unpaved lanes.

"Not this entryway. There's one about forty yards up ahead. Take it."

"What? Why?"

"Because this entryway takes you straight to Faye's grave. Forty yards isn't all that far. Just do it, please."

He shrugged and then jerked the car back into traffic, briefly, until the next entryway was before us. The Saturn kicked up a dirt cloud as we trolled through the red-dirt paths looking for a secluded spot. We finally found one not far from a memorial to eighteen Union soldiers who died in the Confederate prison camp the Rebs built in Montgomery. We dragged Treadface and Twitchy out of the back seat and positioned them against a tree in a spot of shade. It was 115 degrees out, after all. I didn't want them sweating to death.

I was so eager to get back to Red I almost forgot to stick her sign next to the yea-bobs.

"You sure they won't get sunstroke out here?" I asked as we hopped back in the Saturn.

"The maintenance crews come through every hour on the hour. Those two may get a little dehydrated, but nothing serious. I suspect they'll be the top story on tonight's news."

"They were the top story *last night*. Only nobody knew them by name."

"Okay, their *names* will be tonight's top story. I'm going to Tivo it."

I didn't want to admit to him that I had no clue what Tivo was.

As the road bent I threw one last glance over my shoulder, just to make sure the sign hadn't blown over. It hadn't. The letters were as legible as the markers pointing us to Hank Williams's grave.

WE'RE VOTING FOR MAYOR JUSTICE, the sign said. EVEN IF WE DID MURDER HIS DAUGHTER.

CHAPTER TWENTY-THREE

Sure, there were loose ends. There always are. The loose ends of High C's intestines, for example. Ten years ago they got me sent to Kilby. This time there was no blood, however, just cracked noggins and clavicles. If Treadface and Twitchy dropped my name to the police, I could honestly say that Bubba and I had done the city and the mayor a major favor. We had all but put a bow on Montgomery's most wanted.

"I've got something you might need," Bubba said when we rolled into the lot of the Capitol Plaza Lodge. He reached under his seat and pulled out a Charter Arms .38. I suddenly remembered what Eric the ex had said about Lexi cheating on him with Bubba. For a crazy second I imagined that this whole week had been an intricate ruse to get me to the moment when a gun could be turned on me. I had stolen money from Bubba, after all. If what Eric claimed was true, I had also stolen Lexi. Cash and women are two things that a man is unlikely to forget losing.

Or forgive losing, either.

"Take it," Bubba said, flipping the rubber grip my direction. "The serial number's been filed off, so it's untraceable. Even if you have to use it, you can chuck it and it'll never come back to haunt you."

"I get caught with it, though, I go back to Kilby."

"If High C catches you empty-handed you won't be going anywhere but to the morgue."

He had a point. Still, I stared at the pistol, working up my courage. I hadn't held a gun since I shot C. Taking this one would be tantamount to stepping back a decade in time. Only I wasn't the same person as ten years ago. I felt my fingers wrap around the steel.

I swear I also felt the ghost of a hand closing my fingers around it.

"You and me, sweet pea," Faye had cooed. *"Pow, pow."*

"El Rey reopens Tuesday," Bubba was saying. "We'll have people coming in all day after they vote. You won't believe the tips you can make off folks waiting for the election results. I'll need you and Lexi both. Can I put you on the schedule?"

"We'll be there." I checked the .38's cylinder. All five chambers were loaded. I clicked on the safety, tucked it to my back, and gathered up Dixie's money. "I won't you let you down . . . *boss."*

I watched him drive off. Then I dashed up the stairs. Yes, come Tuesday Red and I would be back on the clock. We wouldn't work at El Rey forever, of course. We would only stay there as long as it took for Lexi's art to win the attention it deserved. As for me . . . well, I had no idea what to do with the rest of my life, but I had a girl to love and a surrogate daughter to take care of and a father to make amends with. I had St. Jude on my side, too. Any more seemed greedy.

I was so giddy that once up the stairs I practically tore the door hinges from the jamb. Thanks to the heavy curtains, the room went pitch black as the door crashed shut behind me. I threw Dixie's money down and crawled onto the bed.

Red was napping hard. She deserved it. We had been up all night. The whole plan had been her idea, and it required hours of phone calls to pull it together. We had to track down Bubba and get him onboard, track down the number of Twitchy's momma to get a call in to the goobers, chart the details on

Montgomery street maps, rehearse the mad run to the trap in the alley. We all deserved to sleep until Tuesday. I looked forward to my nap, too—right after Red and I made love.

She lay on her left side, naked. I slid up against her, one hand on her hip. I pressed my lips deep into her neck and curled my other arm under her shoulder to roll her into an embrace. I kissed her gently across her jaw to her mouth, which was clenched tight and strangely unwelcoming.

"We're free," I whispered, but that didn't seem to soothe her. "Relax," I said softly in her ear. "St. Jude didn't let us down."

To prove we had his blessings, I kissed her forehead the way a saint would—one of those anointing kisses.

Her forehead was wet and sticky. I started to wipe the wetness off my lips when a familiar odor filled my nostrils. A taste leaked into my mouth, and I felt instantly queasy. I drew back and groped for the lamp on the endtable. When the light clicked on it gutted me stern to stem.

Goddamn if Red wasn't still beautiful—even with a bullet hole between her eyes.

I leaped from the bed, screaming. It was a sound unlike any I had ever heard. It didn't sound human, and yet it couldn't express the rage I felt. I kicked over the chair, sending loose bills flying. I shoved the TV off the dresser, shattering it on the floor. I drove my fist into the wall, smashing the plaster to flakes. Then I fell to my knees, crying and heaving.

No matter how hard I pounded the floor, she was gone. No matter how many ribbons my knuckles were sliced into by crushing shards from the broken TV, Red wasn't coming back. You don't come back from a bullet hole. She was gone—gone because of me.

When I couldn't cry or scream anymore I cradled her. I held her forehead to my cheek and kissed her face until mine was smeared with her blood.

Then I thought of something else.

Somebody else.

I ran outside to the next room, beating bloody prints onto the periwinkle calm of Dad and Dixie's door. The only answer was a muffled moan. I tried the knob, but it was locked. I tried kicking the door open, but my ankle was more likely to break: the door was steel-reinforced and the deadbolt didn't budge. Finally, I stripped off my shirt and, wrapping my fist, punched in the window.

Climbing inside, I found Dad hogtied on the bed. His mouth was wrapped as tight in duct tape as Bubba and I had wrapped Treadface and Twitchy. He was bucking and rolling, terrified. I jerked the ropes loose and ungagged him as best I could without stripping the skin from his face.

"Who did this to you?"

"I don't know . . . I just fell asleep and woke up this way!"

He gaped at my face. I could read his thinking. He saw in the blood covering me a reflection of the blood that covered him in the famous picture of his beating at the Montgomery Greyhound station in 1961. Only reflection wasn't the right word. More like obverse: the opposite.

"Oh, my God . . . tell me . . . who have you killed?"

I didn't answer. I had my own question. "Where's Dixie?"

"I don't know. . . . We were just listening to the game on the radio, waiting for you, and I don't know . . . I guess I fell asleep . . ."

"You passed out. You passed out!"

A Conecuh Ridge bottle lay on the floor, half its contents staining the carpet.

As Dad rubbed the rope burns on his wrists, I sank into a corner trying not to cry. I didn't want to do that in front of him. Not my father. Not after all I had been through, all I had put him through, all *we were going to have to go through now* . . .

But it was no good. I started blubbering.

"What's happened?" He stood over me, still wobbly, still drunk. "Whose blood is this? What did you do . . . ? Son, tell me, what have you done now?"

It was too much. I bowled myself into him. We fell onto the bed, where I pinned him, my kneecap in his stomach.

"I didn't do anything wrong!" I screamed into his face. "I was trying to make things right! Do you hear me? This time it wasn't my fault!"

My arm cocked back, my fist forming a hammer. I wanted to beat Dad's disappointment in me out of him. I probably would have, too, if he didn't swallow his terror long enough to ask the only question that mattered: "Who then? Who? Who has Dixie?"

I stumbled backwards harder than if he had taken his own swing. We looked at each other for a second. Then I bolted back to my hotel room. Dad followed. "Oh, my God!" he said when he saw Red sprawled on her back, her opal eyes staring blankly into the swirls of the stucco ceiling.

"I—I know you couldn't do this. . . . You loved her . . . I saw that in you. . . . I was proud to see how you loved her . . ."

"Sh—she had a boyfriend . . . an *ex*-boyfriend. . . . He's the only one who knew we were here . . . It had to be Eric. . . . *It had to!*"

I no sooner said it than something on the pillowcase next to Red's body caught my eye. It was thin, almost invisible. Gray, too, so it blended with the white of the sheets. I would have overlooked it if it hadn't been so long—six or seven inches at least. But there it was: a single strand of hair, as long and coiled as a snake.

"Whose is that?" Dad asked. "Is that yours?"

"Not quite." I held the strand up to the light. "I shaved my beard off four days ago, remember?"

Saturday, 2:50 A.M.

"I hope you kept that hair," C said with a rumbling cough. He took his beard down from over his shoulder and poked a shaky finger through the hole that blemished it. "That would spare the mortician a little patching."

"I think I'll shave you bald after you die. How would you like that?"

He let out a bubble of air. It was supposed to be a chuckle, only C didn't have the strength now. His skin was grayer than the beard, and his lids hung heavily halfway down his eyeballs.

"You got it all figured out, don't you, Ennis?"

"It was complicated, but not so hard to sort out. I give you credit for creativity with all that guff about Anarchy Ahoy, but there were spots in your story that strained credibility. Like the idea that you had $100,000 of your own for Treadface and Twitchy to steal. Once Walk told me how much he had paid in blackmail over the years it all came together. You had your boys kill Lister for that money."

"I can neither confirm nor deny that rumor."

"Only Treadface and Twitchy got a little *overcreative* with that autoerotic asphyxiation business. Somebody would have figured out it was murder sooner or later. A rubber phallus in the chalice is like an exclamation point on a sentence—it calls attention to itself."

262

"What can I say? Nobody ever accused Southerners of under-statement."

"The only thing I'm not sure of is how you found out Lister had the Great Man on the hook."

"Shouldn't be hard at all to figure. Dixie herself told me. During lunch at the El even. One morning she walked in on Lister stacking money in his home safe. She asked her grand-daddy where all that green came from, and he told her that Walk was financing her college fund. That's the great thing about having a conversation with the kid. She can't lie. She'll tell you everything. The sad part is that she didn't understand why Lister cracked up over that money. She doesn't know that she's too dumb for college."

"You've done so much for Dixie over the years, haven't you?"

"Faye had her hooks in me, too, remember. It wasn't a week if she wasn't hitting me up for cash. 'The baby needs new clothes,' she would tell me. 'She needs tuition for school.' I'm not stupid; I knew the money was going right into her bloodstream. Faye had me over a barrel, though. She said if I didn't pay, she would go to the cops and spill everything she knew about my chemistry classes. I couldn't fork over $5,000 a month, of course, but I paid her a lot. That $100,000? I was just trying to get my money back . . ."

"Only it never entered your empty head that one of your own goobers might fall for the kid, that Twitchy and Uncle Treadface might double-cross you."

"You don't think Dixie is mine? I'm hurt, Ennis, hurt. Emotionally this time."

"Maybe Dixie is yours, maybe not. Maybe some anonymous jelly bean that none of us ever heard of is the dad. Would it matter? Probably not. In the end, Faye had Dixie so she could inveigle you, Lister, Walk, and who knows who else into her little game of paternity poker."

He shrugged. "All of us except you, huh?"

I smiled. "I want the rest of the money."

"The rest of it? What rest of it?"

"Walk paid Faye for nearly fifteen years before she died. You paid, Lister paid. Regardless of who fathered Dixie, there was a lot of money flying around—$840,000 of it just from Walk. That cake belongs to Dixie. I'm going to make sure the kid gets it."

"You really think Faye *saved* money? Jesus, Ennis. Now you're being sentimental. That money went out as fast as it came in. There was nothing when Faye died—*nothing.*"

When I didn't answer, C nodded toward the body of the mayor.

"You're leaving out half the intrigue. How does he and the daughter figure into this mess? Are you going to tell me that Amory Justice, the Great White Hope of Montgomery, was another mark of Faye's?"

"Not hardly. That would make things too perfect. I've just about fried my brain trying to figure out his and Reese's connection to Dixie. And my best guess is that . . . there isn't a connection, except for Treadface and Twitchy. The bus-boycott picture was a side deal gone sour. You let a good business opportunity slide by when they came to you with Wookie's story about finding the picture of Amory. You wanted in on the deal, but your boys weren't playing. I'm guessing there was a spat and that the three of you traded threats. Most likely that's when they decided to clean out your safe and relieve you of Lister's money. I'm just not clear on when that happened—before or after they killed Reese."

"You didn't seem so unsure about it downstairs. Pretty cute of you to give the mayor that guff. You have to know I never would have okayed them killing Reese. I don't need that kind of grief. Those boneheads, though—they're not deep thinkers. They make Dixie look brilliant."

"They wanted the Justices' money as much as they wanted yours. That was another $25,000, after all. You know the funny part? There is another copy of that pic floating around. Walk has it. It was supposed to appear in the newspaper today, but Walk stopped the presses when Reese was murdered. That tells you what a guy he is. He wasn't going to kick Amory Justice while he was down."

C stared at the mayor's body again. "Looks like that picture won't *ever* make the front page now. What a waste. Some old picture from a history that nobody cares about anymore . . ."

"You're wrong. A lot of people still care about that history."

"Who? Walk Compson? Ha. Oh, wait . . . maybe you mean your daddy. I hate to break this to you, but ole Quentin's caring days are over. Your old man is a drunk."

I cocked my gun. Then I reminded him of somebody who had died for a lot less than Montgomery history.

"You didn't have to kill Red."

C rolled his eyes. "I'm not going to tell you again: I didn't hollow your girlfriend's cantaloupe. Somebody planted that hair there."

"Sure, somebody snuck a hair off your chinny chin chin when you weren't looking. You killed her, C. It's the only way it plays. Don't lie. You don't have much longer. Maybe a minute."

"Hey, here's a theory—" He pointed feebly to the mayor. "Maybe *he* killed Red. It's not that farfetched. All Francis and Yancey had to do was put word on the street that *you* shot Reese. Amory has plenty of boys working for him—or *had*, as the case may be. Hell, if one or two of his cops could Taser a black woman on TV, no telling what they'd do when cameras weren't around. I knew Amory Justice. He wouldn't have settled for arresting his daughter's murderer. Sure, I put my money on him. He was as big a gangster as gangster gets in Montgomery, Alabama."

"Nice try. Don't let your last breath be a lie. Tell me you killed Red. Then you can tell me you're sorry."

He motioned toward the CD player. "How about that Maria Callas now? Let me go out listening to her. Do that, and I'll beg whatever forgiveness you want me to."

I watched him pant. Then I went to the CD player and cued *Tosca*. The room filled with a soaring soprano. High C pinched his eyes closed and tried to jimmy his grimace into a smile.

"It's time," I said again. "Say it."

He laughed. I didn't think he had it in him, but he managed. His laughs were guttural and jagged, like heels crunching gravel. Swear to God, C sounded like he was prying the ghost right out of his own gullet.

"I'm sorry, Ennis. Really sorry . . ."

He swallowed hard. For just a second, his glassy eyes cleared, and he was his old devil self again.

"I'm sorry I *didn't* kill your girlfriend. For that matter, I'm sorry I didn't kill you."

I aimed the gun at his forehead. That only made him laugh harder. I let him laugh at me for about five seconds, and then I shot the CD player. Maria Callas's aria shrieked to a stop, mid-trill.

That put an end to his laughing all right. C thought I had put an end to *him*. He thought I had shot him again.

He would have preferred that.

"Dammit, Ennis! That's art! You don't park a Hornaday in art! That's why you're in this situation, you toothless, brainless wonder! That's why the best you've got to look forward to is going straight back to Kilby. That's where you belong! You'll be back there come Monday morning because you've got no imagination! No imagination—just sentimentality!"

He was killing himself trying to scream.

"Your goddamned sentimentality over a waterhead daughter

of a druggie whore who never loved you. . . . You've wasted your life because you couldn't appreciate what you had going for you! You don't believe me? Go ask Quentin. Ask Quentin why he's a drunk—he'll tell you it's because of you! You ruined a great father by being a lousy son—"

I pulled the trigger again. For a half-second, C's mouth continued to move after the bullet drilled him in the same spot where he shot Red. He blinked once as if he wasn't sure what had happened. Then his head fell forward, and a gooey string of blood spooled down to his bare toes.

"*En-nis,*" Dixie's voice floated up from downstairs. "*Won't you come and stay?*"

"*En-nis,*" she sang softly. "*Won't you come and play?*"

CHAPTER TWENTY-FOUR

I spied on him for hours. I knew I was going to kill him, but I was adamant I wouldn't be rushed. The last time I faced him with a gun I was uncertain, and my haste landed me in hell. So after Dad dropped me off at the opening of C's cul-de-sac, I jumped the back fence to his McMansion and patiently crouched among a tall row of boxwoods, the sweet aroma of the hedges my only compensation for sweating so hard.

To pass the time I emptied the bullets from Bubba's Charter Arms and replaced them in different chambers, over and over, each time tucking the gun to the small of my back. Occasionally I looked at my watch and checked Red's phone to make sure I still had cell service out here in the boonies. "You call me when it's over," Dad had said as I slinked from his truck into the phony sylvan splendor of THE WOODS. "Whatever happens, you call. I won't let you down this time. Two honks and you'll know I'm here to fetch you."

Dad wasn't going to let *me* down.

I kept thinking about it. Hearing him say it filled me with shame. I wasn't worthy of such a pledge—not from Dad, not from anyone. I had failed so many people. Red was gone because of me.

I hoped I could stay alive long enough to not fail Dixie.

When C appeared on his patio, he wore the same Euro-clingy swimsuit as Monday when his boys first shanghaied me to his crackerbox palace. For a guy who had shot a woman in the head earlier that evening he seemed remarkably unburdened. I watched him work on his laptop, flex and prance, swim fifty laps, slather aloe vera over his sun-pinkened belly, drink three beers, and then light his silver grill, which was about as big and boxy as the pool pump that churned only a few feet from me. I listened to him sing along to his beloved opera, which blared from a pair of shoebox-sized speakers that hung like claws from his fascia boards. He cooked a fat dripping steak along with a baked potato the size of a football and ate them both under the still-open umbrella of his patio table. Then he stretched out in an Adirondack chair and slept. I suppose I could have snuck up on him while he snoozed, but that hardly seemed sporting. I wanted C wide awake; I didn't want him mistaking me for some random nightmare. So I waited and waited.

When he awoke it was nearly two A.M. I watched him piss into a flowerpot and then comb his beard like he was raking white sand on a Florida panhandle beach. Finally he jumped back into his kidney-shaped pool, flopped into an inner tube, and gazed like a poet to the stars.

It was my chance.

He was tracing the Little Dipper from the deep end as I snuck up on him. I hopped the diving board. He was just close enough to the edge that I could reach out and yank his ponytail, jerking him off the tube. I caught him by such surprise that all he could do was flail as I dunked him repeatedly, holding his head under water for a minute at a time. When I let him up he gasped and spat until I drove his face into the tile pool trim, leaving a red welt that striped his forehead like a sweatband.

I started to pull out the Charter Arms to press it to his temple, but I thought better of it. I decided I didn't want C knowing I was carrying. Ten years ago when I shot him I waved Faye's gun in his face for so long he didn't take me seriously. The scar on his belly wouldn't let him underestimate me again.

I ordered him out of the water. He crawled onto the concrete, sputtering. "You're a dead man. . . . You, Quentin, Walk Compson. . . . I'll kill everyone who's ever meant anything to you, you junkie loser . . ."

"You already got a jump-start on that threat, didn't you? This is for Red—"

I kicked him in the stomach. Hard, like I was punting a football past an opponent's twenty-yard line. C rolled onto his side and curled into a ball.

"I want the girl." I put my heel to his windpipe.

"What the hell are you talking about? What the hell's gotten into you?"

I pushed all my weight into my foot. His face wrinkled as he grabbed my tennis shoe to pry me off his throat. He couldn't do it, though. I had the leverage. I had him pinned. Even if he got free, he was a goner. I would shoot him poolside if I had to.

"The girl. She's mine. I'm taking her."

I booted him across the chin and then twisted his ponytail in my fist, dragging him toward his house. I pulled so hard a clump of hair came loose and the back of his scalp turned prickly red. C had to scuttle like a crab to not feel the tearing. I yanked open his French doors and drove a toe into his ass to send him across the threshold. He was still on all fours, scampering for the couch, when I followed him inside.

My mistake was keeping my eyes glued to him.

I was two steps past the threshold when the blow caught me on the crown. It threw me left, where I crashed into one of C's Pier One lightstands and fell to the hardwood with my feet tangled in its cord. I felt my spine pop as I landed on the Charter Arms; the pop was so loud that for a second I thought that gun had gone off. I shook my head to clear my dizziness. Somebody stood over me with a book as thick as an attaché case. That somebody was close enough that I could make out the book's title: *The Oxford English Dictionary.*

"No wonder the polls have you down," I told Amory Justice. "I'm not sure clocking your constituents is a smart campaign strategy."

He wasn't interested in talking to me. "This is him?" he asked C as he threw the book aside. The book was so damn bulky that if I trusted what I was seeing I swear it buckled the coffee table when it landed.

"That's your boy." C was on his feet, massaging the spot on his buttock where I had kicked him. "Meet your daughter's killer, Mr. Mayor."

I would have laughed out loud if laughing out loud wouldn't have launched a blitzkrieg in my brain.

"So that's how you're playing this off? Treadface and Twitchy are your boys, not mine, C. I'm guessing that by this point MPD has found them in the cemetery. The dots won't be hard to connect. The dots all draw lines back to you, not me."

"Those boys in the cemetery told me everything I need to know," the mayor cut in. Standing over me, he looked twenty feet tall. The Glock he whipped out of his suit jacket didn't do much to dwarf him down to size. "They told me *you* killed my baby. I have a fair sense of why, but you're going to tell me in your own words. You messed with the wrong family, boy."

"Ennis is big-headed like that," C chimed in. "Famous son of a famous father. He's never known his place."

I wasn't listening. I was realizing we weren't alone. Dixie sat in a corner rocking chair, her knees drawn up to her chin. She was shivering.

"Get her out of here. She doesn't need to be exposed to this."

"See what I mean?" C threw up his hands. "He's giving *you* orders, Amory. What gall. I'd shoot him right now if I were you. Get it over with."

271

"Shut up," the mayor grunted.

His eyes were moving back and forth between me and C. The way they jittered told me this was a marriage of convenience. It was obvious Amory wasn't prone to trust a Euro-swimsuit-wearing meth-cook-turned-publisher who egged him on just a bit too enthusiastically. The more anxious the mayor grew, the more he clenched his teeth, and the more his long Leno jaw seemed to melt back into the glacier of his face.

"Tell him what brought you to my door, Amory. Go ahead. Tell Ennis how you ended up bringing Dixie over here to me. Tell him we've been waiting—what?—Christ, *hours* for him to bless us with an appearance."

C smiled at me.

"We knew you'd show up eventually, but, man, you had to keep us in suspense, didn't you? The mayor here has a busy agenda. He's got a campaign to run—not to mention a funeral to plan."

"Shut up," Amory Justice grunted again.

"Here's how it played out, Ennis: the mayor is sitting at home grieving over his dear daughter's departure when all of a sudden his phone rings. His *private* phone, the number of which is known only to his family and a few trusted assistants. Only on the end of the line it's none of those familiars. It's a stranger, a young lady. Tell him what the snatch said, Amory."

The mayor's face was red as a stop sign. He was either angry or flummoxed—I wasn't sure which. I wasn't sure it really mattered. Either way, his right index finger wasn't going to budge from the Glock's trigger.

"The girl was terrified," Amory recounted, slowly and methodically. "She said she had gotten herself in a situation that she couldn't get out of and that she needed help. She said if I helped her she could tell me who killed Reese. She said to look for a clue in Oakwood Cemetery. I asked how she got my private number. She said she had an ex-boyfriend who was a police officer. Name of Eric. He had text-messaged the number to her. She told me she was at the Capitol Plaza Lodge. She told me the room number even."

I didn't believe him. "I had her cell phone with me. It couldn't have been Red."

"The number came through on my caller ID. She didn't try to block it. She wasn't trying to hide."

Amory recited the number. It was my father's.

"Then what?" C goaded him. "What happened next?"

"Then the line went dead. I called my chief and told him to get to Oakwood. Then I got into my car and went straight to that motel room. You know what I found there. Whoever that young woman was, you left her there just like you left Reese lying up on Lafayette Street."

"I didn't kill Red," I insisted. "And I didn't kill your daughter. You're pointing that gun at the wrong guy. The right guy is right over there."

"Nope, sorry," C went. "You can't pin the death of that snatch on me."

The mayor's head jerked C's direction.

"The girl in the motel, I mean—not Reese. I would never use that word to describe your daughter, Amory. I liked Reese—she was my type of girl . . ."

"I found a hair from his beard on the pillow next to Red's body," I told Amory.

The news made C pucker. "You lying bastard! I was home all day, fighting black algae and working on my new book!"

I nodded to Dixie. "Then how did she end up over here?"

"She was in the motel room when I found that girl's body," the mayor said. "She was in a corner, huddled up just like that, shaking away and singing to herself. I got her out of there."

"And you just happened to come out here to THE WOODS,

did you? How do you even know High C, Mayor? I've been wondering for three days just how his boys hooked up with your campaign. What was the connection between them and Reese?"

"It's called opposition research," C said. "Montgomery is a small town. There aren't a lot of people who can dig up dirt discreetly here. Basically, there's me. I lent my boys out to the mayor's campaign, that's all."

"Sure, out of the goodness of your heart. Don't bullshit me. You give the mayor muscle, the mayor leaves Anarchy Ahoy alone. Unlike Walk Compson, who would shut you down by hook or by crook."

C shrugged. "What does any of this matter now?"

"It matters because it was your boys that killed Lister James. It was your boys that killed Reese."

"That's not the way it played, Amory. Swear to God. Ennis here, he ganged up with Francis and Yancey behind my back. I thought they were trustworthy, but sweet Jesus good help is hard to find. Ennis here corrupted them by flashing all kind of money in front of their eyes."

"There's a simple way to prove I didn't do any of that. The girl in the motel room—I loved her. I would never have put a bullet in her brain."

"Don't fall for it, Amory. Ennis here has left a trail of destruction in his wake since he was twenty. You're a Bama fan, aren't you? You know damn well what Ennis Skinner did to the Crimson Tide. *Cocaine on the membrane*—that's Ennis's contribution to great moments in sports history. Tells you everything you need to know about the crut."

I looked to the mayor. "You and I are meeting for the first time, but you and C here obviously have a previous relationship. You know what he's capable of. He brought meth to Montgomery. He dealt to this kid's mother for a good fifteen, sixteen years until her heart was so weak it just gave up. If your association was ever public knowledge, voters might not be keen on the company you keep."

Then I looked to Dixie.

"Tell the mayor who killed Red. Tell him how you saw C shoot her."

"Stop it, Ennis," C jumped in. "Maybe the mayor here doesn't know what you're doing, but I do. This girl here, Mr. Mayor, she's not star witness material. She has a problem distinguishing fantasy from reality. She really thinks her momma was Supergirl. You can't believe a thing the kid says."

I said it again: "Tell the mayor how you saw C shoot Red."

"Quit it, Ennis! Quit feeding her that lie."

We were all looking at Dixie. She wasn't looking at us, though. She had gone back to staring at her kneecaps, her chin resting on them as she rocked back and forth in the chair, singing softly, distantly.

"You saw him shoot Red, Dixie. I know you did. You remember it all, don't you?"

The mayor looked back and forth between the girl and C. It was working. He was beginning to wonder if he hadn't been rooked.

I said it one more time: "Go ahead, Dixie. Tell us the story."

"Goddammit, Ennis! Stop!"

The mayor's aim suddenly swung away from me. When it landed on C, a look of fear whitened his eyes. He realized all of a sudden how vulnerable he was in nothing but a wet swimsuit.

"I want the negative," the mayor said.

"Negative? What negative?"

"Don't bullshit the mayor of Montgomery," I jumped in. "Reese was buying it from the Wookie when your boys killed them. Maybe killing her wasn't part of your plan—maybe it was. It doesn't matter. Treadface and Twitchy are your guys. That means you're responsible—right, Mayor?"

"The negative," Amory Justice said again.

C looked back and forth between us.

"Ennis is lying, Mayor. I don't know anything about a negative. I don't know anything about a positive!"

"I want it," Amory said for a third time. "Now."

C sized up his options. "Okay," he agreed, holding up his palms. "It's upstairs in my safe. Come up with me and I'll get it for you."

I had a pretty fair idea he was lying. The last I had seen of the negative was when Twitchy fished it from Reese's purse. Intuition told me something else was waiting for Amory Justice in that safe, but I wasn't going to blow the surprise. It might be my only chance of getting out of C's McMansion alive.

"Everybody comes," the mayor said. He was nodding at the girl, not me.

"No," I insisted. "She's seen too much as it is. Leave her downstairs. Look at her: she's so terrified she can't move. She's not going anywhere."

I watched Amory work over the logistics, silently. Then his chin tightened as he grimly motioned me into line behind C. As we started hiking the circular stairway, the mayor kept jabbing me between the shoulder blades with his Glock. I hoped he was too anxious to notice the outline of the Charter Arms at the small of my back.

Upstairs, C went down on a knee in front of his safe. The mayor was behind him, backed up against C's bookcase. I sidled a few inches to the right toward the glass-topped desk with the huge white computer.

"I know you'll be glad to get this negative," C said as he worked the tumblers. "You would take one hell of a beating on Tuesday if it fell into the hands of the Compson campaign. I won't keep on telling you I wasn't in on Reese's murder, though. I wasn't, but what does it matter at this point?"

"Sure, you weren't in on it," the mayor said through his teeth. "You just happen to have the negative. I'm sure it floated into your hands. By carrier pigeon."

"I've got to say, it hurts like hell that you don't believe me . . ."

The last tumbler fell into place. C paused a second before yanking the lever and swinging open the safe door. I slipped a hand behind my back. The safe was stuffed damn near to the gills. Not with cash, mind you, but with a stack of paper—a manuscript. I busted out laughing.

"What were you thinking, C? That somebody was going to steal your next book? Now I know how Treadface and Twitchy nabbed that $100,000! You didn't even have it in the safe, did you? The cash wouldn't fit in there with your magnum opus! Ha ha!"

"I suggest you shut up, Ennis," C said, slipping a hand behind the paper stack. "The negative is here, Amory. I've just got to do some reaching, I promise. I had to tuck it in a corner, you see, because you never know when some feeb may try to rifle your saf—"

He whipped around just in time for a flash of light to discharge from his hand. The mayor flew backwards into the bookcase, a look of surprise slapped across his face. He sort of half-turned as he tried to keep to his feet by grabbing at the shelves, but the shot caught him in the heart, and all his desperate pawing accomplished was to pull a load of Anarchy Ahoy books onto his face as he spilled onto his side, dead.

C didn't have time to gloat. He no sooner hopped out of his crouch to stand over the mayor than another shot sounded— this one from my Charter Arms. As the echo bounced off the walls C looked at the smoking hole in his beard. He dropped his gun to poke a finger through it, just to make sure his eyes weren't deceiving him. Then his legs gave out. He slumped sideways into his recliner, staring at me, too astonished to blink.

Because you know how it is when you get the drop on a guy who thought he had the drop on you.

He gives you that "Et tu" face, like you betrayed him by having more smarts than he ever thought to credit you with.

Saturday, 2:52 A.M.

The first thing I did after killing C was call my father.

I wanted to tell him that I had tried to make my amends, but that sometimes things get so cockeyed that a man will end up hammering himself crooked trying to bend the world back into something even resembling straight.

"You were right," I planned to say. *"I was headed back to Kilby all along. Only this time without the 'attempted' in front of 'murderer.' "*

I wanted to tell Quentin that I would accept my punishment. I wanted him to understand why I felt I neither deserved nor wanted freedom. I wanted him to know that it had nothing to do with C, however. It was because of Red.

"I'll be a lifer now," I would say. *"The sentence I serve will be my amends to her. For never even getting the chance to call her Lexi.*

"I hope you can see this is my way of taking responsibility.

"I hope you won't think you wasted ten years standing by a screw-up son only to lose him again to prison within a week.

"This time is different, old man.

"The only thing that's even remotely the same is that I'll still be sorry to put you through it."

And lastly:

"Take care of Dixie for me. She needs somebody."

Of course, I didn't say any of those things. All I said when Dad answered his phone was, "It's over. Come and get us."

"Two honks," he assured me, and he sounded as sober as I had ever heard him. "You listen for two honks, and you'll know I'm there for you, son."

I hung up and watched a bead of blood gather enough mass to drip from the hole in C's forehead. It seemed to fall in slow motion, tumbling and changing shape mid-air before splattering on the carpet, oblong enough to speckle his dirty toes.

I was so busy staring at the dead man's scuffed feet that I almost missed the sound of others thumping up the circular stairway. I bolted toward the landing, but I wasn't fast enough. Dixie made it into the room before I could block her from seeing the bodies.

"Don't look!" I yelled as I pulled her into an embrace. She broke away from me and squatted in front of C. "Wake up!" she yelled, shaking his slumped shoulders. "Wake up!"

It hit me hard: if what C had been telling me since Monday was true, I had just murdered Dixie's father.

Amends, I reminded myself. *I am making my amends.*

"I'm sorry, Dixie. But you're better off, I promise. Quentin will take good care of you."

I saw her eyes swing to the open safe. She seemed to study it, strangely, before lurching toward it. She began pulling pages from the stack of paper, flipping them over her shoulder until she seemed lost in a blizzard. Finally, she yanked what remained of C's manuscript and threw it against the wall above the safe.

"He said he would write a book for me! A book with Supergirl!"

Then she started sobbing.

She looked broken. I couldn't move. It took two bleats of a horn to kick me into gear.

"We need to go." I tucked the Charter Arms to my back and pulled Dixie to her feet. I led her past the two bodies and the two dropped guns and the two separate pools of blood toward the stairs. I could hear her feet padding the floor behind me. It was a reassuring sound. It meant she trusted me. Well, that was something. I took comfort in that trust until Dad fired off another two honks. If he kept that up he would wake a neighbor. I didn't want any busybodies spying his license plate from a bedroom window. I would make my amends, but I needed time to get Dad and Dixie back home, back to safety, before I would go to the police and confess the whole sorry mess.

Halfway down the stairs, I heard yet another honk.

At least, I thought it was a honk.

Only it was sharper and louder than a honk. Not to mention hotter. It caught me right below my left ear, sending me flying forward into the curve of the railing. The force drove me over the balustrades, and I spilled to the hardwoods of C's living room, my head cracking on the bottom step. Saliva flooded my throat like lava.

Dixie stood over me, Amory Justice's Glock in her hand, a curl of smoke still winding from the barrel tip.

"Where's the rest of my money?" she demanded.

My mouth fell open, but I couldn't speak. The bullet had rocketed diagonally through the side of my neck, severing the bottom plate of my dentures as it exited my jaw. I coughed out the shattered remains of my fake teeth and shakily tried to stanch the blood draining across my throat. I couldn't find the wound, though. My chin was gone.

"Don't tell me that $100,000 is all that's left." Dixie bit her lip and shook her head in disbelief. "Dammit! I should've known you bastards would have wasted it all!"

There was a wild energy in her glare. She aimed the Glock at my face but then dropped it to her side, tauntingly.

"*Pow, pow, sweet pea.*"

Swear to God, that's what I heard her say.

"What's wrong, Joe Namath? Are you shocked? Don't be. If

281

you'd been born with the world telling you that you were nothing but a shortbus you'd get smart about playing dumb, too. That's the first lesson Momma taught me: 'Always make them underestimate you.' "

She smiled.

"That's right. You can thank Faye for my acting skills. I wasn't but a sweet little birdy before she taught me what wool we could pull over the world's eyes. She showed me how much money I could get out of men, how people would house me and feed me. . . . Hey, you want to see something? Say *hamburger.* . . . Oh, wait—what's that? You can't talk right now? Okay, I'll do it: *hamburger!*"

She stiffened, and the wicked smile evaporated back into the shy, scared, vulnerable face I had known for three days. As her eyes blinked rapidly, a dark spot appeared in the crotch of her cut-off jeans. It spread all the way to the fringe ends of the denims before a brief liquid stream trickled down her inner thighs.

"That's what my momma taught me! She loved me so much she showed me all kinds of tricks. She taught me how with a few simple words I could make enough havoc that nobody would know I was getting everything I wanted."

She slipped back into her baby face.

"*My granddaddy takes pictures of me! He tells me he's my daddy!* Bam, I've got my own apartment just by whispering those words to Walk Compson. *My granddaddy has a room full of money he says is mine!* Bam, C sends Francis and Yancey over to Lister's to get rid of that cop-a-feeler creep and get my cake for me in the same swoop! *Mr. C says he's keeping my money for me until I'm old enough to know how to handle it!* Bam, that dope Yancey and his fat uncle are only too giddy to fetch my $100k from that old methmucker . . .

"Those are just the face-to-face games I got to play. There

were all kinds of behind-the-scenes ones nobody would ever think to credit to little old me. You know why? *Because I'm a dummy!* Why, nobody as slow as Dixie would ever post dirty pictures of herself on the Internet, just to send them to C so he would have some reason to wrangle Ennis Skinner into seeking me out. In the e-mail I made sure to use my momma's nickname for C, Scruff Bunny, but C never once thought Faye's daughter might be the only logical person who might know that name. Why? *Because Dixie is a waterhead!*

"Don't think you're any better than C, Ennis Skinner. It never entered your mind that I might plant the name GILBERT in my apartment so you would track me to that photographer's studio. You never once wondered if maybe C *wasn't* the one who drilled your precious girlfriend in the bean, that maybe somebody slipped a hair from C's beard to set it next to her hollowed head. Do you know how I got that hair? You of all people should know! It was Momma. 'Always get a lock of hair from any man you sleep with,' she told me. 'That way you can Delilah any Samson you come across.' I have a shoebox of locks I inherited from her under my bed. There's a curl from you, from Lister, Walk Compson, C, and a ton of others . . . and yet you never put two and two together. Why? *Because Dixie ain't but a retard!*"

She laughed at her own ingenuity before stopping abruptly.

"Oh, Ennis, think of the fun I could've had if I had known about that picture of the mayor! I'd have another chunk of change to roll in! Then again, considering how detrimental that negative has proven to folks' health . . . well, it's best I wasn't too greedy, wouldn't you say?"

She was interrupted by two honks of a horn. *Dad,* I tried to gargle, but I couldn't form words. I could feel air rush out of my throat when I tried to breathe.

"I hope the old man has my cash in the car. I would hate to

have to drag him all the way back to that lice trap of a motel you stuck us in. It might send Quentin back to the bottle if he had to see your girlfriend's dead body once more."

She crouched over me.

"You should have seen how surprised she was. Sure, Red was beautiful, but fear gave her a whole new kind of beauty. I would say you have it now, too, only I'm afraid you're missing the bottom of your face . . ."

She giggled.

"We were lying on that bed, watching TV. She was telling me she was going to take me shopping when it was all over. You would have thought I was her kid sister. Red was so eager to make sure I wasn't worried or upset that she didn't notice me drop a hand into my purse and pull out my gun. . . . Oh, I know what you're thinking: where does a waterhead get a gun? Yancey gave it to me, and the funny thing is you never thought once when you were yanking me out of Gilbert's studio to peek into my purse. Like I said, a girl can get whatever she wants just by acting stupid."

Her eyes tightened as she smirked.

"I kissed her for you. I want you to know that. Right before and right after. When she saw the gun she went as white as a piece of paper. You know what shocked her, right? *The gun had been in that purse all along.* It was in that purse even when you broke the strap. I almost felt bad for her to realize that—she had been so nice to me! I even apologized. 'I have to do this,' I told her. 'Because of him.' *Him* being *you,* of course. She saw it as well as I did. The anger that's in you, Ennis Skinner. When you threw me on that bed and tore those pigtails out of my hair—Red had to know that she would be on the receiving end of that someday. So I shot her and then I kissed her goodbye for you. From there all I had to do was tape up your daddy, which was easy since he was passed out, and then call the mayor. What a dink—it never entered Amory Justice's mind that *I* might have been the voice on the other end of that line. Why? *Because I'm a shortbus!*"

Dad's horn blared again.

"Uh-oh . . . Quentin is getting impatient. I can't keep him waiting much longer. I would hate for the old man to come inside and see you like this. I know how guilty you feel for disappointing him. Famous son of a famous father. It must have been some burden to bear to make you go to pot like you did for so long. I guess I can understand why you came out of prison feeling like you had to prove you're a good guy at heart. It's just too bad some things can't be forgiven. You never had a chance, you know. You were a dead man the minute you walked out of Kilby. This whole week was your payback for what you did to my momma and me. The minute I heard you were getting out I spent every second waiting for the one second that I could look into your surprised eyes and say these words: *In memory of my momma, Supergirl, I am here to kill you. Goodbye . . . Daddy.*"

That last word hit me harder than if she had shot me again. I lurched up with what strength I had and clutched her arm. She just laughed, though. I was too weak to wrestle.

"Go ahead," Dixie said. "Hit me. Hit me the way you wanted to in the motel. Hit me the way you used to hit my momma. Threaten to kill me the way you used to threaten her. Does it make you feel like a man to know that all those years you were locked up she still lived in fear of you? Faye only needed to hear your name and she would start trembling. 'I've known a lot of bad men,' she always told me, 'but the one you come from, En-nis Skinner, he was by far the worst.' "

No! I tried to tell her, but I could only sputter.

"If it hadn't been for you, Daddy, she could have gotten off the drugs. If not for you, Momma never would have gotten hooked in the first place. 'The only thing that man ever gave me that was any good was you,' she used to tell me. I blubbered like a baby when she said it. You know why? Because of what she said next: 'He gave me you, but don't believe it ever meant a thing to him.' "

I tried to tell Dixie that I never even met her mother until after she was born, but I couldn't speak. My voice box was a blendered bowl of Spaghetti-Os.

"I wanted to love you, Daddy. I wanted to, but Momma was my voice of reason. 'Have you ever had a letter from Ennis Skinner?' she would ask me. 'One letter just once in your life?' She wouldn't stop asking until I said 'no' out loud. 'Has he ever given me money to help support you?' Never, Momma would make me admit. 'Has he ever even acknowledged you by having that stuck-up drunk Dad of his come to visit you?' And, of course, I had to say 'no,' which broke my little baby heart. . . . 'There's the moral to your story,' Faye always told me. 'Don't ever try to meet your daddy, darling, because he'll kill you as sure as he tried to Supergirl.' "

For a second I thought she was going to cry, but she didn't. She just stared at me, hard, unrepentant, unforgiving.

"Don't act so surprised to find yourself in this position. I'm just your legacy, Daddy dearest, come to clear your account."

She aimed the Glock at my face again. I stared into the hole. *You're wrong,* I heard myself say. *You don't know how wrong. . . .* But it was all in my head. I closed my eyes. Instead of a shot, however, I heard two more honks from Dad's horn. When I looked again, the Glock was tucked in Dixie's cutoffs.

"Maybe I'll kill Quentin, but maybe I won't. I've already had one granddaddy off'd, after all. I should keep some family around, don't you think? I'm sure Pawpaw Skinner isn't the greedy perv that Grandpa Lister was. Plus Quentin and I have a bond: we both know what it's like to be disappointed by you."

She put her palm on my chest and pressed hard, as if she were squeezing the air out of me.

"That's the only gift I have to give you, Daddy. I'm going to let you go into the next world guessing what your little girl is up to. I hope you're as sorry as I am that it'll be the first time in nineteen years you've ever bothered to wonder."

She leaned in close enough for her black hair to fall across my face. Her bangs dipped into my blood. I felt her lips anoint my forehead. Then she rose and left.

As she strutted toward the door, I reached out, but Dixie never turned, and the only eyes that fell upon me were those of the St. Jude tattoo on my forearm.

His were as vacant as mine.

A short time later (*how long I couldn't say; time was expanding indefinitely*) I heard two sharp metallic raps. By then the world had drained to white and I was nothing but shallow, intermittent breath.

For the life of me—what little life I had left to me—I couldn't tell if the raps were honks from a horn or gunshots from a Glock.

ACKNOWLEDGMENTS

Permission to use epigraph (27 words) from *Song of Solomon* by Toni Morrison, copyright © 1977 by Toni Morrison, was graciously granted by Random House, Inc.

"El Rey Burrito Lounge" logo used by permission of Il Panificio, Inc., 1031 East Fairview Avenue, Montgomery Alabama 36106. Many thanks to Tyler Bell, proprietor.

ABOUT THE AUTHOR

Kirk Curnutt is the author of eleven books of fiction and literary criticism. His first novel, *Breathing Out the Ghost*, was named Best Fiction in the Indiana Center for the Book's 2008 Best Books of Indiana Awards. His other works include a short-story collection, *Baby, Let's Make a Baby;* a fictional dialogue with Ernest Hemingway entitled *Coffee with Hemingway;* and *The Cambridge Companion to F. Scott Fitzgerald.* The winner of an Alabama State Arts Council Grant, he won the gold nonfiction medal in the 2008 William Faulkner–William Wisdom Creative Writing Competition sponsored by the Pirate's Alley Faulkner Society. As a passionate devotee of all things Scott and Zelda Fitzgerald, he serves as vice president of the International Fitzgerald Society, coedits the *Fitzgerald Review,* and sits on the board of the Fitzgerald Museum.

Curnutt lives and writes in Montgomery, Alabama, and may often be found at the real-life El Rey Burrito Lounge, located at 1031 E. Fairview Avenue. He recommends the *hongos a la parrilla* with a sweet, stiff sangria.

Website: www.kirkcurnutt.com
Email: kirk.curnutt@gmail.com

W24
LC 2/12/11
#C 2

Add 12/28/09